"Have you ever had a wife?" Lucie glanced up to find Sky studying her with those hungry eyes again.

He made a sharp sound that could have been a laugh. "I frighten white women."

"You don't frighten me."

"I did the night I jumped through your window. And you ran from me the first two times I tried to speak to you."

All true. "I had a bad feeling about you."

"Most women do." He lifted his water skin and offered it to her. "And now?"

She drank the warm water and passed back the skin. Their fingers brushed and the tingling excitement rushed through her. She rested her chin on his shoulder.

"Feelings change."

HIS DAKOTA CAPTIVE

Jenna Kernan

All the characters in this book have no existence outside the imagination of the author, and have no relation whatsoever to anyone bearing the same name or names. They are not even distantly inspired by any individual known or unknown to the author, and all the incidents are pure invention.

First published in Great Britain 2011
by Mills & Boon, an imprint of Harlequin (UK) Limited,
Eton House, 18-24 Paradise Road, Richmond, Surrey TW9 1SR

© Jeannette H. Monaco 2010

ISBN: 978 0 263 88803 4

Harlequin (UK) policy is to use papers that are natural, renewable and recyclable products and made from wood grown in sustainable forests. The logging and manufacturing process conform to the legal environmental regulations of the country of origin.

Printed and bound in Spain
by Blackprint CPI, Barcelona

Every bit as adventurous as her heroines, **Jenna Kernan** is an avid gold prospector, searching America's gold-bearing rivers for elusive nuggets. She and her husband have written several books on gem and mineral hunting. Her debut novel, WINTER WOMAN, was a RITA® finalist for Best First Book.

Jenna lives with her husband and two bad little parrots in New York. Visit her on the web at www.jennakernan.com, for news, contests and excerpts.

Previous novels by Jenna Kernan:

WINTER WOMAN
TURNER'S WOMAN
HIS BROTHER'S BRIDE.
  (part of *Wed Under Western Skies*)
THE TRAPPER
FALLEN ANGEL
  (part of *A Western Winter Wonderland*)
HIGH PLAINS BRIDE
OUTLAW BRIDE
SIERRA BRIDE

Did you know that some of these novels are also available as eBooks? Visit www.millsandboon.co.uk

To Jim—now and always.

"I do not believe that Indians…who are a perpetual source of expense to the government and a constant menace to thousands of their white neighbors, a hindrance to civilization and a clog on our progress, have any right to forcibly keep their children out of school to grow up like themselves, a race of barbarians and semi-savages."

—Thomas Jefferson Morgan, Commissioner of Indian Affairs, 1889 to 1893

"If the Great Spirit had desired me to be a white man he would have made me so in the first place. He put in your heart certain wishes and plans; in my heart he put other and different desires. Each man is good in the sight of the Great Spirit. It is not necessary that eagles should be crows."

—Sitting Bull (Teton Sioux)

Chapter One

Dakota Territory, September 1884

Sky Fox neared the spring when the first shout brought him up short. An instant later a high-pitched voice spewed a string of first-rate insults in Lakota. Next, he heard a deeper voice speaking English.

"Ow! You little bastard! I'll teach you to bite me."

The crack of an open palm striking flesh made Sky Fox wince. He eased off his horse and slid the rifle from the beaded leather sheath. He wore the clothing of the whites, except for the broad hat that he never did get used to. His blue eyes and pale skin marked him as white, which he was, except on the inside.

He crept silently forward and came upon the white man, struggling with a young Indian boy and the buttons on his pants simultaneously. The boy's bloody calico shirt was torn and the gaping hole showed russet skin and the parallel gouges that could only be from the man's fingernails. His attacker held him by the throat and was doing his best to throttle him with one hand.

Sky aimed his rifle at the white man.

"Let him up."

The man startled and then turned, but kept his hand about the child's neck. His captive glared at Sky with hatred showing in his split lip and black eye. Despite the abuse, the young man was silent. His captor gave an oily smile.

"Oh, hey, there, brother. You gave me a start. I didn't hear you come up. I'm a truant officer—"

"Let him go." Sky placed his thumb on the trigger.

The man lifted one hand in surrender, but kept hold of the struggling lad with the other. The result was that his pants gaped but somehow managed to stay up.

"I'm working for the school, catching runaways, understand?"

Sky snorted. "You planning on catching him in your trousers?"

The man flushed scarlet at the reminder that he'd been caught with his pants round his hips. What was left of his intentions shriveled under Sky's cold stare. He hoisted his pants to cover himself. "Now you listen here—"

The click of the hammer on Sky's gun seemed especially loud. The man fell silent and Sky spoke to the boy in Lakota. "Do not fight, little brother. He will not touch you again."

The youngster stilled and wiped the blood from his chin. The officer let him go. The child moved several paces away and then stopped. Sky released the trigger and lowered his rifle.

"Ah, you speak their lingo. Nice trick. How'd you learn that?"

"From my father."

The man wrinkled his brow in confusion.

"He a trader?"

Sky Fox's mouth twitched. "He was called Ten Horses, a warrior from the Bitterroot tribe."

The man's eyes bugged. A moment later he reached for his pistol. Sky Fox raised his rifle and the officer hesitated, extending his arm away from his weapon.

The two faced off.

"He's gotta come with me," said the man.

"No. He doesn't."

"But he's a runaway."

"Here's what will happen. You'll turn around and ride off alone, or you'll try to take the boy and I'll kill you."

Beads of sweat covered the man's forehead and streamed down his cheeks.

"Can I fasten my trousers?" he asked.

Sky nodded.

The truant officer grappled, fastening the closure and buckling his belt with sweat-slick hands. Then he looked back toward Sky.

"I'm going."

Sky said nothing. The man walked stiffly toward his horse but when he lifted his foot to mount, he went for his pistol.

Sky fired high so as not to hit the horse. Wasn't the horse's fault that he carried such a man. The bullet pierced his shoulder, sending him backward, where he writhed on the ground as blood leaked from the bullet hole. Sky lifted his rifle for the kill shot, aiming between the man's eyes. His prey stilled, staring down the blue-gray barrel at death. Sky's mind flashed back to the arrow notched and drawn, the smooth release and the sound of the tip striking flesh. Sweat blossomed on his forehead and he lowered his gun. *Damn it!*

Seeing Sky would not shoot, the boy grabbed his captor's pistol and aimed the barrel at the man's head, but Sky knocked it from his hand.

The boy glowered at Sky.

Sky placed a foot on the gun. "Killing him won't return what he has taken."

"It is my right."

"Count coup and have done."

The boy hesitated a moment longer, staring at the pistol now securely under Sky's moccasin. Finally, he lifted a sturdy stick, but instead of touching the enemy with it, to prove his bravery, he swung it with all his might. The officer had enough sense to dodge and the branch grazed his temple. He went limp, his head lolling to the side. The boy raised the branch again, but Sky plucked it from his hands.

"Enough."

Sky squatted and checked to see the man was still breathing. Then he looked at the wound. It was ugly, but he wouldn't bleed out. The infection might still kill him but he left that to the Great Spirit. Sky considered tying him to his horse and taking him back to the school. Then he glanced at the lad, seeing disappointment glimmering in his filling eyes. His reaction only confirmed Sky Fox's original guess. This man had abused the boy. The only question was how badly?

Sky stood, determining to leave the man where he lay.

"Come away, brother. It is finished."

The child's shoulders sagged as he stared silently at his tormentor. Sky kicked the pistol several feet away.

"How are you called, little brother?"

"No Moccasins," he answered.

"I am Sky Fox, once of the Bitterroot people."

"I am Sweetwater."

"Did he hurt you?"

He gave one angry shake of denial. Sky Fox wondered about the wounds he could not see because those cut the deepest. He waited for No Moccasins to lift his head.

"He tried, but then you came."

Sky glanced at the truant officer, thinking perhaps he should kill him. He ground his teeth, as he thought of the white man who had taken him from the Black Hills. Like the boy, Sky had stayed only until he was old enough to run. He reached for his pistol and then stopped.

No. As a tribute to the friend he had lost, Sky had vowed long ago never to take a human life and that included this worm of a man.

It was never more difficult to keep his promise than now. He resisted the urge to kill and mutilate the body. It was what his people would do to such a man as this. But the great Lakota had fallen to their knees.

Sky turned toward the boy.

"Where is your family?" he asked.

"They walk before me, except my sister and our uncle. He sent me to the white man's school to learn the stick words, but I ran. My younger sister is still there, I could not bring her."

"Where is your uncle?"

"On the reservation. He's head man."

"His name?"

"He is called Eagle Dancer."

Sky Fox stilled at the name he had not heard in many years. Joy filled him to know his friend and mentor had survived the wars. And sorrow filled him that a great warrior had lived to see his people conquered and penned like sheep. Sky always knew he would come back. He was tired of running and tired of the guilt. The time had come to face his past.

"I know your uncle. I would like to see him again."

He waited. The boy had been taught manners, of course, and hesitated only a moment before extending his hospitality.

He nodded. "We would be honored."

Sky smiled. "We can ride double."

The boy pointed at the unconscious truant officer. "He has a horse."

Their eyes met. Sky knew it was too dangerous. The horse would raise questions. He shook his head. "We take nothing from this man."

No Moccasins gazed longingly at the pistol lying several lengths from his tormentor. Sky placed a hand on No Moccasins's shoulder. The boy flinched and pulled away from the gentle restraint, but nodded.

"I have a fine horse," said Sky. "He is just through there. He is strong and fast."

No Moccasins glanced in the direction of the thicket.

Sky knew it was a shame for a brave to walk and even a boy this age had pride. Women walked, dragging the young ones behind them on travois. Or they did—once.

"You can take the reins. I'll ride behind you."

The boy did not smile, but nodded his acceptance

of the offer. Sky acknowledged that it might be some time before this child lost his vacant expression, but at least he could ride like a warrior until they reached the Great Sioux Reservation.

Sky considered leaving the man his horse and rejected the idea. He should suffer the walk after what he had done. The officer had his gun, also the horse would return to the barn, signaling trouble and triggering a search. Perhaps they would be in time to save this worthless one. Of course, there was a chance the mare would join a wild herd. Sky left that in the hands of the Great Spirit. He removed the saddle and unfastened the bridle. The horse tossed her head and trotted away. He turned to find No Moccasins staring at him.

"How did you come to the people?"

Sky answered honestly. "My people were travelers on the wagon road. They sickened and Ten Horses found them in their wagon. My father still lived and offered his horses to take me to the fort, but Ten Horses took all he wanted and he kept me, as well. He called me Sky for the color of my eyes."

No Moccasins nodded at this. "Do you remember them?"

"No. Ten Horses is my father and I am Lakota. That is all." They mounted and before the evening wind died, they were heading north, to the place the whites could never drive from his heart, back to the people he loved.

Five days passed before they reached the reservation. As they neared Indian lands, Sky avoided the main road. Only full-blood Indians were permitted here. But that was not the only reason Sky skirted the house belonging to the agent from the Bureau of Indian

Affairs. He didn't want to answer questions about his business or how he found his traveling companion. The boy had washed away the blood and now wore a clean shirt that was miles too big for him.

At moonrise they found their way to the small square box that was now the home of Eagle Dancer. His people once blew over the plains with the wind. Now they were scattered about in shabby houses, waiting for government distributions. Such a life was sure to kill a man's soul.

He sent No Moccasins to the door, uncertain of his welcome. It had been years since their parting and there were many reasons for his old mentor to hate him now.

When the door opened again, a man stepped out holding an oil lamp before him. Did the orange flame cast strange shadows or had his face changed so greatly?

Here stood the man who was once the best rider and best shot of the Sweetwater braves. Now he shuffled forward like an old man. Sky recalled watching this warrior ride behind the fleeing bands of women and children, bravely engaging the enemy to give the others time to escape. Sky had worshiped the young man and emulated everything he did. Now Eagle Dancer moved as if each step pained him.

No Moccasins stood at his side, pointing. His friend handed him the lamp and spoke in the direction his nephew indicated.

"Come, brother. You are welcome here," said Eagle Dancer. His voice, at least, had not changed.

Sky Fox stepped into the light and Eagle Dancer smiled. Now he recognized his friend once again. He had maintained the handsome features and his body was still lean and straight. His eyes twinkled as he opened his arms. The two embraced and then drew back.

"Look at you, tall as a buffalo's hump," said Eagle Dancer.

It was true, in his twenty-nine winters, Sky had grown to six feet three inches by the white man's measure, but he liked the Indian reckoning much better. For a moment he felt as if he were coming home.

His friend ushered him in. The interior was a strange combination of white and Indian. The head man had not adopted chairs, keeping to the traditional wooden backrests which sat upon the ground, draped with furs. He had placed four of them in a half circle on the dirt floor before a fireplace made of brick. It reminded Sky of the sacred circle, now cut in half by the white's square dwelling.

Eagle Dancer draped an arm around his nephew. "Thank you for returning this one safely."

They took a seat. Eagle Dancer was a good host. Unlike the whites, he asked no questions, but fed them first.

They dined on pinto beans and bacon with black coffee and a coarse corn bread that crumbled when touched. It was the diet of cowhands, not warriors. No Moccasins could barely stay awake to finish his meal. His uncle bundled him in blankets and he stretched out near the fire on a buffalo skin.

Sky drank his coffee. When he'd had his fill, Eagle Dancer began to talk of the old days and then of their new life here. After a time, he checked the boy and found him sound asleep.

He rejoined Sky beside the fire.

"His face is bruised," said Eagle Dancer.

Only then did Sky report the circumstances of his recovery and his suspicions over his treatment.

When Eagle Dancer spoke, his dark eyes grew vacant.

"They send no food for the children unless they attend the white man's school. What are we to do?"

"I am afraid my shooting this man will not help our people."

Eagle Dancer nodded grimly. "Is he dead?"

"No, though he may die from the wound."

Eagle Dancer's brows descended low over his dark eyes. Did he disapprove of him for not taking the life of a man who deserved death or for bringing such trouble to his doorstep?

"This man is white and so the whites will come."

"We left him alive and took no trophies."

"That was wise."

His friend lifted his tobacco pouch. Sky frowned as he saw the poorly embroidered deerskin sheath. Some of the trade beads had fallen off or sagged on loose threads. It seemed odd that a head man, who should have items of the highest quality, would keep something so awkwardly fashioned.

Eagle Dancer noted Sky staring and handed over the pouch.

"A gift from my wife, the first piece she ever made for me."

Sky Fox held it like the precious object it appeared to be. "She showed great promise."

"I built this house for her, a white man's house, so when she comes back, she will feel at home."

Sky frowned, not knowing what to say to this, but

Eagle Dancer was no longer looking at him. Instead, he stared toward the ceiling. His face had a faraway expression that faded as he reclaimed the plump little bag. Then he sighed and quickly filled his pipe, lighting it with a splinter of firewood. He inhaled deeply as the scent of sweet tobacco rose about them. Instead of savoring the smoke, Eagle Dancer began a deep wet cough. Sky got him some water and that seemed to help. The head man offered his pipe to Sky and they smoked a while.

After a comfortable silence, Eagle Dancer glanced at Sky. "Do you still walk the Red Road, then?"

"My heart is always Lakota."

"I am happy and sad that we are still your people. I had hoped you would find your place with them." He motioned toward the door, indicating the world beyond.

They were silent, Sky Fox thinking back to the last time he saw Eagle Dancer. "I carry that day like a stone in my heart."

His friend studied him for a time. Sky waited for him to cast judgment.

"It is good you do not forget. Perhaps saving *this* boy will help you walk in balance." Eagle Dancer motioned to his nephew.

"I can never repay this debt."

Eagle Dancer did not try to dismiss his opinion, but merely accepted it with a nod. "You feel you must do more and you must do what you must do. So I will tell you that Joy Cat still lives but his eyes are full of clouds now. And your friend's sisters, Forever Flower and Pretty Wren, both lost their husbands in a battle before the Greasy Grass Fight. Maybe you could marry them."

Sky Fox was so stunned, he let the tip of the pipe sag and only just kept it from touching the earth. Certainly he was wealthy enough to keep two wives. Some Sioux warriors had as many as four, but he knew Joy Cat hated him and so he doubted the man would agree. "Would they accept me?"

"I don't know. Many things have changed since those days. The sisters fight a lot now. If they were gone, Joy Cat might marry again. He is a respected head man and we have many widows. Perhaps you can capture a piece of this life with them. But you cannot stay here with them. I am sorry, my brother, but the white men will not see you as one of us."

Sky knew that the treaty allowed only full-blooded Lakota to live on the reservation and Sky Fox did not have even a drop of Indian blood. It was a failing that had always pushed him to be better, faster and braver than his comrades. He had wanted to prove worthy. His eagerness caused him to take the shot that day, to be first to place his arrow in the deer that was not a deer. His head sank as he thought of his friend bleeding in the cottonwood thicket.

"They are good women, strong and pretty."

"Then why have you not taken one?" asked Sky.

They were from the Bitterroot tribe and so Eagle Dancer could marry either or both.

"My heart is not free."

Sky Fox felt a stab of guilt at that. He hesitated.

"Is yours, brother?" asked Eagle Dancer.

"My heart is only broken. I fear it would be a lonely life for a woman."

"You have lost your place in this world. Perhaps you

should take them both and begin a new life from the old."

Sky swallowed hard as he thought of accepting such a responsibility. Would Sacred Cloud want him to marry his widowed sisters? Had his friend lived, he would provide for them. Sky felt the mantle of duty fall heavy on his shoulders.

"Ask her father. If this is his wish, I will marry either or both."

Eagle Dancer smiled and Sky Fox realized he had spoken in haste. He had lived too long with whites and forgotten to consider his words before uttering them. Eagle Dancer still did not know the rest of the burden he carried.

Sky Fox cleared his throat. "There is something more I must say, brother. Then if you still think I should wed the sisters, I will do so. But before you put this question to Joy Cat, I would tell you of my return to the whites."

Eagle Dancer nodded and sat back to listen, putting the pipe carefully aside on the forked wooden holder.

"After you set my feet on the road to the fort, they brought me to their head man and he asked me about other white captives. It was the first thing my new people wanted." He lowered his head in shame.

Eagle Dancer did not ask, but waited, silently.

"I betrayed you, my brother."

Eagle Dancer lifted a brow. It was so different than the way of whites, quick to question, quick to blame, quick to fight. His people were slow to anger, slow to fight. They knew the power of words and so they treated them with great care.

"They showed me a photograph of Sunshine."

The muscles in Eagle Dancer's jaw ticked. Sky hoped he would fly at him, strike him, kill him for what he had done. But Eagle Dancer showed the control of the seasoned leader he had become.

"Why did you do this thing?" he asked in a level voice. Only his eyes showed the agony this news brought him.

Why indeed? Stupidity, arrogance. "We were strong then. I knew the army would not venture off the narrow wagon roads to follow us so far north. They always turned back and even if they did not, I knew our braves would defeat them, for we were many. I never considered…" His words fell off. How could he finish?

Eagle Dancer completed his thought. "That her father and mother would come along and steal her?" His friend gazed off to someplace far away and spoke as if to himself.

"Yes."

"That my own mother would betray her only son?"

Sky's eyes widened. This he did not know and had no response to such a confession. He lowered his head.

"You carry heavy burdens," said Eagle Dancer.

"As do you."

His friend nodded at this.

Sky Fox stood. "I will leave now."

Eagle Dancer extended an open hand. "You will spend the night."

It was a courtesy he did not deserve. It shamed him. He sank back in his seat.

"I have tried many times to die with honor. I do not know why I still live."

Eagle Dancer waited until Sky met his steady gaze.

"I think it is because you walk for two now. If that is so, then you must honor him and lead a worthy life."

The men stared at the dying fire.

"I was with your father when he fell at the Greasy Grass Fight."

Sky's eyes pinned Eagle Dancer. He had heard that his father had fallen at the battle of Little Big Horn, but that was all.

"He fought well and died well."

Sky longed to ask the details but then hesitated. Perhaps it was best to remember him as he had been. "Thank you for telling me this."

"He spoke of you often, worried about you in the world of the Wasicu, just as I have worried over Sunshine. I wonder if she is happy back in that world where she was born." When his friend spoke again, his voice had the faraway quality of wistfulness. "The markings my mother gave her always made my wife sad. But I thought they were beautiful. For a long time after she left, I hoped those marks would bring her back to me. Each morning, when I pray at dawn, I watch the sky turn red and remember the color of her hair. I would give what is left of this useless life just to see her once more."

From behind him, his nephew stirred, crawling out of his bedding and joining them at the fire.

No Moccasins's eyes were wide as if he had been startled awake.

Eagle Dancer quirked a brow. "You have heard all?"

No Moccasins stared. "What color was her hair?"

Eagle Dancer lowered his head and sat in silence, so Sky Fox answered.

"It was red-gold, long and wavy."

No Moccasins ran his hand over his chin. "She bears the mark of the Sweetwater?"

Eagle Dancer now pinned his nephew with a look of intent interest.

"I have seen her. She's at the school."

Eagle Dancer grabbed his nephew's shoulders and stared in astonishment. Then he released No Moccasins and held three fingers beneath his lip and dragged them down his chin. "Like this?"

"Yes."

Eagle Dancer's face lit with joy as he turned to Sky Fox. "My wife has come back to me."

Sky sank to the backrest as if someone had struck him in the stomach. Why would Lucie West return to the Sacred Black Hills?

Eagle Dancer clasped Sky's shoulder. "She is here!" He stood now as if ready to run all the way to the school. Then he looked back at Sky. "I am forbidden to leave the reservation. You must go after her."

Sky gaped, but no words came from his mouth as he rose to face his mentor.

"Please, brother, you must tell her that I still wait, that I have kept my heart only for her."

Sky Fox hated to point out the obvious. "But, my friend, she ran. Why would you want a woman who does not want you?"

"She did *not* run. She was captured, taken where I could not find her. She is searching, too. Don't you see?"

"Perhaps it is not even Sunshine."

"She is the only white woman who bears the mark of Sweetwater. She is here and you are here, just like the time when she was stolen. The hoop has come full circle."

Sky pointed out the other possibilities. "She may be married again or be a mother."

Eagle Dancer shook his head in denial. "No."

"What if she will not come willingly?" asked Sky, dreading the answer.

Eagle Dancer's face grew solemn, but he would not hear the possibility of doubt. "She will come."

"You cannot force her to stay."

Eagle Dancer shook his head. "I will keep her only with the power of my love. It is all the tethers I will need. Go, brother, and bring her back to me."

Chapter Two

The next morning No Moccasins met the older boys at the river. How he envied them. He wished he was fourteen so he would not have to return to the black-robes' school.

The older boys would not normally have shown him any interest, but today they called him over. Their leader used to be called Arrives Late, but he had gone on his vision quest and now had his adult name. No Moccasins wondered how any of them would earn their feathers in a world with no more battles to fight and no more buffalo to hunt.

He knew Red Lightning had seen Sky Fox as he left his uncle's lodge early this morning.

"Why does your uncle allow an enemy into his lodge, Pollywog?" asked Red Lightning, using the nickname No Moccasins hated.

"He is not an enemy."

Running Horse made a scoffing sound. But No Moccasins continued.

"He is the son of Ten Horses."

Running Horse's eyes widened. "I have heard of that one. He killed Joy Cat's son. Joy Cat has only daughters now, very pretty daughters."

No Moccasins did not want the boys to get talking about girls again. He could not understand their endless interest in them, but it seemed to be all they spoke of. Plus he needed their help to find the wounded man.

"He is called Sky Fox and shot the man who captured me."

That got their attention. Both boys now stared at him with such surprised expressions they reminded him of burrowing owls.

"He was..." No Moccasins stammered and then recovered. "He was beating me and Sky Fox shot him." He expanded his chest. "Then I tried to shoot, too."

The boys began to laugh.

"I thought he was serious," said Red Lightning.

"What did you shoot him with?" asked Running Horse.

"I took his pistol."

The laughter stopped.

"Where is this pistol?" asked Running Horse.

"Sky Fox made me leave it behind."

The older boys exchanged a look fraught with meaning.

No Moccasins sensed they were going to leave him here. "I'll lead you."

They were silent for a moment, as if trying to think of a way to do this without him.

"We could follow the buzzards," suggested Running Horse.

"He's not dead," said No Moccasins.

Red Lightning narrowed his eyes. "We'll take him."

* * *

Lucie West eyed the unusual man tying his horse at the hitching post before the blacksmith's shop. His bearing struck her first because it seemed familiar in its supple grace. He did not stand or move like a soldier as he flipped the stirrup over the saddle and loosened the girth. She ran the length of him trying to understand why the sight of this stranger should stop her in her tracks. He was taller than most and broad...what?

Where was his hat? No white man rode in or out without one. Yet, here he stood bare-headed. His shaggy, shoulder-length hair was streaked with gold, bleached by the sun. His face was deeply tanned, but his light hair marked him as white. Perhaps he was one of the many born of both races.

His bare forearm flexed as he untied his saddle-bags and effortlessly flipped the heavy sacks over one wide shoulder. Her gaze caressed his back and powerful legs, the menacing gun belt at his hip and then halted abruptly at his high moccasins. She recognized the style instantly, having once labored to make similar ones, but never with such skill. Was that why she felt the vague sense of familiarity?

They could be a war trophy or trade goods, she told herself. Her objection did not sooth her growing anxiety.

Mrs. Fetterer, who was also a matron at the Sage River School for Indians, noticed Lucie had stopped and followed the direction of her gaze. The woman stood stiff as a starched collar and wide as the paddlewheelers on the Missouri River. Her frizzy hair was tamed in a conservative knot which made her head seem tiny by comparison.

"Ah," she said. "The horse trader. I see he sold the lot."

Lucie kept her eyes on the man. He straightened, his body now tense as if recognizing someone watched him. He turned in a slow circle until he found her and froze with one hand on the saddle pommel. He stared at her with piercing blue eyes, the color of the clear summer sky. Men often stared at her now, but this stare was different. Her breath caught at the connection and then she broke free, looking at the ground that separated them.

The tingling awareness lifted gooseflesh on her skin as she recognized that he was now studying her.

Mrs. Fetterer clasped Lucie's arm and set them in motion.

"Look at the way he gawks at you. No manners at all and wild as the horses he chases." She steered them across the yard. Lucie put one foot before the other, resisting the urge to turn tail and run, which she would most certainly have done if her companion were not compelling her forward. Something about this man screamed a warning. The last time she felt this breathless with uncertainty she had been hiding from the attacking Sioux.

Mrs. Fetterer whispered as they passed the hitching posts before the blacksmiths. "He is a most dreadful man. My husband tells me that he barely utters a word to him, but will jabber in that gibberish to any Indian who wanders in."

Lucie's step faltered. If he spoke Sioux, it was a reasonable assumption that he understood the meaning of the marks on her chin.

"Is he an Indian trader?"

She swore she could feel the man's eyes still boring into her back.

"I doubt he could receive the proper permits. And the Indians are forbidden to buy his horses. I can't see why anyone would want one of those dreadful spotted ponies. If you ask me the cavalry was right to shoot the creatures along with the buffalo. It's the only way to keep the Indians from their mischief."

They reached the trading post and Lucie opened the door, holding it for the older woman and taking the opportunity to glance back.

The man now stood behind his horse, still staring fixedly at her. She hurried after Mrs. Fetterer. Once inside, she moved to the window to keep track of him as he removed his saddle and entered the smithy's shop.

Mrs. Fetterer strolled along the tables, placing a can of peaches in her basket. "Of course, my Oscar believes the man runs guns to the savages."

"Who's that now?" asked Mr. Bloom, the weathered trader that the Bureau of Indian Affairs *did* sanction. Lucie had to wonder at their choice, for he seemed to spend most of his time drinking half of each bottle of whiskey he purchased and then making up the difference with tea. As a result his eyes were watery and his nose had a fine collection of burst blood vessels making the protuberance swollen and crimson in color.

"That horse trader is back. What's his name again?" asked Mrs. Fetterer.

"Oh, you talking about Skylar Fox? I heard he shot a man in Texas and is wanted for hanging." Bloom moved to the window beside Lucie. "He sell that string of ponies?"

"It seems that he has," said Mrs. Fetterer. "Do you

have any good soap, Mr. Bloom? My skin is so fine, it requires quality."

"Right here." He lifted a box from behind his counter. "You got to admire a man that can catch them ponies solo. Wish I knew how he does it. Even the stallions. It just don't make no sense."

"I hope he catches each and every last one of them."

"Say what you like about them ponies. They're fast and they don't need no grain."

"Exactly why we should be rid of them. What about talc powder, Mr. Bloom?"

"None expected."

"Gracious. I'll have to write my sister again." She chose a bar of soap from the crate and lowered it into her basket. "Do you know what the man did when my husband offered to geld his stallions? Well, he laughed, as if it were the funniest thing he'd ever heard."

Lucie glanced back at Mrs. Fetterer as the chill ran down her spine. It bore out her suspicions that he was more than just familiar with the Sioux. No self-respecting warrior would ever ride an altered horse; only full stallions or fertile mares were chosen. Eagle Dancer used to laugh at the cavalry for having to snip off a stallion's bullocks to control them.

"Maybe he's like them wild ponies—just needs civilizing, same as your students."

Mrs. Fetterer sniffed. "That one? He's wild as a wolf, rather. You'd have to be a fool to try to tame that one."

Bloom smiled at Mrs. Fetterer. "Someone for everyone, they say."

She shook her head ruefully. "They also say there's an exception to every rule."

Bloom peered out. "Wonder if he came across Carr? Man should have caught that boy by now."

"That dreadful man," said Mrs. Fetterer.

"He's a good tracker. To him, runaways ain't no different than coyotes. Never been gone this long, though. That boy must be a sly one."

"The man should be fired. I've said so to Father Dumax."

"What'd he say?"

"He dismissed my concerns."

Bloom snorted.

Lucie glanced out the window and was horrified to see the gun-running, murdering, wanted-for-hanging stranger was now heading her way. He stalked forward with his gaze set on the window. She fairly leaped backward and then had the irresistible urge to run out the back door, had there been one.

"Mrs. Fetterer, I'm feeling quite ill. Will you excuse me?"

"I'll only be another minute."

Lucie gritted her teeth, and then stepped behind the door as it swung open. Perhaps it was arrogant to think he came for her, but she had learned by hard experience to listen to the clenching of her belly and the warning shouted by her mind. He took two steps into the room. She slipped behind him, as agile as a weasel, and then darted out into the yard.

She heard the door slam but did not slow as she dashed across the yard.

"Lucie. Lucie West," he called.

How did he know her name?

"I have to speak to you."

Not if she could help it, he didn't.

She had no doubt he could run her down, judging from the length of his legs. But she was prepared to yell her head off if he touched her. And unlike the last time, she was not unarmed. Now she carried the skinning knife that Eagle Dancer had given her.

He did not run after her and she did not turn about until she was safely in her room with the door bolted.

Sky Fox watched Lucie West run as if her skirts were on fire. She had a fine set of legs beneath all that material. He'd never before seen a white woman pick up her hem and bolt like a startled mare, but he'd seen the women of his tribe run like that, fleeing the endless cavalry raids. If she had been a mare, he'd know what to do. Certainly not shout and give chase—though he was sorely tempted to make an exception for her. But that was no way to gain her trust. And he needed that if he were to deliver the message entrusted to him.

He had made a bad start, as usual. Could she have recognized him after so many years? He had been just a boy of eleven then and their encounters had been brief, because he had refused to speak to her. Curious that she should now do the same thing to him.

He followed after her and reached the drilling yard in time to see her slam the door to the girls' dormitory.

He didn't think knocking would do any good. But she'd have to come out sometime and he'd be waiting.

She had been with the blacksmith's wife, so he headed back to see about his girth buckles and Lucie.

The smithy glanced up at him as he entered. "You sell all them ponies?"

Sky nodded.

"Don't know how you break them so quick. Like to see you work sometime."

Sky ignored the request. "You know the new woman here?" he asked pointing at his chin.

The smithy paused the rhythmic hammering to look at Sky.

"I believe that's the most you said to me in eleven months." He moved the iron spike to the coals and pumped the bellows lever to stoke the fire. "Guess you mean Lucie West. She works with my wife, Dora. Powerful odd." He raised one blackened finger to tap his temple, leaving another smudge on his dirty face. "You seen those marks? Indians did that to her. Something like that, well, let's just say we make allowances, is all, on account of her tragic past."

"How long she been here?"

"Come about two weeks back. She's in charge of the younger girls. My wife says she's defiant. Keeps talking to them in that babble whenever she thinks Dora is out of range. She ain't helping 'em. How they gonna learn proper English that-away?"

"She married?"

The man chuckled. "Excuse me, brother, for laughing, but who would want their leavings? I mean she'd be right pretty if not for them fangs, I guess. But them savages had their way with her." He shoved the spike in and out of the coals for emphasis. "Still, fangs or no, I guess they all look the same in the dark." He grinned at Sky.

Sky balled his fists, and resisted the urge to use them. The words of his father floated into his mind like a falling leaf. *A warrior does not strike in anger.* "Saddle ready?"

"Sure is. That'd be fifty cents."

Sky drew out two bits from his pocket and slapped them on the scarred wooden bench, then scooped up his saddle.

"What direction you come from?"

Sky Fox hesitated and then lied. "South."

"Oh, well, I don't suppose you came across Norm Carr, then. He's our truant officer. His horse came back without him. They're out searching now."

Sky kept his face blank.

"Hope them savages aren't up to no good. You know something about them Sioux, don't you?" asked the smithy. "What terrible things do you reckon they done to her?"

Sky pressed his lips together. As far as he knew, her husband had shown her nothing but respect and kindness. It was certain that he still loved her even after all these years. No telling what lay in her heart. Not that he cared to know. Not his concern. He was just the messenger. Hopefully, only that.

"Thank you for the saddle."

The man frowned, moved the glowing spike to the anvil and began hammering again.

Sky took Ceta to the trough and then saw him settled in a stall at the stable. Finally, he returned to the yard to watch the boys marching in lines like infantry. Perhaps the whites thought it fair that they teach the boys to walk after stealing all their horses. The children wore matching steel-gray uniforms and blank faces. Their dark hair had been bobbed as if they were all in mourning. Sky found that fitting, though he doubted their teachers understood the significance of giving their charges such haircuts. They had sheared his hair, too and he had been in mourning ever since.

Sky couldn't save his people, but he tried to save a few of their horses.

The boys finished their useless drilling and strode off to the mess hall. The girls were already at afternoon lessons learning how to stand over stinking cauldrons of dirty laundry. Sky stood in the shade cast by the smithy's shop, waiting for the girls to be dismissed. Then Lucie would escort her charges across the yard to the mess and he'd have another chance to speak to her. He was glad for the excuse because he wanted a second look.

She could not be as lovely as he first imagined. He remembered the girl she had been, hair in a wild tangle down her back, scabby knees and thin as a rail. Even then she had a full wide mouth and lovely vivid blue eyes that reminded him of deep water. Eagle Dancer had seen the promise of what was to be, but even he could not have pictured the blossom that would come from this bud.

If she hadn't been such a beauty, he might have found his tongue when he'd first seen her, instead of staring, speechless as she passed. He'd just never expected her to take his breath away.

She won't want an outcast like you—that's certain.

Knowing that did not stop the stirrings of desire he felt for this woman. He folded his arms across his chest and waited in the shade for Lucie, but when he heard a familiar song, he crossed the dusty yard. It was a couples song, a dance for men and women together. Who would have the courage to sing such a song here?

He listened to the high sweet sound of the clear voice and followed.

Chapter Three

When Lucie had arrived at the Sage River School for Indians two weeks earlier, she discovered that the teaching position she had believed she had accepted was actually a situation as a dormitory matron with assistant teacher duties in the afternoons when the girls' lessons included practical skills training. When she grasped what had happened, she had been tempted to fight for the position she desired, but that would have meant having to speak to the headmaster and now as always, she found her nerve fled at the thought of confrontation. So she swallowed her disappointment and settled for what they offered, mollifying herself with the notion that she could still be of service. But some small part of her wished she could be like her mother, defiant, foolish and brave. It was tiring to be so cautious but it kept her safe and that was most important.

So here she stayed in this isolated school some forty miles north of Moorehead, Minnesota, and the railroad that connected the western edge of the state to the rest of the world. She had not realized that Sage River would be so far from the town, though she was certain that suited the good people of Moorehead just fine. She was also distressed to learn that parents rarely visited the students. Lucie had been here two Saturdays already and seen no one, though she had supervised the writing of several letters, which Mrs. Fetterer also checked for penmanship before they were mailed.

She had admired the work of the priests from a distance and she agreed that reeducation was the only way to prevent extermination of the race. But on arrival Lucie found the theory and practice far removed. Now that she was here, the actual process of matriculation seemed, well, cruel.

Having once been a slave, Lucie now found herself cast in the unlikely role of slave-master and she liked this position little better than the former. Her mind accepted that the alternative to assimilation was extinction, but her heart, oh, yes, her heart whispered words of treason.

Lucie cautioned herself. She knew she must cease her rebelliousness or lose her position. She was a teacher, or she would be someday. It made no sense to jeopardize her place here, so why did she find it so difficult to obey the rules? She had made a bad start with the matrons and priests. But she would do better—must do better.

Today, Lucie had the dubious honor of assisting the lesson on how to properly wash laundry. The older girls were newly arrived and eyed the large cauldrons suspiciously.

One pointed. "They mean to cook us!"

The girls began to scream. Mrs. Fetterer shouted but to no avail.

Lucie raised her voice and called to them in Lakota. "It's for washing the bedding!"

The girls stopped screaming. The ones that were running slowed to a stop and turned to her.

Mrs. Fetterer scowled. "Come back now, all of you."

They did.

The matron turned to Lucie. "I'm reporting this."

Lucie grimaced. How were they to communicate with the students if the girls did not speak English and she was not permitted to speak Lakota?

"They were afraid we meant to cook them."

"Don't be ridiculous." She tugged at her jacket and glanced about at the wide-eyed children, then cast her gaze on Lucie. Her eyes narrowed. "Continue the lesson."

Without another word, she left them, chugging around the building and out of sight. Lucie stared after the woman, knowing she was heading for the headmaster's quarters again.

Lucie bit her lip to keep it from trembling. Despite her efforts, Mrs. Fetterer and the other matrons would have nothing to do with her and spent much time whispering when she appeared. The women here were no different than the ones in California. Well, what of it? She had not come here for them.

Lucie stared out at the girls. They had been slow to accept her. But she still held high hopes. The lesson might be mundane, but learning to do laundry would help her charges to become useful in white society. She set them at their chores washing, wringing and hanging all the sheets. With eighty-six beds, the work was daunting.

Soon the muggy September afternoon conspired against them. The stifling air and steaming water made the task unbearable. The girls perspired in their new uniforms, their cheeks flushed and damp. The rules forbade them to roll up their sleeves or unbutton the collars of their dresses. Lucie looked out at the pink, sweating faces and felt her heart breaking.

Perhaps her compassion made her too soft on them, as Mrs. Fetterer had suggested on more than one occasion. *'Discipline, dignity and diligence,'* her superior had said at every occasion. But those women did not understand the sorrow of being separated from one's family, while being completely besieged by a strange culture and language. Her captivity had given her a deep empathy for her charges. Her compassion warred again with caution.

They looked like flowers wilting on the thirsty ground. The girls kept glancing at her as if for rescue. Something broke loose inside her.

She began to clap her hands in a syncopated beat, one loud beat and then three taps in a steady, even four-count. Again and again she pounded out the rhythm. The girls looked up and then quickly about to see what would happen. Lucie began to sing a round dance song. Some of her charges gasped. One placed a hand over her mouth. Tears sprang from the eyes of two of the older children. The younger ones laughed.

Her students began to smile. Heads bobbed as they swept wooden paddles round and round in the wash water. Lucie felt the first true connection to her students, bringing a glow of satisfaction that resonated in her voice.

The children at the wringers turned the handles, keeping time to the song Lucie sang. Some of the students began to whisper along. Singing was forbidden, except the hymns and the choral pieces they performed for important visitors. Feet began to tap and some moved from side to side, recalling the circle dances they had once joined.

The work became light as each girl moved to the beat Lucie provided. For a little while they were not in a strange place where adults tried to alter everything about them. They were back at the sacred fire, dancing with their people.

Lucie sang from a place deep within herself, until the last of the sheets had passed through the wringer and were hung on the line. The girls hurried to join in an odd ellipse around the cauldrons. They stood shoulder to shoulder, stepping in unison about the yard. Lucie glowed with pride at the smiling faces and nodding heads. Here, now, she had finally connected with them in a tangible way. She sang louder.

The back door to the school flew open and Father Batista stood in the entrance. His mouth hung open a moment and then snapped shut like a trap door. The yard fell silent. Heads bowed, except for Lucie's. She straightened, rising to her full five feet even as her stomach flipped at the dread trickling through her.

"Miss West, what is the meaning of this!"

"I only thought a little music might…"

"Music?" he hissed.

Lucie knew she should apologize. Instead, she stood like the fool that she was, knowing in her heart that what she had done was right. She wanted to ask this man why her students must lose everything that made them who they were. But of course she said none of it. Instead she bowed her head, avoiding his eyes.

"What have you to say, Miss West?"

"I hear the slaves used to sing in the fields to forget their bondage."

His astonishment was equal to her own. Had she really said that? She glanced up and noted the blood rushing to his face as he raised his voice.

"In the drill yard, all of you. Line up for inspection."

The girls hurried into the building to the parade area and she knew she had not changed a thing, but only added to their misery.

"And you, Miss West. Flagrant disobedience. You will come to the headmaster's office immediately."

Batista waited beside her until all the girls had filed through the school and then motioned. Lucie drew a breath for courage and then preceded him. She stepped around the two-story school, now occupied with the boys at lessons, gleaming with freshly applied whitewash. Clearing the building, she stepped into the drill yard. Before her lay the church, in the central position and to the left the priest's private quarters. Behind her and to her right lay the girls' and boys' dormitories, also clapboard. Finally, to her left stood the back of the carpentry and adjoining blacksmith's shops and the stables, which faced the offices of the Bureau of Indian Affairs and their trading post and distribution warehouses for the school. It was a small enclave, but almost seemed a town, with houses beyond the warehouse for the craftsmen paid by the bureau.

Once outside again, she saw the horse trader. He

rounded the building as she reached the yard and headed straight toward her.

"Lucie, hear my words," he said in English.

This time it was Father Batista who stopped him. "She cannot speak to you now, my son."

The man did not stop at the father's words but kept advancing. Lucie looked away.

His next words came in perfect Lakota with no hint of accent. "Please, sister. It is important."

She halted and stared at him.

"A captive, too?" she asked in Lakota.

He nodded once.

Batista clasped Lucie's arm.

"The son of Ten Horses," he said.

She gasped and stared into his cold blue eyes as her skin tingled in recognition. This fierce forbidding man was once a young boy, a captive of the Bitterroot people. She tried to reconcile her memory of that slim boy, adorned with only a loincloth, sitting astride a fine mare, with this menacing stranger. "I remember you."

Batista tugged at Lucie. "English! We speak only English here!" He turned to the stranger. "Go away or I'll have you removed."

The stranger's smile was confident as he switched back to English. "You could try."

Batista went pale, but he recovered with indignation. "I am a servant of God."

"Not *my* god," growled the man.

Batista pressed his lips together and grasped Lucie's elbow. The man looked ready to intercede. He lowered his chin and took a step in their direction. The priest released Lucie and stepped behind her, putting her between him and the approaching threat. Lucie glared a warning as her hand slipped in her pocket and her fingers curled about the knife. The stranger stopped.

"I must speak to you," he said.

She stared up at him. "Why?"

"I carry a message."

Batista hurried away, leaving her alone to face the son of Ten Horses.

Who would send her a message through him?

The answer took the starch from her spine and she swayed on her feet. It couldn't be. Yet who else would choose this messenger but the warrior who had once made her his wife?

"From Eagle Dancer?" she asked in English.

He nodded.

She could barely speak past the cold terror that gripped her throat. "I will not hear it."

Lucie whirled away, half expecting him to grab her or throw her over his shoulder. Had he been sent to capture her again? She lifted her skirts and hurried away, squeezing her eyes shut against the memories of her capture that flashed, like heat lightning, through her mind. Somehow she reached the church offices and sank onto a bench. She was glad to sit, for her head was spinning.

This was the blue-eyed boy who had ridden with Sacred Cloud, the son of one of the war chiefs of the Bitterroot tribe. He would not speak to her, despite her repeated efforts. The People said he was taken from a wagon full of dead people and that was why he had ghost eyes, though they were merely a startling blue. Her parents had told her that he did not remember his real family and none could be located. According to her mother, Sky was the one who had recognized her photo and told them where she was. She owed her rescue to him. She had never even thanked him.

What had happened to the boy after the immigrant had taken him? He'd gone west, but where she could not remember. Like her, he had come back to the plains. Only she had not come to return to the Sioux. Oh, no, not ever again. Her captivity had been too harsh and, although her return to her people had been hard, she had never feared for her life…until today.

How had Eagle Dancer survived the many battles? She thought back to the day she had been taken from her mother and made a slave of the Sweetwater People. For the months that followed, Lucie felt the cruelty of captivity. The beatings, the work and the lack of food nearly killed her. But the hope of rescue had sustained her during that dark time. She knew her mother would not stop looking for her and she had been right. Still she couldn't have survived to see that day if not for Eagle Dancer. His interest in her had proved to be a mixed blessing, for he fell in love with her and had elevated Lucie from slave to wife. The choice seemed an obvious one at the time. Even at thirteen, Lucie had known her life depended on his protection. And although he had never mistreated her, he would not let her go. Her feelings for him were still a raw tangle of gratitude and resentment. Even now she felt remorseful for having fled, knowing her escape would hurt him. But why should she feel guilty? She was a prisoner. It was her duty to escape.

Lucie bowed her head, knowing that was only part of her misery.

Beneath the regret burned a secret shame at having been his wife. She knew what people would say if they knew she had willingly wed an Indian. That was why she never spoke of it, never thought of it, had tried every day for twenty years to pretend it never happened. Her parents thought she had been forced. But the choice had been hers. Wed or remain a slave, live or die. And her great shame was that, despite the cost, she had chosen life.

Unlike the revered heroines of the books and magazine stories who protected their honor above all else. She found the price too high. Lucie's chin sank to her chest as she cursed herself for being a coward.

She felt sick to her stomach. The priest, Mrs. Fetterer, Mr. Bloom at the trading post.

No. They must not learn of it. She would protect her secret as she had always done.

Why did this messenger chase her, haunting her like a ghost from her past? One look at him told her he would not give up. If she spoke to him, made him understand, would he go away before the others found out her shame? She sat torn between two equally bad options. She did not want to go to him, but she could not afford not to. She sat frozen with indecision.

Father Batista opened the door. "Miss West?"

Lucie dragged to her feet, preparing to be contrite, demure and submissive. Lucie had learned from experience that there were many fights she could not win. But she might win if she was repentant and she would do anything to stay here with the girls and protect her position.

What had gotten into her back there? She needed this work, needed to stay here. So why did she jeopardize everything, why couldn't she do as she was told? She had never been defiant before. It baffled her. She had survived captivity only by obedience and she had continued with this course while under her parents' roof, deferring to her mother's judgment up until she had taken this position. Had she made a terrible mistake, as her mother believed? If she had stayed at home, none of this would have happened.

But her parents' home had become intolerable, a kind of stifling prison that wore out her soul. She couldn't go back there. Better to be a spinster schoolmarm than a full-grown woman hiding like a child under her parents' roof. Lucie wanted to find her own place, somewhere where she belonged, was wanted. The girls needed her—didn't they?

Then why couldn't she keep her mouth shut? She clamped her lips together, vowing to be silent, to push down her objections. Lucie squeezed her eyes shut tight.

What had changed? Why was she suddenly rebellious when she knew full well that such behaviors only made her way more difficult? These strange actions exposed her and frightened her. She must stop, do as she was told.

Father Dumax stood at his desk, hands behind his back. His head looked like a melon except for the fringe of hair at his temples and beneath his round jowly chin. The man's bushy brows hung low over his eyes. The deep lines at his mouth seemed more engrained as he frowned at her.

"I have just spoken with Mrs. Fetterer and now Father Batista has made me aware of a serious offense."

She noticed the dust covering his black robe. Everything here was coated in dust, because they had stripped away all the grass to make a yard for marching.

"Is it true? Were you leading the girls in some heathen ritual?"

"It is a song that we danced to. It was just to lighten the load of work."

The men exchanged a look. Batista lifted his brows at her confirmation.

Lucie tried to apologize. "I'm very sorry, Father. I only tried…"

"Yes?"

"They're lonely, frightened and heartsick for their families. I just wanted to bring them a moment's peace."

"Lucie, these are a defeated people. They are wards of the government. You do them no service encouraging them to revert to their aboriginal ways. The only chance these girls have for survival is to learn to be civilized. You of all people should appreciate that."

Lucie rubbed her chin, feeling the echoing pricks of the bone awl Yellow Bird had wielded against her. There was no hiding the dreadful blue fanglike marks.

Even the good father was unable to keep from glancing at her tattoos. She thought it might be different here, but it was worse, because now she was more confused than ever. Somehow she remained standing under the crushing disappointment.

She squared her shoulders.

What this man could not see painted on her face was that her time with the Sioux had taught her fortitude. She knew at a glance she was stronger than this man.

"They need compassion, as well," she said.

His eyes rounded in surprise and he was left momentarily speechless at her audacity. Had she just done it again? She felt her face flush.

He blustered a moment and then found his tongue.

"Miss West, it is our calling to educate these poor heathens. But we must kill the Indian to save the man."

She bowed her head, but the words came nonetheless. "It's wrong."

"You are in no position to judge. I begin to suspect Mrs. Fetterer is correct. These savages have damaged your mind. I cannot permit you to undermine our good work."

She lifted her chin. "They are not uncivilized. Their way is just different, not wrong."

He rounded the desk to face her. "Miss West, we have made allowances for you because of your tragic past. We have spoken to you about using only English around the children. Yet you persist in your willfulness and then, when caught, you are unrepentant. Father Batista says you were just speaking in Sioux to a man, immediately after he intervened."

"That's true."

"So I ask you, Miss West, why you would do something that would jeopardize your position here, when in our last meeting you assured me that you would take all actions required to keep your situation?"

Lucie held her breath. He was going to dismiss her. She could see it in his eyes.

"We brought you here as an example to the children, to show them the results of their savagery and to encourage them to repent and accept Christ, our Lord. But this situation has not worked out as hoped. It is not your fault, child. We will pray for you, but as of this moment you are relieved of all duties at this school. I will, of course, telegraph your parents and ask them to collect you."

Lucie felt her heart squeeze in panic. Why had she

chanted that silly song? "Please, Father. I can't go back there. I have to find my *own* place."

"Perhaps, with God's grace, you shall. But it will not be here." His eyebrows rose. "Be at peace, child. Your parents assured me that you will always be welcome in their home."

"But that's just it. It's *their* home. I need, I want… Please, Father…" Words failed her.

Silence stretched. When she had brushed the tears from her cheeks, she lifted her head to find Father Dumax studying her.

"You have had a difficult journey. Although I do not forgive your disobedience, it does give me pause. If you are truly remorseful and can devote yourself to our mission, I will follow the good Lord's example and forgive you. You have one more chance, Miss West. I pray you will use it wisely."

Behind her, Father Batista made a sound that reminded Lucie of a hog rooting for scraps. She did not need to look to see the man's disapproval.

"Thank you, Father."

"Thank God, for his mercy, and recall that we are not the enemy. We are all trying to save these poor savages, but unlike you, I must worry about more than their bodies. I am also responsible for their souls."

Lucie nodded her agreement and said nothing more.

He opened the door and Lucie slipped out.

She was halfway across the yard when she remembered the stranger. She hesitated, but found no sign of him. She reached her room and sat at her desk to write her parents, to tell them that she was failing here, as well. She must be such a disappointment to them.

It was as if part of her was still out there in the

prairie, still there with the Lakota people and the rest of her was here in this world. But like vinegar and oil, she could find no way to blend the two.

She heard the girls return to the dormitory as Lucie reread what she had written. The letter was too raw and far too sad to send to her parents. She wadded up the page and tossed it on the floor.

She had saved her position, but in doing so she had agreed to do what she felt was wrong. Should she stay here or go back to California and again live like some addled child in her parents' home? Lucie winced. Her gaze wandered out the window to the place where the lawn was not trimmed and the tall prairie grasses swayed. There was a third option. No, she would never go back to him. He'd refused to release her even when she had begged him to do so. She'd escaped, but he'd kept her too long. Now she had no home, no place where she belonged.

The bell for dinner chimed and Lucie rose to collect her charges and walk them to the dining hall. Eating meals together with all the proper silverware was an important step in assimilation. She took pride in her table of the youngest, each of whom used their napkin correctly. She was still working on the proper way to hold the fork and, of course, they needed help cutting some of the larger bits of meat and potatoes. She lined her students in even rows, five across and marched behind the older girls to their place at the tables. Lucie had them all seated and had bowed her head, when she realized the oldest girls, the ones with whom she had been for the laundry lesson, were missing from their place.

She sought out Mrs. Fetterer, interrupting her as she prayed and received a harsh glare.

"Punished," the matron said.

Lucie's stomach twitched. "For the singing?"

"For uttering their gibberish and all of it entirely your fault."

Lucie straightened. "Where are they?"

"The chapel."

Lucie hurried away. Mrs. Fetterer hissed after her. "What about your charges?"

Lucie did not turn or look back. She stormed across the drill yard like an infantry officer only instead of a saber she held her indignation.

She found the girls on their knees before Father Batista, who was administering something to them like communion. It was not until she drew closer that she recognized it was slivers of soap from a large bar used for laundry.

"What are you doing?" Her voice held all of the fury of her ire.

"They need to understand the rules and pray for forgiveness for their heathen ways."

"Father, it's my fault that they were singing."

He placed another wafer of soap on a girl's tongue. She made a face and swallowed hard.

"Oh, Mattie, don't eat that."

Batista cast her a glance. "I told them to eat them. This is all they will have for supper."

It took all she had not to strike the silver dish from his hand and then knock him to the ground. How could they be so heartless and stupid?

"I am responsible."

"I agree. But unfortunately Father Dumax has

absolved you. These children need a firm hand if they are going to give up their godlessness."

Lucie glanced down the line of girls. There were sixteen or so still waiting for their lesson.

"I'll take their punishment."

Father Batista's eyebrows lifted. He opened his mouth and then closed it again, assessing her. A smile played on his lips. "All right."

"And in return these girls will go to supper."

His smile vanished. "But they will stay to watch and if you cannot take all their 'meals' then they will have them."

"Done."

She felt her stomach lurch in anticipation.

"Kneel, my child," he said.

She did and opened her mouth. The first sliver of soap touched her tongue. She tried to swallow and gagged. On the second try, she forced it down, but it tried to come up again. She had to press her hand over her mouth and squeezed her lips shut, focusing all her will on keeping the soap in her belly. At last she opened her mouth and accepted the next.

When she looked at Batista she saw the triumph in the priest's eyes. It was all the inspiration she needed to swallow the next and the next. Her stomach churned. She knew it would revolt eventually and so she accepted the unholy communion with greater speed.

The girls were crying now. Mattie, kneeling beside her, grasped her arm and shook her.

"No, no, missus."

Lucie held up her hand to stop Mattie. The jostling made her stomach lurch. She clamped her hands over her mouth.

"Only three more," said Batista. "But I'd say you've had enough. You're green as a pickle."

Lucie opened her mouth. The taste of lye coated her tongue and throat again as she swallowed the next piece and the next.

Batista's smile vanished as he saw his victory slipping away. His lips now pinched in an angry scowl as he fed her the last wafer of soap.

Lucie swallowed.

Batista set aside the tray as Lucie clutched her belly. He clapped his hands. The girls startled.

"Up, all of you, and off to supper! Hurry now, you are late already."

He turned and left Lucie there on her knees, following the girls out.

Lucie fell forward to her hands. She knew she would be ill, but did not want Batista to have the satisfaction of seeing her. So she staggered out the side door and vomited on the ground. Over and over her stomach expelled the foul contents until there was nothing but bile left to release. Lucie sat, sweating on the stoop. It was many minutes before she could stand.

In those minutes she questioned again her decision to come and to stay. How could she be a part of this? This assimilation was not a gentle, loving hand. They did not offer enlightenment but a cruel discipline.

She kicked dirt over the mess she had made. Lumps of white soap poked out through the sand. She swallowed and still felt sick. In the kitchen she found water, which did not settle her stomach, but only launched her into a new round of illness. Finally, she tried a little bread and this made her tortured stomach settle.

Only then did she rejoin her girls at the table. She

felt the eyes of every student upon her as she entered. Had the word of her actions spread so quickly?

She tried to keep her thoughts on her students, but instead she came again to the feeling that she had made a mistake coming to this place.

Lucie remembered the blue-eyed stranger and wondered at the message he carried. She rose to her feet, feeling pulled in two directions at once.

All afternoon and evening, Sky Fox had followed Lucie. He'd heard her singing on the laundry yard. She had a fine, clear voice, full of passion and joy. The sound had made his insides jump and twitch like a rabbit caught in a snare. But the blackrobe did not like her song. Disobedient, he called it. Sky Fox had wondered how it was disobedient to follow your heart. Would it lead her back to the Sweetwater People?

Perhaps Eagle Dancer was right and Lucie did belong with the Lakota. He was sure of only one thing. She did not belong here.

His opinion had been confirmed later as he'd watched her at her writing desk composing something. She'd paused often, pressing the end of the pen to her lips as she stared up to the ceiling. He'd considered climbing through the dormitory's low window to tell her what he must, but something held him back. He'd realized then that Lucie entranced him and made him entertain ridiculous possibilities. He of all men should know better. He did not want to enter her world and he could not return to his own.

Now, once she left to join her charges for the evening meal, he retrieved the page she had tossed aside. The letters were slanted and joined together in a long looping scrawl. He could not recognize them. His disappointment was deep as he sat on the floor to study her writing. Gradually, he recognized the letters, joined by the ink, one to the next. *Dear Parents,* it began. So, the two who had stolen their daughter back from a Sioux warrior still lived.

He read on, and with each word his heart broke a little more. Here on this crinkled page were the very things he kept locked in his heart: longing, hope, despair and loneliness. Sky stood and folded the page, then slipped it inside his shirt, pressing it against his chest.

He wanted more. He scanned the room, taking in the tidy washstand holding a tortoise comb and wooden brush. A small glass jar held several hair pins. Several black ribbons draped the rack beside the wash towel. She certainly wasn't a fancy woman.

He turned next to the chest of drawers, surprised to find each one empty. Where did she keep her clothing? He checked the wardrobe. She had only one dress and a bulky wool overcoat hanging on the pegs. He stood in puzzlement. A check under the bed revealed no other belongings. What about her underthings and woolens?

Sky returned to the wardrobe and drew the dress aside. Below, half-hidden at the bottom, lay a trunk. He smiled and drew it out into the light. The container was locked. What was she hiding? He used his knife to pry open the lid.

Inside, he found a gray wool shawl with matching hat and mittens, several pairs of long socks and some underthings. Each item was not folded but neatly rolled. It struck him that she stored her possessions in a box like a Sioux woman, instead of hanging them on pegs or placing them in the drawers like a white woman. She was packed, ready to leave at a moment's notice, just like the People.

He lifted the shawl and inhaled, smelling lanolin instead of Lucie. Beneath the shawl lay a red blanket. He noticed the cardboard next and drew out a small rectangle she had tucked against the back of the case. It opened like a book. Inside he found two matching photographs, portraits of a man and woman. The couple smiled out at him and he recognized them at once.

Lucie's parents. Her mother had dark hair, but Sky recalled it was a deep red. She smiled stiffly for the camera. His gaze flicked to the man. Lucie had inherited much from Thomas West: his eyes, the shape of his chin and the pale color of his hair. They were handsome people, but neither was as beautiful as the sum of their parts. Lucie shone with the best of both.

He replaced the photo and lifted the blanket, but paused as he noted something secreted within. He searched and could not have been more astonished at his discovery. There, carefully protected in the wool, lay a worn pair of beautifully embroidered moccasins. Had Eagle Dancer given her these?

He drew them out and found another surprise. Inside, near the toe of one, hid the sheath for a woman's skinning knife. Sky stared down at the symbol of a woman's coming of age. The cord had been carefully wound around the cover. It was common for a woman to wear her knife about her neck. Sky uncoiled the necklace to reveal that Lucie's sheath was adorned with a red-and-white sun pattern.

Where was the blade?

Sky sat back on his heels as a notion took him. Could

she be still carrying her knife? When she'd faced him in the yard, one of her hands had vanished into her skirts. Had she reached for the weapon? He felt ill as he realized Lucie was frightened of him. What must it be like for her, having this stranger appearing, following, watching?

He must speak to her. It was cruel to delay any longer.

He stood and looked about at the picture that did not fit. She dressed as a white woman. She kept a tortoise comb and boar's hair brush. She wore leather shoes with stiff soles and her hair in a tight, constraining little knot. In all visible ways, she appeared to be a white woman. But here, hidden in her personal effects where her precious belongings were kept, beside her parents' photograph, were these things.

He wound the cord back about the sheath. A moment later came the tap of heels upon wood planking. He had time to leave, but did not. Sky would deliver his message now.

The latch clicked. He faced the door as it swung open and Lucie stepped into the room.

Chapter Four

The boys had been away from the reservation for four days, trotting along on sturdy legs, when they reached the spot where the officer had been shot.

No Moccasins shouted and the others stopped. "This is the place."

A quick scout of the area showed the torn grass and gouged earth, where he had struggled with the officer. Blood, now dry and brown, spattered the brush behind them.

"You see?" No Moccasins pointed. "I told you, Sky Fox shot him."

"Why would a white man shoot a white man over a scrawny Indian boy?"

"Because he is Ten Horses's son."

Running Horse snorted. "He lost that right before we even walked the earth."

Red Lightning studied the ground. "He went this way."

They did not find the man until the next day. He

was within ten miles of the school, walking slowly and favoring his injured shoulder. The boys gave a war whoop and set off at a run. No Moccasins felt his stomach flip, but he would not turn back. This man had tried to violate him. He wanted him dead, didn't he?

Norm Carr turned at the war cry and drew his pistol. He broke into a run, firing wildly at them as he bolted in the opposite direction. He was heavy and slow. Running Horse already had his bow notched and let the first arrow fly. It struck its target, piercing the man's thigh and protruding out the other side.

The truant officer howled and toppled, trying an ungainly crawl using his one good leg and his uninjured arm. Water Snake reached him first, being the fastest. Running Horse had tried to avoid telling his little brother about their raid, but he had followed them off the reservation. Water Snake was a year younger but taller and faster than his elder. But Running Horse was the better shot and he let a second arrow fly, hitting the man's good leg. Carr went down, lifting his gun and pulling the trigger. The hammer clicked uselessly against the empty chamber.

Red Lightning now caught up with Water Snake and together the two boys fell on the Wasicu. The officer had time only to roll to his back and scream before Water Snake had the man's scalp. No Moccasins's stomach heaved at the popping sound of the skin releasing from the bone beneath. Water Snake lifted his trophy, calling his triumph to the sky.

Carr was begging for his life now. No Moccasins had to recall the rough hand upon his neck as the man forced him to his knees. He could still feel the erection rubbing against his face. Shame burned deep as the first war cry erupted from No Moccasins. He lifted the club he had taken from his uncle's home, the one made of cottonwood and the filed elk bone that made a fine point. He swung the club above with all his power and came down hard upon the man's forehead. Bone struck bone and the fanglike elk point broke off in the man's skull.

Norm went slack. His eyes stared fixedly up at No Moccasins. The boy lowered the broken club and stared down at his attacker. No Moccasins's shoulders heaved with the force of his breathing as he waited for the sense of justice to fill him. Instead, he felt more afraid than before. New worries gripped him. He looked at the club. His uncle would know he had broken it.

"Take a trophy," said Water Snake.

No Moccasins did not want any reminders of this day.

"Step aside," said Running Horse. He leaned down and sliced off the man's ear. "Here. Take this."

Running Horse had to clasp No Moccasins's hand and force the bloody lump into it. No Moccasins gripped the ear, still warm and sticky. He turned his back and vomited in the tall yellow grass.

Something was amiss. Lucie sensed it without knowing what was wrong. Her skin prickled and her ears grew hot as her eyes swept the interior of her room.

Everything was still and quiet. The curtains didn't even stir. She cocked her head to listen.

She took one cautious step into the room and then realized what was wrong. It was difficult to see at first because it was not something moved, but rather, something removed. Her letter!

Lucie walked to the place beside the window where she had tossed the wadded page. Her step faltered. Missing! She crouched to peek under the desk and then to peer under the bed. Nothing.

Someone had been in her room.

She immediately suspected Mrs. Fetterer. The woman had an unnatural interest in her business. Lucie turned a full circle and then spied the wardrobe. Her hands lifted to her cheeks. She wouldn't, would she?

Lucie rushed to the door and slid the hook into the eye, locking herself in, and then she hurried to the wardrobe, threw open the doors and dragged her trunk out onto the floor. She fingered the latch. Someone had pried open her trunk.

She cast back the lid and gazed down at the contents. They looked untouched. What if they had found…Lucie threw her belongings onto the floor. The red blanket still covered her secrets. She set it aside and lifted the beaded moccasins, pressing them over her heart. She bowed her head and breathed again. They had not found this, at least.

She burrowed a hand into the soft, supple deer hide and retrieved the beaded sheath, looping the cord about her neck. She then retrieved the knife from her pocket and slipped it into its holder. Eagle Dancer had given her these things, a gift to his wife. Lucie squeezed her eyes closed and lowered her head as the mixed emotions ripped through her again.

She hated him for keeping her, for forcing her to choose between the wretched life of a slave and that of a child-bride. But beneath all that she recognized that he did love her in his way. Why should she feel guilty for leaving him?

It made no sense. Why couldn't she put her captivity behind her? Why was it so hard to be a white woman again? If not for the outward marks she might have slipped away, gone where no one knew her and started again. But that path was closed to her the day Yellow Bird used her awl to mark Lucie as Sweetwater. Now she could never leave this time behind. One needed only to glance at her to know who she was and where she had been.

She was forever changed, both inside and out.

The hairs on Lucie's neck prickled. She dropped her moccasins and drew her knife. She came about, spotting him standing just outside her window. How long had he been watching her?

And then it made sense. It was not Mrs. Fetterer who had invaded her room, but this man. She stepped back, nearly tumbling over her open trunk. When she righted herself, he had already vaulted through the window. He landed, catlike, in a crouch, one hand brushing the floor. There was no sound, as he did not wear the thick-soled boots of the whites, preferring the soft, supple footgear of the Sioux.

"Lucie," he said.

She held her knife out before her.

His next words came in the soft rolling cadence of the Sioux. She understood every word, despite the shaking of her head.

"Your husband has sent me to you. He has a message he would have you hear."

She answered in English. "Leave my room this instant."

He held his hands wide, not in surrender, but rather in a fighting stance she recognized well from her days watching the boys train to become warriors. He meant to disarm her. She glanced at the door, judging its distance and finding it too far. She would have to fight.

When she glanced back he was three steps closer and just beyond the reach of her blade. She aimed for his midsection, struggling to keep him back as she inched toward the door. He did not need to dodge, but as her arm passed him, he captured her wrist. With a twist, the knife fell from her fingers and clattered to the floor.

"Will you listen?" he asked.

Lucie used her last weapon. She opened her mouth to fill her lungs with air and scream. But he spun her against him and she struck his chest with a force that jarred the breath from her. Before she could inhale again he had his large palm clamped against her mouth. Two of his fingers locked beneath her jaw, preventing her from opening her mouth to bite him.

The next second she was facedown on the bed. He used his body weight to hold her as he stuffed a wad of fabric in her mouth and then secured a gag, pulling the bandanna so it sliced across her mouth, holding her jaw locked open. He wrenched her arms behind her back and tied them with a speed that terrified her.

It was happening again. Lucie's brain ceased to function. She kicked and writhed as he trussed her like a turkey.

No, no. Not again. How could she be captured again?

When he had finished, he sat her on the bed and returned her skinning knife to its sheath about her neck. He stood before her, his arms folded as he glared.

"Now you *will* listen."

His head turned. An instant later Lucie heard it, as well. The murmur of voices grew louder as the girls returned to the dorm. Then came the distinctive heel tap of Mrs. Fetterer's shoes in the hallway. The knock made Lucie jump.

"Miss West? Are you in there?"

Lucie glanced at the tiny latch she had thrown when she entered the room and prayed Mrs. Fetterer would sound the alarm. The matron tried the door. Lucie's heart stopped.

"Oh, for heaven's sake." Her footfalls retreated.

Lucie's shoulders sagged. Skylar Fox might have returned to his natural race, but Lucie knew by his stance and his drawn knife that he was still every inch a Sioux warrior. And, although she wanted Mrs. Fetterer to bring help, she did not want the woman to be taken. Lucie had known other captives. Few had lived to see rescue. Lucie knew with cold certainty Mrs. Fetterer would not survive such an ordeal. She turned her attention back to the warrior. If she could just speak to him, she'd tell him that she would listen now. He did not need to take her from this room.

His voice was low and gruff as he spoke to her in Lakota. "We cannot talk here."

Lucie shook her head, but to no avail. Skylar Fox removed her shoes and replaced them with the moccasins. Then he wrapped her in the red blanket and tossed her over his shoulder. She heard the window squeak as he raised it to its full height and climbed to the sill. He hesitated long enough to transfer her from his shoulders and into his arms. Then he jumped, carrying her from the safety of her room and out into the moonless night.

* * *

Sky carried her into the darkness, as she writhed and squirmed in his arms. Lucie felt like an earthworm trapped in the beak of a robin. Eventually exhausted, sweating beneath the wool blanket, she stilled. A moment later he slung her over his shoulder and mounted his horse.

The school was not a fort. Although most visitors arrived through the gate, there was no barricade that prevented a rider from going in any direction.

He nestled her in his arms and drew the blanket off her face. Cool evening air rushed about her as she twisted but she could not slip free. His arm clamped about her waist, drawing her tight to his body, trapping her in place. She saw the lights from the girls' dormitory retreating until they had ridden down the hill and into the valley. Was he taking her to Eagle Dancer?

But the warrior could no longer keep her—could he? A terrible thought sprung upon her. What if he was not one of those on the reservation, but a hostile, raiding, or one of the many who had bolted for Canada with Sitting Bull?

The words of her mother came to her. Sarah West had been horrified that her daughter would even consider returning to the Dakotas. She had forbidden Lucie from taking the teaching position, claiming Minnesota was too close to the Sioux lands. Lucie rarely argued, but she did this time, reminding them that they had let her little brother, just nineteen, join the cavalry. David was stationed less than a hundred miles away at Fort Sully. But her mother was unyielding in her edict. Lucie's lip trembled as she realized her mother had been right.

The pommel dug into Lucie's hip and she squirmed. The steely grip tightened further, cutting the air from her lungs. She willed herself to relax, listening for some sign that she had been missed. But all she heard was the unceasing wind blowing through the grass and the dull thud of the unshod hooves of his horse. The horse's white patches gleamed gray in the darkness. Everything about her was bathed in shadows. Above, the sky glistened with a shimmering glaze of stars. Lucie breathed deeply. The arm about her waist relaxed by infinitesimal degrees. She did not try to escape because, with her legs and arms bound, all she would accomplish was falling off the horse. Once again, she must be patient and wait.

As the horse continued on, her arms went numb. Gradually the ropes of muscle that constrained her relaxed, until he held her in a gentle embrace. She refused to look at him, instead focusing on the horse's neck, which bobbed with the gentle rhythm of its steps. Half the mane was white and the other dark. He rode a spotted mustang. Exactly the type of horse an Indian would favor and precisely the sort of creature the whites abhorred. Hadn't General Crook shot as many as he could catch after the Big Horn? The general had rightly surmised that without their horses, the Sioux could not make raids and without their buffalo, they could not feed their families.

Lucie's head began a steady pounding that seemed to echo the horse's steps. Dark shapes appeared before them, blocking the stars on the horizon. Trees, she realized. The cottonwood and willow grew near water. They must be near the wide muddy creek that ran northwest of the school. They entered the thicket. Sky paused to let his horse drink. When the mustang raised his head, Sky slid Lucie from the saddle and deposited her on the ground, sidestepping with the horse as her legs gave out. Had he expected her to be able to stand after this ordeal?

He was beside her now, whispering her name as he drew her from the blanket.

She saw the gleam of the knife and could not understand why her heart did not at once leap to her throat. Was it his purposeful expression or the absence of malice in his movements?

He sliced the cords at her wrists and her hands sprang apart. He rubbed her arms vigorously until they prickled and ached. She drew away and reached for the gag, but he spun her and released the knot. She spit out the wadding he had forced in her mouth.

Sky offered his drinking skin. Lucie had enough experience with captivity to know never to reject food or water. She drank as much as she could hold and then handed back the half-empty pouch.

Only then did she recall that he had returned her weapon. He was bigger, faster and stronger than she was. He'd already proven he could disarm her. So she remained seated as he released the bonds about her legs.

Why had they stopped so close to the school? The last time she had been taken, the Indians had ridden three days with barely a pause before stopping to eat and rest. They were within a mile or two of the school, too close to avoid pursuit, but far enough away that no one would hear her scream.

Lucie waited, uncertain of her situation or his purpose, for him to speak. He stared at her a long time, his face cast in shadows that made him all angles. But even in the starlight, his eyes glowed ghostly pale. His expression was serious. Did she see regret in his eyes? She hoped so, for she planned to pounce on any weakness like a kitten on a beetle.

He lifted his hand. She did not shy or flinch as his thumb brushed her cheek in a feathery touch that seemed too gentle for such a large man. Now her heart accelerated. There was no mistaking the caress. It made her wonder if his intentions did not run toward abduction but rape. Many white men thought she should count herself lucky if they took this sort of interest in her. Why had she thought him any different?

She'd learned that a man would say anything to have what he wanted. The boldest tried to take her by force. Until today, she'd always had her father or her brother, David, to protect her.

His eyes remained constant and his expression nearly pained as his hand dropped to his side.

"I've marked your face."

Lucie lifted her fingertips to feel the creases on her cheek. Slowly she touched the skin beneath her mouth. "My face is already marked."

She lifted her chin as if daring him to maintain the contact of their eyes. Here most men would flush and look away. But he did neither. Instead he cupped her jaw in his palm and studied her fanglike tattoos.

"It only adds to the beauty of your mouth." As if to prove his point his thumb grazed over her lower lip.

The contact sent off a shimmering ripple of excitement inside her that alarmed her further. What was happening here?

He released her and her jaw dropped open. Had he said *beautiful?* No one had used that word to describe her since before her capture. Back then she was beautiful and darling and a joy. Afterward the words she heard to describe her were *hideous* and *tragic* and *ruined*.

She closed her mouth and straightened at his mockery. "It's ill-mannered to say such a thing."

He squatted back on his heels, resting his forearms casually on his knees. "Have you let them convince you that you're not beautiful, Lucie? Have you let them take away your power? Don't listen. They're wrong."

He seemed so sincere that she almost believed him.

"You *are* beautiful, no matter what you think."

Lucie folded her arms over her bosom and glared. "Why did you bring me here?"

Her skin prickled again, but not in warning of danger. This was a different kind of warning, one that only happened when he drew near. She did not have experience with this feeling, but she recognized it— the pounding heart, the rapid breath, the light-headed feeling that came to her like a child spinning in circles. Somehow, against all reason and good judgment, she found this man exciting.

"Did you murder a man in Texas?"

"In Texas?" His brows rose and his smile did nothing to reassure. "No."

That left a great deal of territory where he could have murdered.

"Are you a wanted man?"

His smile faded. "No. No one wants me. I am just like you."

That stopped her and it took a moment to recover her thoughts. "But you left with that family. You don't look different. It would be easy for you to…"

"To what? Forget who I am? Deny everything I feel inside? No, that is not easy."

Lucie could not meet his cold gaze. After an awkward silence, she found the courage to look at him once more. "You didn't stay with that Mormon?"

His lips drew into a thin line and he lowered his chin. He looked as dangerous as a bull buffalo defending the herd. She eased her hands to the blanket, preparing to flee.

"I did not bring you here to speak of him."

Lucie allowed him to steer the conversation away from a sensitive subject. "Why *did* you bring me?"

He stood and extended his hand. She didn't need it, but found herself slipping her fingers into his callused palm and allowing him to draw her up. He held her a little too long. She stood a little too close.

Sky released her and stepped back, but continued to gaze down at her, unwilling, it seemed, to break the contact of their eyes.

"I promised your husband that I would find you and deliver his message. I owe Eagle Dancer a great debt and could not refuse."

Lucie turned her back on him, stepping off the blanket and into the tall grass that lined the bank. Beside her, the stallion yanked great mouthfuls of grass from the ground and crushed them rhythmically between his back teeth.

"If I listen, will you take me back?"

He stepped so close she could feel his breath on her neck. She had an almost irresistible urge to lean against his broad chest and wrap herself in the strength and comfort of his arms. Would he be a gentle lover or as fierce as his reputation? Lucie could not keep her mind from wandering, even though she knew she could not have what other women took for granted—a husband, children, a home of her own. She'd resigned herself long ago—hadn't she?

His voice broke her musings.

"If that is your wish."

She spun to face him. "Of course it is."

"Why would you want to go back to such a place?"

"Because I am needed and…"

He cocked his head as if doubting that she was needed. Hadn't he already said as much—no one wanted her, just like no one wanted him. She glared.

Her words stabbed out like a sword thrust. "And I am happy there."

His snort made it obvious he did not believe a word. She drew herself up, preparing to defend her fib. But he reached into his pocket and withdrew something. Slowly he unfolded a wrinkled piece of paper. Sky extended the page so it was just before her nose.

Sky watched her face and could tell by the lifting brow and the sudden widening of her eyes that she recognized that this was the letter she had written to her parents.

"You lie," he whispered.

To Sky's ear, the words seemed more an embrace than an admonishment. She had captivated him since the first moment he had seen her at the school.

"Did you read it?"

He recited from memory. "I have made a terrible mistake coming here. Nothing has changed."

She made a grab for the letter but he was too quick.

He folded it and returned it to his pocket. This small piece of her he would keep.

"That does not belong to you," she said, her voice a growl between clenched teeth.

"I only stole what you did not protect."

"Just like an Indian."

He nodded and smiled. "If only that were so." His smile disappeared as he stared into her shimmering eyes.

Her eyes widened. "You'd go back to them?"

He could not speak past the rock of pain now choking him. It was his one unreachable desire, to return—back to that moment in time and change what he had done.

Sky swallowed hard and nodded his answer. Then he took her hand. She allowed it. It required a purposeful effort not to stroke the soft skin on the back of her hand or to rub the tender mound of plump flesh at the base of her thumb.

He knew he could not allow himself to want her. Everyone and everything he loved had been taken from him. He knew better than to try again, especially with this woman.

She is not a maiden, but your friend's wife.

Sky led her back to the blanket and drew her down beside him. He faced the water, listening to his horse grazing and the crickets singing, as he shut his foolish longings back away.

"I have great respect for your husband. He was everything I wanted to be. It is only because of him that I am here today. I have not repaid his kindness. In fact, I am shamed by my actions toward him, for I—" He broke off. Why would he speak of this to her? She was not here for him to share his burdens. But somehow he felt connected to her in a way that he had not felt since before his exile.

Sky released her hand. "When your husband asked me to deliver this message I could not refuse." It helped to say it aloud, to remind himself that this one could never be his. "Are you ready to hear his words now, Lucie?"

She stared straight forward but he could see her head bob once in the starlight.

"He asks that I tell you that he has kept his heart only for you. He has never married although there are many widows who desire him. He does not believe you ran, but insists that you were captured and have been searching for him all this time, just as he prays each day for your return. As he predicted you are not a wife or mother."

Lucie's head hung at this as if his words hurt her deeply. He resisted the instinct to wrap her in his arms. Did she also long for a family, a place where she belonged? It would be too easy to bring this woman into his heart. But this he must never do. He was an honorable man, not some seducer of a friend's wife. His past mistakes had already cost him his people. He would not lose his honor as well.

Without even realizing it, he slipped into Lakota, the tongue of his birth. He cleared his throat. "He still loves you, Sunshine. He asks you to return to him so he can cherish you as his first and only wife once more."

Chapter Five

Lucie sat before him in silence beneath the gentle glow of starlight.

"Do you hear?" said Sky. "He sends me because he is not permitted to leave the reservation to come himself."

She grew brittle inside, like the fragile layer of ice that first forms on the edges of a lake. Eagle Dancer had summoned her.

"Lucie, he still loves you." His voice was low and his tone gentle, almost as if he spoke the words to her himself.

Her anger erupted and her tone was sharp. "Yes, yes. He loves me. He has loved me since he first laid eyes upon me." She spoke in English. "He wanted me, he took me and kept me against my will. I begged him to let me go home to my mother, but he refused." She leveled him with a glare of cold disdain. "Does that sound like love to you?"

"He cherished you."

"Like a lapdog."

His brow wrinkled in confusion. "But…he could not marry you without your consent."

Her chin sank to her chest as all the defiance drained away. Her sigh was deep and long, but still her shoulders sagged. Finally, she lifted her gaze, peering at him from beneath her lashes, cautious as a deer at a watering hole. "Please don't tell them. I couldn't lift my head up if they knew."

There was no dishonor in being the wife of a great warrior. Sky scowled, not understanding this woman. Her husband was head man, a leader, war chief and he loved her. What more could she want?

"If it shames you, why did you marry him?"

The defiance was back, flickering hot in her eyes. "The first night of our capture one of the women killed herself. That was *her* choice. Months later, another captive and my only friend, Alice French, learned her master would marry her. She ran. That was her choice. A few days later he brought back her bloody scalp. My choice was to remain the slave of his mother." Lucie touched her chin. "She gave me these when she thought I meant to run. So you are right, the decision was mine. I picked life and paid the price."

"You speak as if you hate him."

"I do. I hate him for not loving me enough to release me before I was ruined. I hate that he sought to bind me against my will. And finally, I hate him for saving my life and showing me tenderness so that I could not kill him when I had the chance."

His mind reeled with all she had said. No wonder she did not go back.

Lucie drew her knees to her chest and hugged herself. "Without him, I would have died. Because of him I have lost the life I might have led." She stared directly at him in a focused stare that disconcerted him. "As you pointed out, I have no husband, no children, because no decent man will have me. I cannot even get a proper teaching position."

She stared out at the water and said no more.

He stood, feeling hollow inside. "I'll bring you back to the school."

She did not rise. Instead, a strangled sound came from her. "Likely they'd be glad to see my back. What would you do, Mr. Fox, if everywhere you looked you were met with curiosity, abhorrence or pity? How would you like it if you were welcome only because it is the Christian thing to do?"

He wouldn't. Bad enough to feel different on the inside. He had thought them the same, but they were mirror images. He looked white, but inside felt he was Sioux, while Lucie believed she was white, but everyone could see she was no longer one of them.

"Then I will bring you to California. To your parents."

Her eyes widened. "You would do that?"

He nodded. "Or I will bring you to your husband. The people would accept you there. You would hear no insults. You would have a better life—be his wife again and you could have children."

"No."

"Then he deserves to know you do not love him."

Her voice was so quiet he had to strain to hear her. "Will you tell him?"

What she asked, he could not do. Only she or Eagle Dancer could break this marriage. He shook his head.

The whites thought divorce a shame or sin, but the Sioux understood that time and trouble could draw two people together or apart. There was no sin in that. Lucie need only say the words before a witness.

He squatted beside her.

"You must say it," he whispered in Lakota.

She drew a breath. "Eagle Dancer is no longer my husband. I am a single woman."

He scowled, not sure if she did not know the proper way or only pretended not to know. "You must say these words to him."

He did not know what to expect, but he didn't think she would lower her forehead to her knees and weep. The tortured cries pierced him like the tiny thorns of a rose briar. He clutched his own knees, not knowing what to do. Her shoulders shook as she gasped for breath.

Sky lifted one hand and rested it gently on her shoulder. She did not pull away. Instead, she reached for him, taking his wrist in her small hand. Her fingers did not quite circle him, but her grip was strong and warm. Her shoulders still heaved as if she could not draw enough air past the cries of anguish.

His palm circled her soft, slender neck and he drew her forward, cradling her against his body. She remained huddled to him, not resisting his embrace but not wrapping her arms about him, either.

They were strangers, born of common experience. But she had been a slave, while he had enjoyed the privileged position of being only son to Ten Horses. If he had not made that one mistake, he would have fought with his people at the day the world ended. The day the Sioux won and lost the battle to control their destiny.

Her body shook against his. He rocked her slowly as the summer breeze rocks the cottonwood. His throat burned and he lowered his cheek to the top of her head and let the tears fall. He understood regret and loss. In that, they were well matched.

Her sobs rasped on. Was it so hard to say aloud the words that broke the bond of marriage? She did not sound like a woman happy to regain her freedom.

"Enough now, Lucie."

She gripped the front of his coat, small pale fingers glowing like bone in the starlight. He rocked to his heels, drawing back. She let him go instantly, using her hands to brush the tears from her cheek, succeeding only in spreading the water, making her face glisten. She stared up at him.

How could she not know how beautiful she was? Even in her sorrow, she touched his heart. He rose, knowing he must take her back now.

"No one knows," she whispered.

He did not understand.

"I tried to tell my mother once but she said I mustn't speak of it and I never have—until now. I pretended it didn't happen, but inside, I knew what I had done." Her voice dropped to a whisper. "That I was married."

Sky nodded. "And you are still married until you speak these words to him."

She gaped. "But I need only speak these words before a witness."

He shook his head. "You must say them to your husband before a witness. He deserves that much."

She lowered her chin to her chest. "No, I won't."

He sighed away his disappointment that she would not do what was right. "Then you remain his wife, for I will not tell him."

Lucie stared up at him with big round eyes. She chewed upon her lip a moment. He could almost hear her debating with herself, do what was right—do what was easy.

She dropped her head again and he knew her decision. Why was he so disappointed in her?

He sighed. She would not do what she must to free them both, so they would remain tied together forever. "Where would you go now, to the school or to your parents?"

She struggled to untangle her long skirts from her legs and then stood. "I can't go back to California and let them see that I have failed again."

"Your mother fought hard to steal you. I don't believe she would easily give you up."

She wiped her fingers beneath her eyes again. "She didn't. She forbade me from coming."

He scowled. "Then why did you disobey?"

Her lips pressed together and her shoulders went tight with her displeasure. "Because I am not a child to be ordered to my room."

Yet, she sounded like a child now. He recognized this anger as the defiance he used himself when challenged.

"Is that the real reason?"

Her shoulders slumped. "Why should I tell you?"

He nodded. Why, indeed? "Because I might be the only person walking the earth who would understand."

She considered that, searching his face. What did she see?

"My parents reunited after my rescue. They began

the life that had been interrupted by a mistake. I have three sisters now and two brothers and I am old enough to be the mother of them all." She swallowed and glanced away. "They are happy now, except for one thing."

He waited but she spoke no more.

"What is this one thing?"

She glanced about as if fearful she might be overheard. Then she spoke in Lakota.

"Me. I am their sorrow—the symbol of the years they lost and the mistake they made, the stone in their hearts, the daily reminder of one they could not protect. They wish to make my path smooth, but cannot. Each time the Wasicu cut me with a word or look, it cuts them twice. I will lie to them rather than go back and witness again the pain in their eyes."

Sky had always thought of Lucie as brave, but never more than at this moment. He resisted the urge to draw her in. Instead he nodded.

"You wish to protect those you love. It is the natural way. You are a good daughter to spare them this."

Her chin quivered, but she held back her tears.

He gathered up the blanket and draped it around her shoulders, tugging it tight. He imagined Lucie in braids and could see the woman she might have become, had she stayed with the People.

"The school, then?"

"Yes. The girls still need me. Although…"

"What?"

"It isn't what I imagined."

He nodded his understanding of this. It was the first honest thing she had said about the place.

He collected Ceta's reins and held his stallion still.

Lucie needed no leg up to mount. She was agile as a bobcat as she swung up into the saddle, then removed her foot from the stirrup so he could use it to mount behind her.

They did not speak as they rode back, but he was distracted by the sweet scent of her body and the graceful curve of her long, thin neck. He already knew the softness of her skin and the arousing warmth of her body. She leaned against him as Ceta walked steadily along and he found himself wondering what she would do if he did not take her to the school, but instead rode off with her.

He cast off the foolish impulse. Even if it were suitable for him to pursue his friend's former wife, he still could not do so because he knew in his heart that he didn't deserve such happiness, not when Sacred Cloud lay rotting on his funeral pyre.

His head knew these things but his heart felt the pull of this woman. What did she think of him?

"Lucie?" Had he just spoken?

"Yes?"

How did one form a question around such an unfamiliar feeling of need? He had spent his entire adult life by himself and had never felt as isolated as he did at this moment. The squeezing in his chest reminded him of the ache he once felt before parting from his family.

"What do you do about the loneliness?"

Lucie thought on his question, choosing to consider carefully instead of saying the first thing that popped into her head, as she once might have done. It was an important question and deserved a considered answer. At last she spoke, in English.

"My way is to find something more important than myself. I found these girls at this school. They are also lonely, missing their family and the Red Road. That road is fading now. They need skills to survive as a defeated people. I hope that one day they will forgive us."

"Is that why you came back?"

"And to give my parents peace with their new family."

"It is your family, too."

She sighed. "No. It's not. I lost my family on this prairie. The only father I ever knew, died of sickness and then I was captured. I never even met my real father until after my rescue. Thomas West left my mother for the gold fields with a promise to return, but he never did. My mother only tracked him down after my capture. That's when she discovered he had come back to find her married to his brother. He thought I was their child and that she'd abandoned him as soon as he'd left her. Apparently his elder brother deceived them both. My mother never told me the truth."

Lucie thought about Samuel West, the brother of her real father. She missed him and wondered if her mother ever thought of the man she had married and lived with for fourteen years. Lucie had wondered why she never had any brothers or sisters. Now she had David, Julia, Nelly and Cary and the baby, Theodore. It was obvious that her mother was capable of having children. Had they even shared the same bed?

She wondered if her father's life had been more lonely than hers was now.

She felt the rumble of Sky's voice as he spoke behind her.

"You rescue people. I rescue horses."

"I heard you were a horse trader."

He switched to Lakota once more and she realized it was his first language and the one where he felt most at home.

"I call to them and tell them their old way is gone. Their land is gobbled up and they will go as the buffalo. So they come to me and I teach them so they will find a new way of living."

Lucie smiled. It was exactly what she tried to do with her students.

"Yes, I understand that. Do they listen?"

"Some do. Others do not wish this change. They will not take a bit and so I let them go with a prayer to protect them from the Wasicu's bullets."

So he didn't even consider himself white. How odd. But if that was true, why did he come back?

"Sky? Why did you leave the People?"

He did not answer for a long time, so she turned in the saddle to glance back at him. His face showed strain, as if her question caused him great distress.

"We are almost to the school. Quiet now, or they will hear us."

Lucie recognized the avoidance tactic. Clearly he did not want to speak of it. It broke the intimacy and common experience they shared. They had much in common, but she did not really know him at all.

At last they topped the hill behind the buildings and crossed onto the plain where the dormitory lay, a dark outline on the pale prairie. He took her on horseback along the back of the residence, stopping beneath her open window. All seemed quiet.

Was it possible that she had not even been missed?

"I'll lift you up," he whispered.

His strong hands circled her waist, plucking her from the saddle as one pulls up a weed from a garden. Would he be glad to be rid of her?

His duty was discharged. He had no reason to linger.

Sky rested her gently on the window ledge. Lucie swung her legs inside and then leaned out over the sill. Her new position brought her nose-to-nose with Sky.

"Will I see you again?" she asked.

"I must tell your...Eagle Dancer that you will not come."

Lucie felt a stabbing regret pierce her. She knew the way of the People. To break their union, she must say the words to him before a witness. But this she would never do, for it would require that she see him again and she was far too frightened for that. All these years she had pretended that it never happened, but it did and she was ashamed. Ashamed by her weakness at agreeing to wed a man she never loved. She knew what others would say if they knew. Better to be a captive than a... She knew what they would call her, knew what this revelation would do to her family. My God, David was an officer at Fort Sully, on the very doorstep of the Sioux Reservation. What would his comrades say if they knew?

"Must you tell him that you saw me?"

"He knows you are here, Lucie. You cannot keep from hurting him with this." He kept his gaze on her a long silent moment, then added, "I'll be heading out in the morning, in case you change your mind."

He laid the reins across the horse's neck and his stallion turned away. He did not look back, but left her there with her feet on the solid wood of the dormitory planking and her head and shoulders outside under the wide-open sky.

When Eagle Dancer woke, his nephew had returned after many days' absence. He had hoped the boy had gone back to the school, as he had asked. But when he realized that three older boys were also missing, he grew concerned.

Outside his box-house came the once-familiar sound of riders approaching. No Moccasins stirred and rolled toward his uncle, bringing his hands up to cover his eyes. It was only then that Eagle Dancer saw the blood beneath his fingernails. He shook his nephew awake.

"Up!"

The boy's eyes widened. A moment later they heard the men's voices. He cast off the sleeping robe and sprang to his feet.

"Clean your hands and stay inside."

"Yes, Uncle."

The pounding on the door caused No Moccasins to jump. He scrambled for his skinning knife and began to scrape away the dirt and blood.

Eagle Dancer studied the boy. He looked pale and his hands trembled. Had he been seen off the reservation?

"Eagle Dancer," came the call in English. "Open this door."

He did, stepping out to face the mounted soldiers and BIA agent.

Lucie had taught him a little English and he could understand most of what was said, if the speaker did

not talk too quickly. But he did not understand the jab-
bering of the man before him. He wore two stripes on
his sleeve and had gray-and-white side-whiskers that
made him look like a coyote.

When Eagle Dancer did not answer, the soldier
called back to a man still mounted. Eagle Dancer recognized him at once. Thornton Lewis, the translator.
He had to be helped off his horse. He swayed from
side to side, rocked by a breeze that stirred only within
himself. The red-rimmed watery eyes and the stench
marked the man as drunk.

"Tell him what I said," said the coyote-man.

Lewis tugged up his trousers and staggered.

The officer spoke more quickly now. "Names. Get
those names. We're setting an example. These bas-
tards…" Eagle Dancer could not understand the words
that ran together like raindrops. "…treaty and have to
stick…want names, goddamn it."

Lewis spoke to him now. "He see four warriors on
prairie, carrying weapons. You tell us who."

Eagle Dancer shook his head.

The officer snorted, but this time he spoke more
slowly. "Ask about the boy."

Eagle Dancer felt the fear that filled him only when
one of his family faced a threat. Why was it so much
easier to meet danger than to watch this happen to one
you love?

"Your nephew ran away from the school one full
moon away. School man track. Both no see now, many
days."

Eagle Dancer scowled. The man was a drunken fool
who spoke like a child two winters old.

"You seen the boy?"

Eagle Dancer shook his head.

"Treaty say all children go to school."

Eagle Dancer turned to the coyote-man and spoke in English. "This man is drunk."

The bluecoat ignored him and spoke to Lewis. "What about the truant officer—Norm Carr? He seen him?"

The translator asked him about a man who chased runaways.

Again he shook his head.

"You believe him?" asked coyote-man.

The drunk laughed. "He's an Indian. 'Course I don't believe him."

"Tell him that if the boy shows up, I want to know."

Lewis relayed the message. Then he turned and tried to mount his horse. He failed, landing on his ass in the road. He needed a leg up to gain his saddle. The armed contingent turned around and retreated toward the river.

Eagle Dancer waited until the fall of the hooves was obliterated by the murmuring of his people's voices. Many had come, following the riders to his door. The elders were already gathering. Eagle Dancer glanced back toward his log house and saw the worried face of No Moccasins.

What had his nephew done?

Lucie closed and locked the window, for fear Sky would change his mind and carry her back to Eagle Dancer. She lay in bed with her knife in her hand and when she did sleep her dreams were of her capture.

Eagle Dancer still waited, had never remarried. Where did Eagle Dancer live? On the reservation, she now knew, but did he have a house and farm? That was the agreement of the treaty. Subsistence rations issued to each head of household if they were willing to farm. She tried to picture Eagle Dancer wielding a hoe, but she could not seem to conjure an image of him without his horse.

They took that, as well. And now he had lost her forever. She tried to shake away the image of Eagle Dancer humbled and heartbroken, because the thought brought her a physical pain.

Her mind turned to Sky's arms around her. How long would it take Sky to return to the reservation? She realized she did not know the distance to their lands. Would she ever see him again?

Color trickled across the sky, the gray dissolving into a pink glow. Soon the vivid orange bands blazed overhead. Birdsong rose into the air. He would be gone soon and she could forget the entire thing, bury it back inside. Sky would not tell and so she could again pretend she had been forced, when the truth was she had given herself away. Lucie found it hard to breathe past the knot in her throat. She rose and dressed, braiding her hair in one long rope as she had once done and then coiled it properly on her head.

She crept to the window. Had it really happened? Had Sky carried her off and then returned her? She rolled her shoulder feeling the pain and stiffness caused by being bound.

The rapid woodpecker-like knocking on her door made her startle. She stood facing the door, knife in hand.

"Miss West, enough pouting, you must open this door at once."

Her shoulders relaxed and she sheathed her weapon

as she recalled that the other matron had come to her room last night and knocked. How could she have imagined that Lucie sat bound and gagged just beyond? Instead she must have decided Lucie was being difficult.

Lucie lifted the latch and opened the door. "Yes, ma'am?"

Mrs. Fetterer held a lamp and stared at her with a look of puzzlement. "You are already dressed?"

Lucie could think of no quick answer.

"Never mind, come along. Something dreadful has happened and Father Batista has sent for us. We are to bring the sister of the runaway to his office."

She had heard of the boy, of course, but did not know he had a sister. The children were separated from their family groups on arrival and arranged by age and gender.

"Which girl is it?"

"Maud."

The child was in Lucie's care as she was not yet seven. All she knew of the girl was that her mother had died. Her Indian name was Hummingbird, which was what Lucie called her, but in English.

"I'll be just a minute."

Mrs. Fetterer nodded. "Bring Maud with you."

Lucie hurriedly scrubbed her face with the freezing-cold water and retrieved her shawl from the bed. The rest of her scattered belongings she had set right before retiring late last night.

Once she had her shoes buttoned, she carried her lantern to the younger girls' bedroom. The interior was still dark, though she saw some of the children already stirring. She headed straight for Hummingbird and crouched beside her bed.

She laid a gentle hand on the girl's small shoulder and called to her in Lakota.

"Wake, Hummingbird. We need to go see the big father."

Hummingbird threw herself into an upright position, looking up at Lucie with wide frightened eyes.

"Shh, quiet now or you'll wake the others."

"Are you taking me home?"

"No, darling, the big father wants to speak to you."

"But I haven't done anything wrong. I say my prayers to Baby Jesus and wash my hands and face."

"You are a good girl. Come along." Lucie ushered her out of bed and into black stockings and the gray dress. She finger combed the child's hair and found that many of the other girls were now awake and staring wide-eyed at Hummingbird.

"Come." Lucie stood and offered her hand.

Hummingbird gripped it like a girl on a cliff and clung with both arms wrapped about Lucie's.

Lucie saw Mrs. Fetterer in the doorway and switched to English. "No reason to be frightened."

This did nothing to relax Maud's grip as Lucie steered her out the door.

"I've just discovered the trouble," said Mrs. Fetterer. "They found Mr. Carr's body. He's been butchered by Indians."

Lucie stumbled and then righted herself. "What?"

Where was the horror she would expect from a woman relating such nightmarish news? Mrs. Fetterer seemed wholly unaffected in her tone and bearing. "They mutilated his body. Sliced off his hands and used him as a pincushion. It seems he forgot that young boys have parents—savage parents."

Lucie's heart began pounding, but she didn't know why. She had not done anything wrong, but somehow she felt as if she had.

"When?"

"Several days ago, from what I've gleaned. And they still haven't found the boy. What's his name again? Wait, I'll think of it. Phillip, no, Charles Phillip. He's no more than twelve. But it runs in the blood, the savagery."

Lucie and Mrs. Fetterer met Father Batista, who waited just outside the girls' dormitory. Here the lantern was no longer needed. The world was already bright and awake, while Lucie's head spun from fatigue and worry.

"I don't know why Father Dumax thought I was incapable of bringing one little Indian girl to him," muttered Mrs. Fetterer to Father Batista.

"Perhaps he will enlighten you when we see him."

They did not have to wait, but were ushered into Father Dumax's office to find four cavalry officers flanking his desk, before which the Father waited, hands folded, and face strained. Lucie searched the faces for her brother, David, but did not find him there.

Hummingbird took one look at the army officers and screamed, completely disappearing in Lucie's skirts. Was she old enough to remember the dawn raids and bloodshed? It occurred to Lucie, only now, to wonder how her mother had died. Was it at the end of a bayonette or with a bullet in her back? Had Hummingbird seen these men destroy her village?

Lucie wrapped a protective arm about the girl, cutting herself short before she spoke to her in Lakota.

"Miss West, Mrs. Fetterer, thank you for coming so promptly. Have you heard about our truant officer, Mr. Carr?"

"What happened?" asked Mrs. Fetterer.

"Taken from this world and gone to a better place."

Mrs. Fetterer pulled a face. It was no secret she despised the man, but for what reason, Lucie had failed to ascertain.

Father Dumax motioned toward the grim officers. "These men are interested in finding the boy he was pursuing. This one is his sister?"

She glanced at the soldiers and did not like the way they stared at her charge. Lucie found herself reaching into her pocket for her knife. If the headmaster thought she would turn a child over to the army he was mistaken.

"Yes, Father," said Mrs. Fetterer. "Just as you asked."

"Miss West. She is in your charge?"

Lucie nodded.

"How is her English?"

"She understands very little." Her palm grew sweaty on the horn handle of her knife.

"These men have misplaced their translator and so for this one instance we would like you to apply your language skills for us."

Yesterday he had forbidden her to ever speak Lakota, but it seemed she could when it suited them.

Lucie nodded demurely. Captivity had taught her how to hide her emotions.

"Of course, Father."

The man to the priest's right took over. "Ask her if she knew her brother would run."

Lucie squatted before Hummingbird and held one of her trembling hands. "These bluecoats are looking for your brother because he ran."

"Will they shoot him?" she whispered.

"No. They just need to talk to him. Did you know he was planning to leave?"

She shook her head.

Lucie glanced back, the answer obvious.

"Well?" asked Mrs. Fetterer.

Lucie clamped her teeth together to keep from sighing aloud. It seemed she must translate head gestures, as well.

"She did not."

The man standing to the Father's right barked at Lucie as if she were a new recruit.

"Ask where he's gone."

"If she didn't know he was leaving, what makes you think she might know where he has gone?"

He narrowed his eyes on her. Did he think her an "Injun lover," as well? She *did* love this little girl enough to stand between her and the officer.

"Ask her."

She faced Hummingbird again. "Where do you think he would go?"

Hummingbird removed her thumb from her mouth to answer. "Home to uncle."

"What is your uncle's name?"

"The People call him Eagle Dancer."

Lucie bolted upright.

"What did she say?"

Lucie's head was spinning. The boy, the one that ran

and this little girl, they must be the children of Eagle Dancer's only sibling, his sister—Midnight.

It was Midnight who had discovered that Lucie had her monthly flow and taught her how to take care of herself. It was Midnight who took Lucie in at her brother's request, when he grew concerned that his mother would kill her.

Midnight never liked her, but she did keep her alive and treated her with dignity because she loved her brother. And now her daughter was in Lucie's care.

She thought of the Lakota notion of a hoop, a circle that never ends and how all things are connected. Lucie began to tremble.

"Miss West! What did she say?" barked the officer.

Lucie blinked at them as she remembered where she was. Her surroundings all came back and she recalled her purpose here.

"She thinks that the boy would go home to his uncle."

"That's all?"

She nodded, feeling light-headed as a patient just risen from her sickbed.

"Then why are you shaking like a leaf?" asked the officer.

She glanced to Mrs. Fetterer and found no ally there. Father Dumax kept his expression carefully concealed. She looked back at the ruddy face of the officer in charge.

"Because I did not know that this child's mother was my..." Her what? Her captor, her sister-in-law? "She was my friend."

Mrs. Fetterer gasped and then succeeded in looking more disapproving than usual.

"Father, do you know what happened to her mother? Is she alive?"

Father Dumax rounded his desk and removed a ledger from the side drawer. He seemed to know exactly where to look.

Midnight had been alive seven years ago. That was clear from the little girl now gripping Lucie's hand.

"We don't have time for this," said the officer.

"She is an orphan. Her only living relative is...oh, dear." Dumax stared hard at Lucie, putting it together. He knew the name of the warrior who held her. Anyone who read the papers would know.

"When did she see him last?" asked the officer.

Lucie's heart broke as she thought of Midnight. How had she died? Lucie kneeled before the motherless child and asked when she had last seen her brother.

"In the yard, marching."

"Did he speak to you before he left?"

She shook her head. Lucie folded Hummingbird into her arms and lifted her up onto her hip to stand and face the men. Only then did she translate the child's words.

"She doesn't know anything about this. I'm taking her back to the dorm."

"We haven't finished yet."

Lucie was not afraid of this man. He had no power to strike her or kill her. The worst he could do was raise his voice like a wind storm. She took a step toward him, moving close, forcing him to retreat. He bumped into the desk behind him.

"We *are* done, sir. We most certainly *are* done."

Lucie turned to go, but before closing the door she heard the officer speak to Father Dumax. "That's the one they captured—Lucie West. You'd think she'd want them all dead after what they done to her."

She closed the door and carried Hummingbird across the yard. The bugle sounded, calling the children to assemble like good little soldiers. Lucie disliked the military training; in fact, she was beginning to dislike everything about this place.

Before her, Father Robert, one of the younger priests, made a beeline in her direction.

"Miss West, did you hear?"

She paused, impatient with the delay. She wanted to take Hummingbird…where? There was no place the child would feel safe. Her mother was dead. She was exiled to this strange place. Lucie had the urge to run toward the woods with the girl and carry her all the way back to her parents' home in California.

Instead she stopped. Hummingbird hid her face in Lucie's neck.

"About the murder? Yes."

"No. Not that. About the arrests being made on the reservation."

Icy fingers squeezed her throat as possibilities raised ugly little heads. She paused, resting a hand on Hummingbird's small back and rocking from side to side.

"Who?" she breathed.

"Some of the chiefs. They'll be held at Fort Sully until they turn over the ones responsible for Carr's murder. They say they'll hang them if the guilty don't come forward."

"Eagle Dancer?" she whispered.

He nodded. "Yes, he's among them."

The world she had sought to avoid had collided into hers once more. Perhaps it was the hoop, spinning, but it felt more like a locomotive rumbling toward her. Eagle Dancer would be in prison at the fort where her younger brother was a commissioned officer. She did not know if she could help Eagle Dancer, or if her brother would assist her, but she did know that she was white, she was famous nationwide for her ordeal and that her brother was at the fort where they would be holding the Sioux leaders. Those three things may not be enough to help Eagle Dancer, but then again they just might. Eagle Dancer had kept her alive. Here was her chance to do the same for him. And with the debt repaid, perhaps she could finally be rid of him and of the guilt she had lived with for all these years.

She had to go to him.

The decision was surprisingly easy. There was no deliberation or dithering as she turned in a slow circle, already searching.

Sky—was he gone?

Lucie searched the grounds as if he might appear among the children pouring out of the dormitory and lining up for roll-call. It was Sunday, so there would be no lessons but choral practice in the morning and church all afternoon.

The morning, he had said. If she changed her mind, he'd be leaving in the morning.

She glanced up at the sky. The sun had already risen above the roof of the dorm. She took Hummingbird to her place in line and eased her to the ground.

"I am going to help your uncle," she said in Lakota.

Instantly, Hummingbird released her neck. She stared up at Lucie.

"Tell him I work hard to learn the stick writing."

Lucie smiled. "Yes. I will tell him."

"Miss West?" It was Mrs. Dwyer, the eldest matron at the school. She had shown Lucie no kindness here and stepped forward to block Lucie. "What do you think you are doing?"

Lucie straightened and tugged at her short jacket. Then she spoke to her in Lakota. "Mind your own business or I'll mind it for you."

The girls covered their mouths to avoid being seen laughing. Lucie turned and hurried toward the stable. She reached the side door just as Sky, already mounted, left the barn.

His horse stopped without her seeing any movement from Sky, as if the horse and man were of one mind.

"Did you hear they've arrested him?"

Sky nodded. "I'm headed to Fort Sully now to see what I can do."

"I'm going with you. Just let me gather my things."

Sky swung to the ground beside her. "I'll wait."

Lucie hurried to the dormitory. She transferred all her possessions from the trunk to the blanket and tied them with a rope into a bundle. Then she changed out of her shoes and left them behind. She released the bun that held her hair, letting the single long braid swing down her back. As an afterthought she snatched up a pen and set out a piece of paper to write her resignation. This act gave her pause. She had fought her parents and opposed her mother to accept this position. It had been the most important thing in her world, to come back here. To look in the faces of these children and know that they were giving the best her people could give. She had failed again, but was she ready to throw away the security of this place to follow Sky across the prairie into the heart of Indian country? She began to tremble.

It was clear she was not helping the children here. In her heart she knew she should go, that this was her only chance to assuage her guilt and shame. Still, it was hard to step from the shadows and back into the light where people would ridicule her once more.

She thought of Eagle Dancer in a cell and was ashamed, not for her actions but for those of her people. She dipped the nib and wrote the words that would sever her ties to this place. Lucie stood, blowing on the wet ink before folding the page. Instead of the fear she anticipated she felt an unexpected surging sense of freedom. The sensation eroded rapidly as she wrapped her shawl about herself, drawing it close. Was she really setting off with a near-stranger to help a man who had once held her captive—a man who had once kept her alive?

In her heart she knew it was right, but it hurt to leave her students and it troubled her to imagine what her parents would think of this action. Her mother did not believe her capable of making sensible decisions. Was this yet more proof that her mother was right?

She thought of what Sarah West was willing to do to save her daughter and knew that she must be that strong if she were to gain Eagle Dancer's release. Did he know who killed the officer?

Lucie lifted her bundle and left the room. On the way through the yard, she found Mrs. Fetterer.

"Please tell Father Dumax that I have a family emergency and give him this."

The matron pressed the letter to her bosom. "What has happened?"

Lucie squared her shoulders, preparing herself to speak the words aloud. "My husband has been arrested."

Mrs. Fetterer cocked her head and gaped. When she recovered herself she said, "Your husband? But you're not married."

"Tell him I am going to Fort Sully to see about his release."

"Whose release?"

"My husband, Eagle Dancer."

Chapter Six

Lucie had no horse and the stable had none to rent. "I'll pay double your rate."

Mr. Fetterer owned both the smithy and the stable. He stood before her now and Lucie noticed he'd singed all the hair from his arms by his work at the forge. What was left was coiled, melted lumps or red hairless patches. He had a bad habit of picking at the healing scabs on his forearms as he talked, causing them to bleed. "Double won't help. Those ain't mine. Only ones we got have owners."

She eyed the chestnut mare.

"That one belongs to Mr. Bloom. Carriage horse, mostly, though it does take a saddle."

"Would he sell it?"

"Doubt it."

Sky, who had been standing back by the entrance, dropped the reins of his stallion. The horse followed as he walked back to them.

He spoke to Lucie, ignoring Fetterer altogether. "Ask if he'd take forty dollars for that old horse."

Lucie headed for the store and returned with Mr. Bloom. The man would have been a fool to refuse, though he did mutter something about stolen money as he hurried ahead of Lucie. Sky managed to get him to include a saddle and bridle, before producing two twenty-dollar gold pieces that shone bright even in the dim stable. Bloom fairly snatched the bounty from his hand. The exchange complete, Sky tied her bundle behind the saddle.

Lucie thought of a time she had been happy to ride on just a piece of buffalo hide rather than walk the miles the women walked, carrying the belongings to keep the men's hands free for their weapons. On more than one occasion she had witnessed the wisdom of that method.

She saw them all before her, the women and children hurrying ahead and the men turned back to hold off attack by the cavalry.

"Lucie?" Sky stared at her. She had not seen him mount. But he now sat beside her on his horse.

She had to shake her head to bring herself back to the here and now. Men didn't just throw forty dollars away on a horse, especially men who made their living catching and training mustangs. Lucie was not naive enough to believe he purchased the animal out of Christian charity. Did he act out of duty to Eagle Dancer or did he want something in return? Her stomach clenched at the thought.

His brow wrinkled as he stared at her. "Don't you like the horse?"

She managed to find her manners. "Yes, thank you for buying her."

Sky's smile made her insides tremble. But now she recognized that the sensation she initially thought was dread had somehow changed to an excitement she did not understand. Sky was a stranger, wasn't he?

But he wasn't. Not in all ways, at least. They shared a past and common experience. That alone brought them together. But this nervous jumping of her insides and the rush of blood to her face, that was something else entirely. She was setting out alone with Sky and she was unreasonably thrilled at the prospect. What the devil was wrong with her?

His smile faded and she realized she had stolen any pleasure he might have had at the gift by her odd reaction. Her cheeks burned now with embarrassment.

"Have you changed your mind about going, then?" he asked, venturing a guess at the cause of her befuddlement.

She shook her head, when in fact she had been thinking just that. She was afraid of leaving the safety of the school, of riding out with a near-stranger onto the prairie where she had been taken. But most of all she was afraid of this rolling anticipation within herself and where it might lead. She knew better than to be enamored with a man who was as wild as his horse.

Lucie wavered between what was right and what was safe. She stared out at the vastness of the plains, knowing better than most how tiny she was by comparison.

"Lucie? He needs our help."

She swallowed hard and met Sky's steady gaze. He held himself with a kind of confidence she admired.

This man knew what was right and he only waited for her to recall her duty…to her husband.

She nodded. "I'm ready."

Mr. Bloom stepped up to hold her horse as she climbed the mounting block and swung her leg over the saddle. Once seated she glanced at the stallion that had carried her last night, noticing now in full light that he had one blue eye and one brown one. "What is his name?"

"Ceta," answered Sky, "because he can fly."

Falcon, she thought. He had named his horse after the fastest of birds.

She lifted the reins and looked at him. He smiled his approval.

"Ready," she whispered.

Mr. Bloom raised his hands to halt them. "Aren't you forgetting something? Bacon, coffee, beans?" As the owner of the only trading post within miles, it obviously pained him to see an opportunity to make money riding off.

Sky shook his head.

"You'll get mighty hungry before you reach Fort Sully."

"No," said Sky. "We won't."

The man snorted. "Suit yourself." He turned to Lucie. "You sure about this? Might be better to stay here where it's safe, especially if they're raiding again."

"I'll be safe with him." She believed it, but her words caused Sky to snap his head around and stare. She just was uncertain if she would be safe *from* him. Was it only yesterday he had abducted her? If he had meant to use her that way, then surely he would have done so last night.

She bit her lip at the truth she now recognized. She was fascinated by Sky in a way she had never been with any other man. If someone had told her that today she'd be willingly riding from the school with Sky, placing herself in his care, she would have called them crazy.

Crazy—yes, perhaps she was. But she knew she could trust him to keep her safe. It filled her with the confidence she needed to take this step.

"Good day, Mr. Bloom." She nodded to him and the smithy. "Mr. Fetterer."

The smithy cocked his head and gave her a sly smile. "It's true then, 'bout you marrying one of them savages?"

Sky prepared to face Fetterer, coming to her defense without her even asking. But Lucie lifted her hand, and Sky hesitated.

"Yes, Mr. Fetterer. Eagle Dancer is my husband."

"That why they fired you?"

Is that what they were saying? It made sense, of course, making it appear to be their decision, rather than hers. It wasn't as though she hadn't given them cause.

"Just one of a litany, Mr. Fetterer."

"My wife said you was an Injun lover."

Why did she care when the man leered, his gaze slithering up and down over her? Shouldn't she be used to such treatment by now? But somehow it always caught her off guard.

Sky dismounted and the smithy scuttled back like an enormous crab, recognizing the lethal threat Sky posed. Here was her proof that Sky would protect her, even from so slight an insult. Sky glanced back at her, his eyes begging for permission. His look held such longing it nearly made her smile.

She shook her head, denying the approval he sought. He returned to his horse and executed a smooth jump into the saddle that epitomized strength and grace.

She'd had such high hopes on arrival, while trying to hide the truth that was written on her face. Thinking she had finally found a purpose and a place of welcome, but she had made a mess of it. They *should* fire her. And she *was* ruined. Pretending otherwise didn't change a thing.

Lucie had a moment to reflect that she had veered badly off the course she had chosen. Yesterday she would have been mortified for anyone to know her secret and today she was speaking about it in public. There was an unexpected feeling of freedom attached to her revelation, coming, she decided, from the fact that she was no longer hiding. She had never realized what a strain she had felt until the burden was lifted.

But she feared the consequences of her revelation and how it might hurt her family.

The last time she had felt so great a sense of foreboding, she was a captive. But now she rode willingly out to meet her fate and for reasons she could not even begin to articulate.

For good or ill, she had broken her ties here and could only move forward, to Fort Sully. Their roles were now reversed. Eagle Dancer was a captive in her world.

Sky lifted the reins and Ceta bolted forward with such speed that Fetterer had to leap backward to escape being trampled. He landed on his fanny in the road.

Lucie touched her heels to her new mount and followed Sky out across the prairie.

The sun shone in their faces as they rode southwest. Sky tried to listen to the wind and watch the hawks that floated effortlessly on the current of wind. But instead his mind could not break the tethers that drew him back to the woman. She rode upwind and so he drew in the fragrance of her skin with each breath he took. He tasted her on his tongue.

Nothing he said had made any difference. But today, at the word of Eagle Dancer's arrest, she'd changed her mind. She did not even look like the same woman he had captured yesterday. Then she'd trembled and tears had filled her eyes. Her hair had been tied up in a tight knot, as one ties a horse's tail for battle. Her dress had included many petticoats and her shoes were stiff.

Now she wore no shoes. The moccasins sheathed her in soft bleached deer hide. Her long hair hung in a loose braid down her back. There were no bits of metal holding it up in the knot now. And her skinning knife and sheath adorned her neck, there out in the open, for all to see. The shawl about her shoulders reminded him of the blankets worn as any proper woman would do. The transformation shook him. Which person was she—the prim white woman or the proper Indian woman?

The changes did not end there. He breathed deep again and then glanced at her once more. Her face was now relaxed, her posture confident. She did not radiate uncertainty and fear. There was a determined lift of her chin that made her look fierce and serene all at once. Last night she was beautiful. Today she was magnificent and he could not take his eyes off her.

"Do I have dirt on my face or are you staring at my chin?" she asked.

He startled. Her voice was not gentle, and it held a certain edge that cautioned him to be careful.

"You look different."

"Yes, facial tattoos will do that to a woman."

"Different from last night."

"Ah," was all she said.

Yesterday she had tried to set Eagle Dancer aside. But today she admitted to the mangy blacksmith she was his wife and she was riding to his aid. Would she remain his wife? He pondered the change of heart as he fixed his eyes on the horizon and kept them there, until the sun shone in his eyes. She did not complain at the heat or fuss that they did not stop at midday for a meal. He had expected her to act like a white woman on this trip, but somehow, she had changed back to the girl he had first met on the prairie, walking along the trail north.

He thought of how arrogant he had been then and felt a pang of regret.

"I am sorry I did not speak to you then."

She did not pretend not to know what he meant.

"You were afraid what your friends might think. I didn't know them, those Bitterroot boys, but you were never without them."

He nodded. Time made the memory sweet and bitter all at once. "Yes, my friends. I thought if I tried hard enough I would be Indian." And he had been, until that mistake and then he had been white once more—an enemy, hated.

He felt the hole in his heart growing.

"Were you rescued or were you released?"

When he did not answer, she stared at him.

How could he tell her of the circumstances of his exile? He never spoke of it. He and Lucie had much in common, but not this.

"In my heart, I never left them." He pressed his legs into Ceta's sides and his horse broke into a trot. "We'll camp up in those trees," he said as he passed her, leaving Lucie and her questions behind.

Lucie watched him go, keeping her horse to a steady walk. There was no need to rush; she could see all the way to the grove and these plains were no longer the dangerous place they once had been. She watched him break into a canter. He certainly was in a rush to be rid of her, or was it her question? Rescued or released? Had he been forced to leave like the Commanche captive Cynthia Ann Parker, ripped from the only family she had ever known? Was he the same as her students, stranded by circumstance in the white world?

He was a mystery. She had some of the pieces, but was determined to gather the rest until she knew him. If that meant revealing some secrets of her own, she was prepared to do so, for if anyone could understand her, it was this former captive. He knew the People and he knew the whites. But unlike her, he had not chosen to return to his race, not completely. Instead, he pined like a dog whose master is not coming home. The path he chose to walk had vanished, not just for him, but for all those children back at the school. They must have a new way of being. She understood that and still thought assimilation the answer. She glanced at Sky. He had certainly made his thoughts clear on the matter.

He completely rejected the schools mission, but then again, he had not really assimilated himself—had he?

She considered the quandary. How could her pupils find a place among people who would judge them on sight and hate them?

The only good Indian I ever saw was a dead Indian. General Sheridan's sentiments were the norm. Would a proper education change that?

Lucie set her jaw and followed Sky Fox toward the cotton grove. By the time she found him he had his horse hobbled and a fire struck.

"How progressive of you," she said.

"What?"

"Not expecting the woman to carry the wood and set the cooking fire."

"I'm used to doing for myself."

"I see."

Was he, or did he just want to exclude her, even in this? She wondered if this was just another way to keep his distance. Why was he so adamant about his solitude that he took such measures to remain apart from everyone? She watched him move about, setting a wood pile here and his saddle there. Instead of driving her off, his behavior only increased her curiosity.

Finally he faced her.

Lucie thought they had traveled better than thirty miles this first day. A reasonable amount for a late start. She wondered if they had entered Dakota Territory and could not quite suppress a shiver. She knew Fort Sully was just south of the lower reservation, the one recently named Cheyenne River, and that Eagle Dancer resided in the northern reservation that now was called Standing Rock. But where exactly this tract lay, she was uncertain.

"How far to Fort Sully?"

"The Missouri is a hundred and thirty miles southwest, maybe."

Lucie's jaw dropped. "What? Why is their school in Minnesota if their parents live halfway across the territory?" No wonder she had never seen a parent visit. "I had no idea they had to travel so far."

Sky snorted again. She was getting used to the sound.

"The parents who visit have to walk all that? It must take weeks."

He said nothing, but his muscles still bunched as if he held himself back.

"Then why didn't the government allot land for the school closer to the reservation?"

Sky gave her a look of incredulity. Whatever he saw caused his look of aggravation to transform into astonishment.

"Lucie." He began with the tone one uses when educating a child or someone who does not have all her faculties.

She narrowed her eyes in offense.

"They don't want the parents to visit or for the children to hear the stories of their ancestors. They want them to know the Ten Commandments. There was no mistake. The summer apprentices, the lack of holidays. Do you really think weeding turnip patches will teach those boys to be farmers? It's all to trap them in the white world, so they'll forget how to be Lakota."

"But learn how to be American citizens."

Sky shook his head. "Stop telling yourself this is for

their good. It is for the good of the people who want their land. That is all."

Lucie fumed. "They what would you have them do?"

"Return the children they stole, for starters. Allow them the seasonal hunts. They can provide for themselves, if you'd let them."

"They use the hunts as excuses to raid."

Sky threw up his arms. "What use is a man when his family does not need his protection or the food he provides? They have no purpose now, so they cross the river to the whiskey camps. What else is there for them to do but drink to forget?"

She hadn't thought of that either. A shadow of doubt crept below her wall of certainty and she could not meet his eyes. He rested a hand gently on her shoulder. When she glanced at his long fingers splayed from her neck to upper arm, he drew it quickly away. He stared at the fire now.

"Will you be all right for a little while?"

"Hunting?" she asked.

He nodded and he lifted a familiar object from his saddle bags. The beaded buffalo bladders were connected by a tether so they could both be carried over one shoulder. At the sight, her mind flashed back to her morning routine all those many years ago. She was the first up and off to the river where the spring joined the flow to fetch water. Then she returned to the tipi and set the fire, all before her mistress had crawled from the buffalo skins. Tedious and terrifying, that was the life of a Lakota slave.

Sky lowered the skins to his side, his face now showing concern. "I can do it."

"No." Her voice sounded sharp. "You go. I'll get the water."

He held the tether looped over one finger. She snatched it off and headed toward the bank.

"Watch out for rattlers," he called.

She already had a stick in her hand and beat the brush before her. How naturally it all came back. While at the river she stripped out of her dress and corset and then waded waist-deep into the warm water. She splashed the dirt and sweat away. Lucie sank to her knees using the mud to scour her skin. Finally she rinsed her hair and then stepped out and shook off. She was only damp when she slipped back into her dress, leaving the corset behind on the bank. The day's ride had proved how impractical the garment was.

Lucie made her way cautiously up the rise and back to the fire, adding more wood. Then she sat in a patch of sun with her head thrown back to dry her wet hair. She did not hear him coming, but sensed him, somehow.

"You had a bath?"

She smiled, the answer evident.

He held out a long rattlesnake. "Can you cook this?"

She stood to accept the snake.

"I will go bathe, as well."

She smiled. After he left she skinned and gutted the snake. She skewered the snake and was about to rake coals over to roast it, when she decided instead to walk down to the riverbank. The girls would often spy on the boys bathing. When she was a slave, she did not dare and when she was a wife it would have been unseemly, though she was only thirteen at the time. She slipped through the long grass, as quiet as a hunting lynx, following the splashing.

She found a place where she could see him standing in muddy water up to his navel. The harmless prank turned serious the instant she beheld him. His hands were raised as he rubbed his wet hair, turning his arms into corded ropes. His back was an anatomy lesson of well-defined muscle. She rooted to the spot, fixed by the beauty and power of this man. He glistened, his muscles bunching as he stooped and cording as he stretched.

Her belly fluttered and her fingers tingled in anticipation of what was not hers to touch. Until this moment she never allowed herself to fancy a man because she never expected to find one who would overlook her flaws…call her beautiful, spend the entire day stealing glances at her.

Whatever it was that drew them, it was stronger now than when they stood beneath the stars and it was growing by the minute. How long until it was too powerful to set aside, too powerful to ignore?

Her pleasure at her delusions burst like a soap bubble in the sun. Of course he called her beautiful and stared at her. She knew what he wanted, what they all wanted. The only difference was that she nearly believed him, wanted to believe him. But she knew otherwise because no one could ever think her attractive now.

She shook her head in disgust. Perhaps it was because she longed so to be wanted by a man like Sky. A man of her own who would court her and love her. She slashed at the green blades before her with her open hand. *Stupid woman. You may find him attractive, but never the other way around.*

It took a moment to recognize that he had finished and was using his hand to scrape the excess water from his body. In a moment he would leave the river and give her a view of him in his entirety. That was the sort of sensual image that would keep her up at night. The kind of thing that once glimpsed is never forgotten.

He turned toward the bank, paused and stared in her direction. She hunched down in the grass. Her hand came upon a small flat stone, smooth and red. The kind of weapon one uses to stun a rabbit. Lucie palmed the stone, measuring its weight.

It had been a long time since she had taken aim at a frog or rodent, and an even longer time since she had done something foolish or brazen or bold. But this was not small game, in fact, Sky was large and the game she considered was dangerous. The temptation to reveal herself bumped against the fear that by doing so she would leave herself vulnerable to the sting of rejection.

When had she grown so cautious? During her captivity, of course, when she could not afford such a luxury as impulsiveness. Once back with her people, the hard looks and harder gossip had turned her into a grim woman.

The stone warmed in her hand as she turned it over and over. The wiser course was to withdraw.

Lucie stood and threw the stone at Sky.

Chapter Seven

Something bounced off Sky's shoulder. He swore in Lakota as he turned, glancing at the bank for his gun belt and knife.

A woman's giggle came from somewhere in the deep thicket above the water's edge. He scowled. How had she managed to get so close without his hearing? Ah, but she was not a white woman, not totally. Lucie knew how to hide and how to move silently. He knew her location now only because she wanted him to. But why?

Was she playing a game? It had been so many years since he had engaged in this kind of foolishness, he barely remembered how.

A smile spread across his mouth as he dived under the water. Two could play at such mischief. Sky came up before her, holding a handful of river mud.

Lucie shot to her feet.

"I surrender!" she called.

Sky did not pursue her as she turned tail, using the

stick to beat a safe path before her. He took a moment to scrape the water from his body and wring the moisture from his hair before dressing and following the way she had fled.

He found her still laughing when he appeared at the fire a few minutes later. The sound had such an unexpected effect upon him, he froze in his tracks. His skin tingled, not from the bracing water, but from her. Every time he got close to her his blood pounded in all the wrong places and his belly twitched like a speared fish. He recognized this feeling, though he had not experienced it in many years. He wanted Lucie.

That recognition made him break out in a cold sweat. There were many reasons why he could not pursue her. His mind instantly supplied the objections and countered them all just as quickly. *Married—to a friend.* But she will divorce him. She told you so. *Eagle Dancer is making an offer to the daughters of Joy Cat on your behalf.* He won't want you and you don't even know those women. *It is the right thing to do.* Ha, you don't want her because she could make you happy and you can't allow that, now, can you?

Sky cleared his throat and Lucie glanced toward him, smiling broadly.

"You have no manners," he said.

"You are only angry because I snuck up on you."

His mouth quirked. "Perhaps."

She turned the green stick that held the roasting meat. "Would you like me to stretch the skin?"

"I can do it."

He ignored her frown at his rejection of her offer. But he did not want her keeping camp as if she were his woman.

Sky made a circular frame from a cottonwood branch and sewed the rattlesnake skin in place, using thin strips of moose hide. He set aside the project when she offered him a skewer. She used her own stick to flick something out of the fire.

Sky recognized it immediately and was so pleased he forgot his dark mood as he spoke in Lakota. "You found potatoes!"

His outburst brought another tinkling of her musical laughter before she answered in English. "It's been a long while since I cooked groundnut. It's not really a potato."

"It's the only kind I like."

She drew a breath and straightened, looking pleased at his reaction. Then she fished five more tubers from the coals. Their skins were burned black, but the inside was white and fleshy.

"I like the seeds the best," said Lucie.

"Roasted."

They shared a smile and then were silent as they ate their meal. With her, he forgot that he preferred his own company. She didn't make him feel awkward or unwelcome. She no longer stared at him as if she feared what he might do. Oh, he could get used to the company of such a woman.

"It's nice to sit with someone who doesn't stare at me," she said, voicing his very thoughts.

He lifted his eyebrows at that. "Is that what men do?"

"They either stare or try not to stare. But you make me feel like there's nothing wrong with me."

"There isn't."

Her smile seemed sad. "Well, of course there is.

They're hideous, I know. But my point is that you seem to see past them and see me."

He was about to object. To tell her how lovely she was in the firelight, but then he remembered himself. To tell her this was to tell her that he could not control himself. It was bad enough that he recognized his weakness. He would not let her know, as well. So he focused on his meal.

The riding and the absence of lunch gave Lucie a hearty appetite. She ate all of her share of the meat, but only two of the six groundnuts. The others did not go to waste.

After the meal, Sky leaned back against his saddle and sighed contentedly.

"Been a long time since I shared a meal with anyone."

His comments wiped the smile from Lucie's face.

Every night since her arrival, she ate in the dining hall, surrounded by her girls, reminding them how to hold the fork, helping them grow accustomed to the napkin and cutting the meat for the littlest of her charges. Before that she shared a table with her family.

All that time, Sky had eaten by himself.

"You live a lonely life."

"By choice. Rather be in my own company than with most folks."

"Because you feel different?"

"Because I *am* different."

She nodded. "Yes. I feel like that, too, sometimes."

He stared at her. "Only sometimes?"

She gave him a commiserating smile. "I was not with them so long. Not quite a full year." She moved a little closer, wondering if he might feel more inclined to talk when his belly was full. She steered clear of asking him the whys and hows of his departure from the Bitterroot tribe and tried another path. "Where did they take you, after you left Fort Laramie? Last I remember Mrs. Douglas was trying to teach you to use a fork for a berry cobbler. You had juice and pulp all over your hands and face."

Sky flushed. Somehow she thought he did not embarrass easily. But she knew things about him most didn't. She had seen him then, when he was a frightened boy, alone in a strange place. He raked his fingers through his hair.

"That was long ago."

"Yes, and not so long ago. Will you tell me of your life since then?" When he did not answer she offered bait. "I'll tell you of mine," she coaxed.

He pressed his lips together and glowered, but his glare had no effect whatsoever. Now he was the one off balance and he did not like it. If her fear of him was gone, then one more barrier between them had fallen.

"Come now, is it so bad?"

He lifted his unmasked gaze to her, allowing her to see the pain that remembering that time always caused him.

She dropped her teasing tone and grew serious. "I'd still like to hear."

"You like sad stories, then?"

"Well…let's say I'm accustomed to them."

"The ladies at the fort made me their project. I hated the shoes and threw them off whenever I could. I liked the pies. That first night I snuck out the window and started for home, but then I remembered…" He fell silent and shook himself. "I didn't have one. So I crawled back inside. I think Captain Douglas was jealous of me, because his wife spent more time fussing over me than him. He was the one that arranged for me to go with Eli Sutton."

"Was that his name? I never knew it. He seemed very serious."

He clenched his teeth as he remembered. "Yes, beating the devil out of me was serious business to him."

"He beat you?" Lucie did not try to hide the horror in her voice. An instant later her shock dissolved as she pressed her lips flat, looking ready to spit nails. It touched him that she should be so outraged on his behalf.

"Regularly, and he didn't feed me much. I learned how to work a plow and recite the Lord's Prayer and that he was stronger than me. But I was growing. He didn't stay stronger very long."

Lucie's eyes widened. Did she think him a murderer? Well, so he was, but not in the way she imagined. He scowled as his mood darkened.

"Sky?"

He made a face. "I didn't kill him. Should have, but didn't. I stole his horse."

"In Texas?"

"What? No, Utah. That's the second time you mentioned Texas."

Was she blushing? Certainly she could no longer meet his gaze.

"Mr. Bloom at the trading port said you were a murderer and a wanted man. He mentioned Texas."

Bloom couldn't know about Sacred Cloud. But he'd been half-right, just the same. He was wanted, but not by the whites. He glanced at Lucie. This was why he kept to himself. Too many questions without answers. Too many mistakes that could never be righted. He was only worthy of his own miserable company. He didn't deserve her, never would. Not after what he'd done.

His voice sounded wooden. "Only thing I did in Texas was drive cattle."

"You were a cowboy?" She sounded delighted. Obviously, she'd never been on a drive or she'd know it was about as romantic as any fall butchering. Just took longer.

"I worked a few drives after I ran away. Found I had a knack for catching horses. I liked saving animals better than driving them to their deaths, so I quit riding for the cattlemen."

"I'd like to see you work with horses sometime."

A few had asked him that, but he'd never been inclined to let anyone see him work—until now. Training horses was the only time he allowed himself to feel free and connected. His method was deeply personal, but he discovered he wanted Lucie to know that part of him. It was the very reason he should tell her no. Instead, he found himself nodding. "Sometime, maybe."

Lucie smiled during the silence that no longer felt strained.

"You said you'd tell about your time away from the Dakotas," he reminded her.

"Yes, well, where to begin? My parents remain together, even now. They have five other children. There's David, born within the year of their marriage. He's a man of nineteen now, a soldier at Fort Sully. I hope he can help us, though I am not certain. He doesn't understand the People and holds them a grudge."

"Why?"

She gave him an indulgent look. "You don't understand whites very well, do you? In any case, David has a promising career before him." Her proud smile died a slow death. "I'm certain my mission will embarrass him. You don't think it will damage his career, do you?"

"I don't know." Sky still considered soldiers as the enemy and did not like Lucie connected to a man who shot women and children in the back.

She thought on that and a crease formed between her brows. He resisted the urge to touch the furrow there. After a moment, she seemed to mentally shake herself. Lucie forced a tight smile. "Then Julie, born the following year. She's engaged to a fine man."

He noticed the hitch in her voice and wondered at the cause. She glanced away now, not wanting him to see—what? Did her sister's impending marriage remind her of what she did not have? Did she also long for those connections? Looking at Lucie, he wondered if she might be different from the other Wasicus and more like him.

She rattled on now, as if nothing had happened, filling the silence with empty words. "Julie's fiancé is a naturalist who means to drag her off to the Alaskan territory. Cary is thirteen already and wants to be a painter. Nelly is ten. It took Mama six years to get her to wear skirts. Then there was Melissa, who passed away from a disease of the lungs. That was very sad. She was just three and everyone loved her. Then last year Theodore surprised everyone, a late blessing. I call him Beaver because when he was teething, I watched him gnaw through the handle of a wooden spoon." She laughed.

He tried to hold his smile, but his heart wasn't in it. She had family, brothers, sisters, parents. Why did knowing she had kept them all through her captivity make him feel so alone? Her bounty somehow made him feel solitary as a tortoise gazing at a family of rabbits. He may want what they had, but he knew he'd never cast off his shell, no matter how much he longed to. He tried to picture them all about her.

"All with red hair?"

"Yes, some dark, some coppery."

"Any like yours?"

Lucie's smile failed her. "Melissa's was just the same."

He'd made her sad again. He tried over. "You were much older, more like an auntie."

Lucie could not hold her smile. Unintentionally he'd touched another source of sorrow. He seemed to have a knack for making her miserable. He sat forward, interested now, to understand her.

Her voice was so low he had to strain to understand her words.

"I sometimes pretended they were mine." She swiped at her eyes, dashing the offending tears the instant they dared breach her lower lids.

Why would that make her cry? He shifted back, drawing away from the pain that was too raw and too similar to his own.

"Sometimes when I was tying a shoe or braiding hair, I'd realize that this was as close as I would come to motherhood."

He denied it. "You could have a family."

"As if anyone would want me." She glanced at him, keeping a brave face, despite the tears that brimmed in her eyes. "I hope you aren't shocked to hear that I did not have a flock of beaus following me about."

"White men are foolish," was all he said.

"I'm lucky to have my family. I know that."

He nodded.

"But sometimes…"

"You don't have to be alone to be lonely." How had he read her emotions so perfectly?

She stared at him, seeing a new openness there in his eyes. "Yes, that's right. It is hard to watch them leaving. First David, and now Julie. She'll have a husband soon and children, God willing, while I just—" Her voice broke again. She squeezed her eyes shut, refusing to say aloud that her life had stagnated like a pond robbed of fresh water. They would all leave home, one by one, all but her. That recognition had given her the push she needed to leave the safety of her parents' house, but that had worked little better. She drew a long breath of the crisp air and found the courage to face him again. She could not expect honesty from him if she would not give him the truth in return.

Lucie scraped her palms over her skirts as if wiping away her misery. "I did have one proposal."

Sky's brows descended low over his eyes. "But you are already married."

"My mother said my Indian marriage wasn't real."

"What do *you* say?" he asked.

Lucie stared into the fire, watching the flame embrace the logs. Finally, she lifted her gaze to his. How could she make him understand?

"Eagle Dancer loves you. You are first in his heart." He watched her, intent as any hunter. "He could give you a family."

She pursed her lips. "But I do not love him. I was always, and only, his captive."

"His feelings for you are strong."

"They always were. Nothing I said could dissuade him. But are those feelings love?"

"They are."

"You think it is love that made him take a girl that was terrified to marry, keep her against her will and prevent her from ever seeing her family? Is that how you think of love, Sky?"

"It was a war."

"If he loved me, he would have done what was best for me, what would have made me happy."

Sky nodded. "Perhaps he loved you too much to bear living without you."

"And so he made the decision for both of us."

"If he was so selfish, why do you care what happens to him now?"

Lucie drew her knees up and hugged them. "I would like to help him, if I can."

"Why? You say you will break the bonds that hold you to him. So why do you tell those Wasicus that you are his wife and then tell me you will break your marriage?"

Her eyes grew even wider. "You must not tell anyone I spoke those words."

His body stiffened at that. Didn't he want her to be Eagle Dancer's wife?

They stared at each other, her with speculation and him with a stormy look.

"Why not?"

"Because I can only help him if I am his wife. Wives

have certain rights. I can visit him and argue on his behalf."

"So now you will be his wife?"

Lucie shook her head. "No. I will not—never again. But you must not tell them, or him. Not yet."

Sky stood to add more wood to the fire. When he settled himself Lucie spoke again.

"Who do you think killed Norm Carr?"

Sky tried not to shift under her focused gaze. Should he tell her the truth? He played with a stick as he debated the question.

"I don't know."

"But not any of the head men. They were miles west on the reservation."

"It's just a nasty trick to force them to hand over the culprit, don't you think?" Lucie said.

She looked at him for reassurance and he wondered how much he should tell her.

"Likely. But Carr did catch Eagle Dancer's nephew. He beat him. He was preparing to…to use him as a man might use a woman."

Lucie's eyes widened in shock. "What? Are you saying he was going to rape a child—a boy?"

Sky nodded.

Lucie sat back, still and pale. She remained motionless so long, she looked carved of wax.

"But how could you know that?"

"Because I am the one who stopped him," said Sky.

Lucie nodded her understanding and then her breath caught. He saw the instant the possibility crossed her mind. She didn't know him, didn't know that he was not a killer, couldn't kill, not since that day.

"I didn't do it, Lucie."

Her stiff posture told him she was unconvinced.

"I used my gun to stop him. When he was mounting, he drew on me and I shot him through the fleshy part of his shoulder. Here." He pointed his index finger to the fleshy part of his upper arm, marking the path of the bullet.

"You shot him?"

He nodded. "Then I sent his horse back to trigger a search. It was less than a hundred miles. He should have made it."

"But he didn't."

"No."

"What did you do with the boy?"

"I brought him to the reservation—to Eagle Dancer. No Moccasins told him about you and he sent me back to the school with the message. I looked for Carr, but when I didn't see him, I assumed he was already back. At the school I learned his horse returned, but he did not."

"You don't know what happened after you left him?"

"No."

"But you shot him and then abandoned him."

She made it sound like it was his fault.

"He hurt the boy. He did not merit help."

Lucie glanced toward the horses. What would he do if she tried to leave him now? The overpowering urge to keep her sprang on him with such force it momentarily stole his breath. Was this what Eagle Dancer had experienced, this possessiveness?

"You should have told the school what happened."

Going to the BIA had never occurred to him. In his eyes they were still the enemy, not to be trusted and certainly to be avoided.

"They could have investigated. Found Carr and arrested him. At the very least they would have dismissed the man."

"You only say that because you trust them to do what is right."

"You do not?"

"I see what they do at that school. There is nothing right there. You should not be a part of that place."

"We are teaching them to be civilized."

"You are making them ashamed to be what the Great Spirit made them."

"No. We're teaching them useful skills, converting them to American citizens."

"Stealing all their land and making them farmers."

"The reservation is a huge tract of land."

"Bad land, useless land."

"Well, we can't let them run about killing people and capturing women and children." She dared him to argue with that by lifting her painted chin at him.

He cast out a long sigh. "It is a war, Lucie. Do not be fooled. Instead of shooting them or starving them, they are stealing their children, stealing their future."

"It is better than extermination."

"Better is not right."

She rose. "How dare you judge me? I was trying to help these poor children. I was trying to ease their way. They need an education and vocational skills." She folded her arms before her in a gesture she knew was defensive, but could not seem to help. Was she trying to convince him or herself?

He stood now, making her feel small and ashamed.

"Eagle Dancer failed to make you an Indian. What

makes you think you will do better making his children white?"

"That's *not* what we are doing."

He said no more, but instead glanced up at the sky. She followed his example. They had talked and argued through the setting of the sun and as the stars grew bright above them, but now the stars were gone and the air held the feel of rain.

Sky glanced to the river. "We have to move west, away from the water and these trees."

"Will it be bad?"

He did not answer at first, just listened to the rustle of the leaves as he studied the wind. One moment the wind was warm and dry and the next the direction changed and the temperature dropped, blowing past her with icy fingers.

He gave a low whistle and Ceta trotted into the clearing. He was sorry she had to leave the fire, but knew it would do her little good when the rain came. She had been through many storms on the plains. Surely she remembered their power. Too bad they did not have a tipi, where the destructive winds could find no perch and simply whistle past. But barring that, he knew the trees were the very worst place to wait out a storm.

Lucie packed quickly as Sky saddled the horses. In a matter of a few minutes, they were riding west, diagonal to the approaching storm.

Sky cocked his head as the first rumble reached him. Soon the thunder increased until it sounded like the running hooves of stampeding buffalo. The sky was alive with flashes of light exploding, one after another beneath the huge storm clouds that swept down on them.

"Dismount," he called, straining over the wind now.

Lucie did not argue, but did exactly as he asked. Before he could say so, she had the saddle uncinched and was dragging it and the blanket down. He had chosen a small depression in the earth, one that sloped slightly to the east. It was not the high spot, but not so low as to fill with water. He hobbled the horses tightly, so they could not escape, and then moved Lucie away from the taller animals. The horses' eyes rolled white and they reared up in fear, but they could not bolt with the tethers joining their front feet. Instead they crow-hopped about in restless motions that only assured Sky that they were in for a terrible storm.

Lucie followed carrying her bundle. The wind was so strong it lifted her braid. He worried for a moment that the thunderbirds were swirling in a whirlwind, but such storms usually came from the south. When they were well away the horses he stopped. Lucie sank to her knees, just as any Sioux woman would do, and waited.

He crouched beside her.

She leaned forward to speak. "This will be bad."

He nodded and looped his arm about her. The skin on the back of her neck was cold.

"Do you want your blanket?" he asked.

She shook her head and clutched her bundle to her chest. "I'll try to keep it dry."

It would be better to have a mostly damp blanket after the storm than a soaking wet one. So rather than drape herself in wool, she would drape herself around the folded bundle and hope the water did not pool beneath her. Sky reached in his bag and drew out one old oilskin duster and dragged it on. Then he pulled

Lucie before him, nestling her between his legs, and sat with his back to the wind.

Her heat warmed his chest and belly. He wrapped his arms about her and held tight until she stopped shivering. Gradually she relaxed and sank deeper against him. The wind buffeted his back, throwing his hair across his face. Stinging pellets of ice beat against his exposed neck and head. He rested his chin on Lucie's wavy hair, closed his eyes and waited.

Chapter Eight

Lucie did not notice the moment when the hail changed to sleet, but she was certain when the sleet became rain, pouring down in torrential sheets. Sky remained fixed to the earth like a boulder, her shelter from this raging torrent that flattened the grass all about them.

She could no longer see the horses. The lightning continued to flash. She counted as her father had taught her.

"One Mississippi, two Mississippi, three…"

The crack and boom vibrated through her chest. Less than a half mile away now. Her boulder moved, bringing her down to the wet grass as he opened his slicker over her. He lay half on top of her, pressing her to the earth as the rain beat against her legs. But Sky's body protected her head, torso and much of her upper legs. Not that she wasn't wet—she was—but she was warm, too.

They stayed down as the electrical storm crashed about them. Sky flinched only at one strike. It was not the closest, but it did sound different, as if connected to a cannon blast. She felt his chest vibrate and knew he spoke, but she could hear nothing past the caterwaul of the storm raging above them.

Gradually, Lucie began to count again. When she could consistently reach six Mississippi, Sky moved off of her and rolled to his feet. Lucie rose more slowly, weighed down by sodden petticoats and her heavy wool dress. He offered his hand and drew her up.

Sky was whistling now, not the ordinary come-here whistle but the perfect imitation of a male oriole. He stopped and then began again. She listened when he paused but heard nothing.

Was he calling his horse?

He cocked his head and set off at a quick trot. Lucie lifted her saturated hem and hurried behind. Wet petticoats stuck to her legs. She missed her buckskin dress that was naturally resistant to rain.

Sky disappeared into the night for a moment, but she hurried on. She could see him now, silhouetted by the flashes of retreating lightning and then she saw the horse. It was down on its side kicking. Somehow it had managed to get one rear foot stuck between the two front ones. Sky reached the beast and rested a hand on its neck. The horse stilled. Sky cut the hobble. Falcon rolled up and shook his head so furiously its mane flew up and down. Sky laughed and stroked the creature's wet hide.

His horse, then. She glanced about. Where was hers?

It could not have gone far. Sky was obviously thinking the same thing because he was also craning his neck, this way and that.

"Where is she?" called Lucie.

Sky walked up the small hill. Sky began a string of spectacular curses in Lakota as he charged out of sight.

When she reached the hilltop she saw her mount, still and sodden, her neck stretched at an unnatural angle, as if she had died in some horrible contortion of agony. Sky knelt beside the creature, pressing an ear to her chest. By the time Lucie arrived he was already standing.

"Is she?"

Her answer came from Sky's mount when he moved within ten feet of the other horse before shrieking a wild whinny and galloping off.

"Lucky it didn't kill Ceta, too. Maybe he was down when that bolt hit." He glanced at her. "Don't know why the heavens would want us both on one horse, but that's the way it will be, I guess."

It was one thing to be pressed up against Sky while lying facedown in the mud, quite another to rest, cradled in his arms while riding horseback. She thought of the night he took her from her room and her stomach began to jump. Then memories of another warrior intruded. Eagle Dancer used to carry her, sometimes, on his horse, but only when no one could see them. It was wrong for a warrior to carry a woman. His hands must be full with weapons to defend his people. But he had broken convention for her and she recalled that his horse had been fast as the wind. It was an intimate act, riding so close that you could feel the other's warm breath, hear the beating of your heart and his.

"Will you eat horse meat?" he asked.

There was a time when she would have eaten anything. It was not so long ago that she had forgotten.

Food was to be savored and cherished, for it was not always provided.

"I will," she said, hardening herself for what he would do.

Lucie moved forward, seeing the black hole now, in the horse's haunches. It looked as if someone had taken a spear and stabbed it, but there was no blood, only blackened flesh. She leaned close enough to touch her mount. The stench of scorched hair surrounded her.

"Lightning came out her hoof. See?"

Lucie saw nothing unusual. She leaned closer.

Sky pointed behind her. "Shoe's gone. Lightning likes metal."

Sure enough, the shoe was missing, while all three others were in place.

"Poor thing."

Sky unsheathed his hunting knife and lifted it to the heavens offering a prayer of thanks for the nourishment the horse would furnish. Lucie bowed her head and prayed, as well.

She found herself using the old words, the ones Eagle Dancer had taught her. She heard his voice on the wind, chanting as Sky thanked this four-legged one for carrying her and giving this final gift. When Lucie opened her eyes, Sky was already at work. His movements were quick and efficient. This man knew how to use a knife and knew anatomy. He gathered the liver and then a fine strip of red meat from the haunch. He bundled the meat in long grass and carried it to his horse.

"We have to go, before the wolves find this kill. They'll smell the blood now. When we are away, we'll stop and change."

He saddled Falcon and swept up into the saddle,

offering his hand to her and tugging her up before him. She sat half across the saddle horn and half in his lap, clutching her bundle before her and shivering. It was a miserable ride over the wet grass. He kept on until the stars reappeared. She did not know his destination. She only knew she could not rest for the cold wet clothing and the chattering of her teeth. She thought back, recalling a time when she had been colder, in her light summer dress, then torn and ragged.

When you are my wife, I will give you the best of hides to make a dress and wolf furs for a cloak.

Eagle Dancer had kept every promise. But she had not kept hers. She had not been a good wife. She had wanted to run. He knew it and so he watched her always. Now she was running again, only this time she was running to him. How had it happened, this change of heart? How could she feel this ache and worry over his safety, while at the same time, dread seeing him again?

Did she dread this reunion because of fear of what he might say or do or did the trepidation grow from guilt at leaving him, when she knew he loved her with his whole open heart? His love was possessive and selfish and generous and kind. She didn't understand him. She didn't understand herself. Lucie wrapped her arms more tightly about her waist and waited. Waited for the ride to end, waited for the warmth of the morning light, waited for answers to questions she could not even form in her tired mind.

At last they reached a grove of trees, dark against the prairie. She might find dry wood there in the dead branches that still clung to the trees. Falcon stopped and Sky slid from the saddle, dropping the reins. He reached for her. She clutched at his shoulders as his hands encircled her waist. She floated through the air for a moment like the white fluff released from the flowers of the cottonwood. Then her feet touched the earth.

He did not release her. She glanced up at him and found an expression she recognized, for she had seen it often enough in the face of Eagle Dancer. It was a look of possession.

She was so startled that her instinct was to flee. Had she again fallen into the hands of a man who would not let her go? She stepped back and his grip tightened so that his fingers bit into her skin.

"Sky?"

Sky's instinct was to hold her, but the look of fear on Lucie's face struck him like a slap. The cold and the accident gave him a right to wrap his arms about her as they rode over the prairie and he had taken full advantage. Breathed in her scent, nestling her close, warming her with his body—her proximity made him entertain wild notions. But the fear in her eyes struck him like a slap.

He had to let her go. He knew it, yet his hands still gripped her. He had not expected this battle within him to come to the surface. But she had seen it, hadn't she?

"Let me go, now," she urged.

He didn't.

She placed her hands on his wrists and pushed, urging him to release her. He relaxed his fingers and she slipped from his grasp.

Lucie stepped quickly away, escaping him as she had her husband. "I'm going to gather wood."

A moment later he heard the crack and snap of branches being torn from the trees.

Sky unsaddled Ceta and led him to the spring. There he removed the bridle, leaving his stallion as the Great Spirit had made him. He did not worry over his friend disappearing. Falcon stayed because he wanted to, not because he was made to. He glanced into the darkness in the direction Lucie had vanished. That was how a real marriage must be. Both parties agreed to stay. Why did Eagle Dancer, who was so wise in so many ways, fail to see that?

Sky found Lucie arranging firewood. She had torn the inner bark into paper-thin strips, encouraging the fibrous hairs away from the core. These delicate threads would take a spark and create the ember that would light their fire.

"I didn't bring my flint," she said, looking up at him. "You still have it?"

She hesitated and then nodded. "Yes."

That information warmed him. He retrieved the sharp-angled stone and used the blade of his knife to create a shower of sparks. Eventually a few caught. Then he blew, carefully coaxing the fire to appear. Once he had a flame, he fed it the twigs that Lucie handed him. When the fire caught, they both sat back to exchange expressions of gratification.

"That's a welcome sight."

Sky nodded. "Did your clothing stay dry?"

She retrieved her bundle and found her things only damp. "Mostly."

Sky knew it was more the shield of their bodies than the wool's natural water repulsion that protected her things. She stepped away from the fire to change. Sky did not need any such privacy. He stood and stripped out of his shirt and moccasins. Then he peeled out of his clammy dungarees and tossed them aside. Had he been alone he would have stood beside the fire to warm up before dressing. But instead he went to his saddle-bag and drew out a green, three-point Hudson Bay blanket and looped it about his waist. Then he squatted by the fire to await her reappearance. Anticipation tugged inside him, tight as the head of a drum. Was she standing naked out there? His mind furnished images of her in cotton underthings, made transparent by the rain.

"Lucie? You there?"

He heard a hiss. "Don't you dare come over here."

Sky laughed and stared in the direction of her voice, listening to the rustle and the mumbling that he could almost make out. At last, she emerged from the night, fully dressed in a dark skirt, white blouse and a shawl draped about her shoulders, carrying her moccasins. Her feet were bare and her long wet hair flowed over her shoulders like a waterfall soaking the back of her blouse.

She stopped at the sight of him. "Please tell me you are wearing trousers."

"Only got but one pair." He thumbed at the denim now draped over a bush and dripping copious amounts of water onto the soggy ground. "Got a breechcloth, though. If you're still cold, I can give you this blanket. It's mostly dry."

He stood and reached for the roll of scratchy wool that encircled his waist. Lucie shielded her eyes.

"No! That's quite all right." She placed her moccasins by the fire and then retrieved her wet things, stretching them out over branches and brush. When she was done she fidgeted with her wet hair, which showed its natural proclivity to wave.

"I make you nervous?"

He didn't talk much to women, but when he did he found them to rarely answer a question directly.

"Exceedingly," she said.

He smiled. "Straight as the shaft of an arrow."

"Excuse me?"

"Come sit by the fire, Lucie. I won't bite you."

She did, but chose to stay as far from him as she could without sitting in the smoke.

"You want to eat again?"

She shook her head. "I'm tired."

He glanced up. The violent storm had passed. But the storm was still here, rolling inside him every time he got near her. Sky stared up at the stars, appearing now between the sweeping clouds. "Going to be a cold night."

"Mr. Fox, if you think I will come crawling over there and beg you to hold me, you are much mistaken. My parents raised me better than that."

"And if you think I'm going to let you sit up all night shivering, you're mistaken, as well. My parents raised me better than that, too."

He returned to his bags and exchanged the blanket for his breechcloth. He traveled light and had no buffalo robe, but he did have the slicker.

He folded her damp blanket for a mat, thinking it would make her more comfortable. Then he motioned to her. She remained shivering where she was.

He frowned. "If you don't come over here, I'll come and get you."

"No, thank you."

"Not a request, Lucie."

She glared. "I won't be ordered about."

Like a slave, he thought. The woman had good reason to be cautious of possessive men. He tried reason, but was disturbed by his eagerness to convince her. "You're cold."

"You'll take advantage of me."

"I'd sooner cut off my own hand than offend you."

Lucie's brows lifted in surprise at that.

"I was sent to retrieve you. Do you think I would risk our friendship for a woman?"

Now she glared at him, her skin flushed gold by the firelight. His head knew his words were true, but then why was he holding his breath in anticipation of her acceptance? He was a hypocrite, happy for this excuse to possess her again.

Lucie stood. He indicated the pallet he had made and she lay stiffly upon it. He moved in beside her and covered them with his blanket and then the slicker. Sky slipped an arm about her and pulled her to his naked chest. It was like hugging an ice maiden. Her body trembled and her teeth clattered together like finger bones in a bag. But he held on.

She curled against him, pressing her back to his chest and gripping his arms. Gradually his skin grew warm again and then her trembling eased. It was as though she was melting into slumber. He felt her slip away to dreams.

Sky rested his chin on her wet hair and closed his eyes. How would it be to hold this woman in a lover's embrace and lie with her every night beneath the stars? It would be so easy to nestle his hips against hers and then from there, a short step to stroking her, being lost in her heat.

Sky did not move until she did. He allowed her to roll to her back and followed, keeping her pressed to his side, telling himself he only meant to warm her.

He resisted sleep as long as he could, knowing that he would not soon again have an excuse to be holding her, while hating himself for betraying his friend in his heart. He wanted her, he would admit it only to himself. He wanted his friend's woman. Sky squeezed his eyes shut, grinding his teeth against the urge to take her.

When the larks began to call the dawn, he tried to ignore them. When she roused, would he have the strength to let her go?

He realized that given the chance, he would do exactly what Eagle Dancer had done. He would steal this woman for himself and keep her with or without her consent. It was that realization that finally shook him from his bedding.

He moved away from her, each step as difficult as the last. All he wanted to do was run back to her side. How had she captured him so completely in so short a time? But he knew how. It was her beauty and her plainness. Her courage and her fears. Her power and her weakness. Everything about her called to him, except the one truth that shouted above them all. He couldn't keep her.

He thought he had accepted his path long ago. Outlaw, outcast, loner. He was all this and worse. And even if she was not Eagle Dancer's wife, even if he gave his blessing, Sky could not have her. Because if he did, he knew that one way or another, he'd lose her, too, just like he'd lost everything and everyone he ever cared about. It was what he deserved but after a while it was easier not to care at all. And that was exactly what he had done. And then she had come along.

Sky crawled away from the bedding, from Lucie and her warm, sweet body. He made it to the edge of the small clearing.

"Where are you going?" she asked. Her low voice, made sensuous by sleep, made his body twitch like a rabbit caught in a snare. And just like the rabbit, he struggled to breathe as he fought to regain his freedom.

"To find my horse." All he need do was whistle and Falcon would swoop down upon them. But she did not know this.

"Oh." She frowned at him.

He remained frozen by her attention. If she called him back, he knew he would go, but what he would do then sent him back several more steps. He wanted to cry out from the silent torture of being captured by those rich, blue eyes. Did she see him resist the desire roasting him alive from the inside?

"Will we eat first? I can rouse the fire."

She already had.

He broke the contact of their eyes. "Yes. Do that."

Sky turned and trotted away, trying to act indifferent as he resisted the urge to run like the coward he had become. He had to break this wanting, for it shamed and weakened him.

Sky had reached the spring and was throwing ice cold water on his face when he heard Lucie scream.

Lucie had gone a little ways from camp to relieve herself and was returning when the thrashing in the brush stopped her. She thought it was Falcon or Sky trying to catch his mount. But instead the three warriors stepped from the wall of green and stood motionless before her. She sat beside the fire, in plain sight, knowing they had seen her already. It was too late to run. So she did the only thing she could think of. She opened her mouth and screamed at the top of her lungs.

One of the men sprang forward, capturing her upper arm. He pressed a big solid hand over her mouth.

Another moved beside him. "Are you crazy? Let her go. We'll run."

The third peered at her. "Did you see her chin? Why does she bear the marks of the Sweetwater?"

No Indian was allowed off the reservation. Yet here they were. Lucie struggled and kicked, managing to land one good blow to the shin of her captor. He released her.

"How do you say *quiet* in English?" asked the man.

"I don't know."

The three stared at her and she inched back. She could make no sense of them. The last time she had come face-to-face with a warrior, he had her tied and gagged in a matter of moments. Yet these three simply stood and stared as if she were some dangerous creature. She drew her skinning knife, holding it out before her.

"The little kitten has one fang," said the second.

"Let her run off, then. I won't stop her."

"But she's seen us. She'll tell."

Sky sprang into the clearing before her, facing the warriors. But to Lucie's dismay, he had not even bothered to draw his pistol. Instead, he held his arms out before him as if to stop them or perhaps offer to wrestle them.

The men went for their knives, and still Sky did not reach for his gun. Instead, he spoke to them. "What are you doing here, brothers?"

The three glanced at one another with startled expressions.

One lowered his knife. "We are not your brothers."

"I am Sky Fox of the Bitterroot clan."

The third stepped forward. "We are of the Village-at-the-End."

"This woman is under my protection," said Sky. "She is the wife of Eagle Dancer."

The three made sounds of astonishment.

Their representative nodded and all weapons were lowered. "I fought with Eagle Dancer. I will not stop you. Take her."

Sky pulled her behind him, but he did not lead her away as she had hoped.

"Have you eaten, brothers? My horse was struck by lightning last night and I took her liver. I also have some of her flank."

Lucie wanted to pound his back and pull his hair. Was he insane?

The men exchanged glances and then the eldest nodded. "We would be honored to share a meal with you and the wife of Eagle Dancer."

"Come." Now Sky motioned toward their camp.

Sky tried to move away from Lucie, but she clutched at him, grasping both arms around his waist and pressing her head to his chest. She knew she was making it difficult for him to walk and embarrassing him, but she could not keep herself from clinging like a frightened child.

She was making a hiccupping sound now and found tears streaming down her cheek.

His voice came only loud enough for her to hear. "You're safe with me, Lucie. Trust me."

She shook violently now. "It's like the first time, when they took me."

"Those times are gone, Lucie. There are no more raiding parties. No more captures."

"What about the truant officer, then?"

He hesitated. "I don't think these men did that."

"You are risking our lives on a hunch?" She glanced back to see them following, silent as three wolves on the hunt.

"They carry no weapons of war. They're only a hunting party."

She shook her head. "Hunting? But they aren't allowed to hunt. The government provides for them now."

"Have you seen the provisions?"

She fell silent.

"If you had, you would know why they sneak away to hunt."

"But that is dangerous. They could be arrested or shot."

"Or they could stay on the reservation and see their women starve."

She eased back enough to look up at him to judge if he was serious. "It can't be as bad as all that."

Sky said nothing. His silence made Lucie wonder. If he felt no compulsion to defend himself, his words might very well be true.

"Why didn't you just speak to them?"

Terror. She hadn't been able to breathe past the panic

pressing on her chest, let alone think. "It reminded me...I...just...screamed." She fiddled with a lock of hair, winding it around her finger until the skin turned white and then releasing it as they stepped closer to the fire. "Just hunting," she whispered to herself and felt a little better.

Before them, the fire now merrily burned the wood he had added. Sky seated Lucie on the blanket and had to peel her fingers off his arm.

He laid out the second blanket near the first and offered it to his guests. Lucie did not help him prepare the liver. She sat motionless as a stone, trying to be invisible as she had long ago, recalling the warriors who first begged for food and then...she pressed her hands over her eyes, to shut out the images. The wagon boss had been unwilling to feed them. The begging turned into angry demands and then an arrow shot that pinned their leader to the sideboard of the lead wagon, triggering the massacre. Lucie opened her eyes, determined to remain vigilant.

"Lucie?" Sky held out a portion of liver to her.

She glanced at him. Women ate last, yet he offered her this. She couldn't eat in any case, and shook her head in refusal. She watched as the men used their fingers, knives and hands in a carefully choreographed dance of slicing and chewing. Sky had been right; they were hungry. As she stared, she noted the differences from the braves she had known. They were thin, perilously so, but that was not what struck her most sharply. It was their carriage. They did not sit or eat like warriors. Instead they had a wary look about them, a caution instead of the confidence she was accustomed to seeing in such men. It was almost as if they had lost their place in the world. These were the parents of her students, she realized, but also the sons of the men who attacked her wagon.

"What are your names, brothers?" asked Sky. He was more relaxed with these men than he was with her. It nettled her to no end.

"I am called Black Horn," said the eldest. "This is my brother-in-law, Eye Lance, and his eldest son, Small Hawk. Thank you for the meat. It is much better than the beef rations."

"You are hunting?" asked Sky.

He nodded. "Eye Lance has two young daughters. He refused to send them to the school and so he and all in his family have lost their rations."

Lucie straightened at this and glanced at Sky.

"Can't he have some of yours?" asked Sky.

"Yes, but there is not enough. Our women are already skinny as weasels. Holding my wife is like rubbing two sticks together. There is not enough fat on either of us to keep us warm." He smiled at the joke that broke Lucie's heart. Black Horn looked at her as he spoke to Sky. "Is she really the wife of Eagle Dancer?"

"Yes. She worked at the school."

"The school?" said Eye Lance. "Does she know a little girl named Little Rabbit? She is the child of my wife's sister. Only six winters old now."

Sky turned to her, the question on his face, and she realized he was waiting for her to admit that she understood every word of this conversation.

Lucie drew herself up and faced them. "They give the girls American names. I don't always know their real names."

They stared at her in astonishment for a moment, then Eye Lance nudged his son.

"See, I told you they took their names with their hair."

It was only one of the things they took, thought Lucie.

"Do they get enough to eat?" asked Eye Lance.

Lucie thought of the soap. "Yes. The girls make fresh bread every day and beef for supper."

He nodded. "Beef again." He looked up at her. "And they learn the stick words?"

Half of the day, she thought. The rest was supposed to be vocational training, which turned into chores that ran the school—cooking the meals, doing the laundry, sewing the uniforms as if all that could be expected of her girls was the most menial of domestic positions. Sky had asked if she thought weeding turnip patches would make the boys farmers. Was Sky right? Had she only been part of a more subtle war against the Sioux?

Her heart twisted in apprehension as a flush of shame heated her cheeks.

"Yes, they are very good students. You should be proud of them."

"Their mothers wonder, when they cry, who will comfort them and when they are sick, who will bathe them?"

Lucie looked at their earnest faces. It was the first time she considered the trauma of having a child forcibly removed from a mother's arms. She had been so busy comforting and trying to act as a surrogate mother, she had forgotten the children had willing mothers who were deemed unfit to raise their own children. Although she had none of her own, it was not her place to take theirs.

Lucie's voice cracked as she answered. "They have doctors to look after the sick and women to bathe the girls. I am one of them, or I was."

"You left to come to your husband."

"Yes."

"That is good for him, but bad for our children," said Black Horn.

Sky watched Lucie as she struggled to defend the school. He thought he witnessed the moment of her surrender with the sagging of her shoulders.

Lucie turned to Eye Lance. "I think the children of your wife's sister would be safer and happier with their families, even if there is less to eat. With you, they will not be made to feel ashamed of who they are."

The man's eyes widened and then he nodded. "Thank you for speaking from your heart."

Sky offered more food and they refused but when pressed accepted another helping of the horse liver. After they had finished, Black Horn changed the direction of the conversation.

"Have you heard of the white-man killing?"

Sky nodded. "Do you know who did this thing?"

Black Horn shook his head. "It was not from my people, but they still took Iron Bear to the fort."

Sky thought again about the truant officer. He thought his punishment was just. But who had killed him? Certainly it was not a seasoned warrior like these men because the job had been clumsy. And why hadn't they removed his male organ? That was a final insult to an enemy, to send him to the Spirit World without his manhood intact. Sky had seen the body. The officer had not been touched there. It was almost as if the killers had been inexperienced in warfare or perhaps pretending to be warriors. And who would want to kill him knowing the trouble it would bring?

He stilled as a possibility struck him. It would explain all of it, the awkward butchering, the chance meeting on the plains that was not chance after all and the lack of understanding of the hornets' nest of trouble such a murder would stir. Could the boy have come back and done such a thing?

Chapter Nine

Sky's mind still reeled with his suspicions as Lucie attended their visitors. No one noticed his preoccupation and after a moment he recovered enough to hear Lucie.

Lucie seemed much more at ease as she spoke to Black Horn. "We have more meat. Please take it."

"You have been generous already," said the warrior.

Lucie insisted. "A gift to your wife and the children, from the wife of Eagle Dancer. Please. It would honor me."

He nodded his acceptance.

Sky watched the exchange with a welling feeling of pride. She was becoming a woman he admired before his very eyes. She handled herself with such poise and compassion. It was a rare thing in this lonely world.

Sky handed over the remains of their food stores, unconcerned about providing for Lucie. He had a fine rifle and a horse. They would most certainly not go hungry. But these men went on foot and without firearms, which they were forbidden to carry, and all because their skin was the color of the fine red pipestone.

He shook his head at the idiocy of the White Father's plan for his red "brothers".

At least Sky could provide some small comfort. "We butchered our other horse late last night after it was struck by the thunder gods. It was a good horse, healthy and fat."

The men discussed the location and then set out leaving Lucie and Sky alone by the fire.

"That was well done," said Sky.

"What?"

"He couldn't accept all our meat until you mentioned his children. You made it a blessing instead of charity. I think you are beginning to understand now."

Her smile faded. "Is that what this is, some grand lesson to teach me the error of my ways?"

Sky realized too late that his compliment had become an insult. He tried to correct his mistake. "I only meant to say that I see now why Eagle Dancer elevated you to wife. He would be proud of his wife this day."

Her eyes narrowed and her face grew flushed. Sky recognized the boiling fury and had the foresight to prepare to duck, but when she stepped forward, she only aimed a finger at him.

"Let me tell you about my elevated life. Before my wedding, my mother-in-law beat me with a cord of wood as big around as her wrist and she gave me this." Lucie pointed to her chin. "I begged Eagle Dancer for my freedom, but my husband wanted to 'elevate me,' a thirteen-year-old child, to wife. He took me the same month I became a woman."

Sky frowned at this, wondering why Eagle Dancer hadn't protected the one he claimed to love.

"Don't you presume that my time with the Sweetwater in any way resembled the romping free life of a beloved son. I was a captive and I did what I did to survive."

Sky met her angry stare, taking in all the pain that filled her face, refusing to look away. "Do you hate them, Lucie? Is that why you worked at their school?"

She threw up her arms. "No. They're children. I wanted to help them adjust. I wanted to keep them from feeling the terror that stayed with me every day of my imprisonment. And I failed. I can't protect them. I can't save a single one of those girls. They are as much prisoners as I was. All I did was make things worse for them, bring punishment to them that…"

She burst into tears. Sky braced, trying to comprehend the lightning-like transition from fury to tears. Was she sad now or was this still the anger? He started to back away, as he would have done had he startled a skunk on the way to the outhouse, but something stopped him. He did not know if it was the rounding of her shoulders that made her look defeated, or the trembling of her body, but he could not abandon her. He hesitated a moment longer trying to decide how to bring her comfort. It was an area he had no experience with. And then he remembered when he was a very little boy, how his mother, Many Flowers, would gather him up in her lap and stroke his head or rub his back until he felt at ease again. The unexpected longing for that comfort combined with Lucie's pain and he felt his own throat close. Oh, no, he'd sooner run off into the brush than let her see his tears.

But she was still crying, head down, shoulders jumping. He reached out and clasped her upper arms. She bit back a sob and glanced up at him as he drew her into his arms. She stiffened for a moment and then seemed to melt into him, pressing her wet cheek to his bare chest.

He enfolded her in his arms, rocking like a willow in a summer breeze, gently to and fro. Gradually she reached around his middle and clasped her hands behind the small of his back. He stroked her head, cascading down her tangled hair to the middle of her back and then repeating the tender touch, while wishing he could see her face. Were her eyes closed? Did she know that by allowing him to comfort her, she was also comforting him?

How many nights had he lain awake with longing, wishing simply for a woman to hold him like this, in an easy, gentle embrace that told him he was no longer alone? He had found women to relieve his sexual needs. Those kinds of females were in every town and camp. But to find a woman who smelled of springtime and who would allow him to press his nose into the fragrance of her hair, take in the soft wonder of her skin; this was something rare—something to be savored. Her grief had lowered her defenses enough for her to allow him to give her something so simple, so complex and connect them for a few precious moments.

Her slick, wet cheek warmed his skin and her scent filled his nostrils like all the blossoms of spring, coming to him at once. Her fragrance was delicate as wild cherry and earthy as the bark of the white birch.

As she wept out her frustration and her disappointment, he let his eyes drift shut, wishing he could hold her like this forever. But already her trembling had ceased and her breathing grew less halting.

"You were right about everything. It *is* a war—a war against children." She pressed her nose into the juncture between his shoulder and his chest as if trying to hide her face in shame at ever having been a part of such a place. She had changed, because of what he had said and what she had seen. She could no longer defend the school or its subtle brand of extermination. *Kill the Indian, save the man,* as if one and the other were somehow not two parts of the same whole.

At last she cried herself out and eased away. The internal battle to keep her lasted less than an instant, for he knew already that Lucie hated to be held captive. He forced a blank expression, shielding himself so she would not see the need she had awakened. Would she ever let him hold her like this again?

"My mother was right. It was a mistake, another mistake."

He spoke in the low rhythmic waves that Many Flowers often used, as soothing as water flowing over rocks, but instead of offering empty words, he offered a tiny piece of his soul. "It is not a mistake to go and see for yourself how things are."

"I wish I'd never accepted that position."

He nodded. "I have ridden far with such regret. It is a hard companion."

She lifted her head to stare up at him with speculation. "Regret? Do you mean at leaving the People?"

Lucie gazed at him with hope in her eyes, wanting more than he had already given. He paused, assessing the risk. He did not speak of his regrets to anyone. They were too big, too dangerous. He feared that if he did not keep them down, they might burst from him like maggots from a rotting corpse. Could she understand what he could not? He nearly dared tell her of his friend.

Then he realized that she only thought she wanted to know. Already she was reconsidering her question. He could tell by the way she pulled back, releasing him and stepping clear. What had she glimpsed in his face that had sent her fleeing? The connection between them slipped away like minnows through the shallow water.

"The Mormons taught me of penitence, or at least they gave it a name. Sin, repentance, damnation, all the things I could not name before I came to the Wasicu. When I had walked the earth seventeen winters, I left the Mormon and his skinny wife and headed for Texas. I was good on a horse and driving cattle was easy, boring work. I tried to befriend the other cowpokes, but they made fun of my accent and my poor English. They called me the 'chief.'"

Stray tears still slipped down her cheeks.

"They were fools."

"Just boys mostly. We ran into trouble, rustlers. They pinned us down and stole the cattle. I was the only one who didn't fire his weapon."

She leaned back to look at him. Was she trying to judge why he did not defend himself?

"Because the others were cruel to you?" she guessed.

"No, it was just the day I learned that I would die myself before I would kill. It means that I will never become a war chief. For a time in my youth that was all I wanted. But after I left the People, I wanted to die."

Death seemed easier than walking with the burden he carried.

Lucie turned a critical eye on him, judging…what?

"When I was a new captive, one of the other girls said she would die before she would let one of the men have her. It was the only way to keep her honor, but it is also a mortal sin. She did end her own life, while I…" Lucie bit her lip and Sky wondered if she also struggled to release what was trapped in her heart. At last she drew a heavy breath and continued. "I knew it was expected of me, the brave thing, but I was too much of a coward."

"Dying's not hard."

She smiled. "No? I found it so, but it also seemed a kind of escape, a peace of sorts. But then I had to consider the damnation."

He didn't believe the Wasicu's version of the afterlife, all damnation and retribution and flying corpses with wings. She met his steady gaze and he felt the link again, even without touching her. She was sharing a hidden part of herself. And his need to keep this feeling made him try to do the same.

"It wasn't until I started catching horses that I found any peace."

She gazed up at him and nodded. "I hoped that teaching would be like that. Maybe it could be, but not there." She set her jaw in a look of stubborn determination that he knew was only the merest indication of the wellspring of strength that had sustained her during her captivity. Gradually her gaze drifted away. He wondered what she was seeing, for it was clearly not their surroundings.

"I'd like to watch you with those wild horses," she said.

He was about to deny the fancy. He worked alone, or he always had worked alone. Now he allowed himself to entertain the possibility of a different way of being, a way that included Lucie. He could picture her there, on the prairie, beside him as he rode toward a herd of wild mustangs. She had a wildness in her, too. He felt it as clearly as he felt the air change before a rain.

Something rustled in the underbrush. Sky recognized the sound instantly, but Lucie clearly did not, for she inched closer to him. He chuckled and then gave a low whistle. Ceta nickered in reply. Sky lifted his brow at her and she let her shoulders sag in relief.

"Falcon?" she asked.

"You aren't the only one with a broken heart, Lucie. Mine broke the day I ran."

Questions alighted in her mind like butterflies on a honeysuckle. She knew he wasn't rescued or released. They had told her that he had run away. But why would a boy run from the family he loved? She waited, sensing he was struggling to reveal something important and fearing if she pressed him, he would shut down once more.

"Did you know Joy Cat's son?" he asked at last.

The fact that he did not speak the name of the boy aloud made Lucie wonder. It was the People's way not to speak the names of the departed. Was Sacred Cloud dead?

"He was one of the boys you rode with—the son of the head man." Lucie avoided saying Sacred Cloud, though she recalled the boy distinctly.

"Yes. I wouldn't speak to you for fear of what he and the others might say. It was wrong and I am sorry."

"You were trying to make them forget you were white."

"Yes. But I tried too hard."

His face brightened in shame and she knew something terrible had happened.

She took his hand. "Sky?"

He drew a long breath and then spoke. "We were hunting a black-tailed deer in a thicket. I went one way and my friend the other. We planned to flush it out and...I saw it, moving in the brush." Sky shielded his eyes from her. When he began again, his voice was gravel. "I shot and he fell. But it wasn't the deer. It my friend. I put the shaft right into his chest because I wanted to plant the first arrow in the kill."

It was Lucie's turn to clasp him. She drew him down so his head rested on her bosom. "Oh, Sky. How terrible."

"He died there in the thicket, before I could even reach him. He was my best friend and I killed him."

He was silent a long time, but his body shook with emotion. Finally, he pushed away and stared at her with haunted eyes.

"Eagle Dancer heard me crying and came. He said that Joy Cat might forget that I was an Indian when he saw what I had done. He took me near the fort and told me to run. He saved my life, but made me a coward. I never faced them, never accepted the punishment that was mine to bear. So, you see, I'm still a coward, because I haven't been able to kill anyone since that day—not the rustlers and not Carr when he was abusing that boy."

Lucie recalled what Sky had told her and then something else. Mrs. Fetterer's dislike for the truant officer. Her reason raised suspicion. Did she know? Was it why she had spoken to Father Dumax? Lucie tried to recall her words. The Father had dismissed her concerns and later, when she heard about Carr's death, Lucie had been surprised that she had said that the officer had forgotten that boys have parents. Now she understood. The matron must have known or suspected. Lucie was certain. She had gone to the head of the school, who had done…nothing. Lucie's heart clenched with her jaw. What would she have done, if it had been her brother Carr had molested? She didn't blame Sioux for using him as a pincushion.

Sky continued his tale of self-loathing. "I didn't even draw my gun when you screamed."

"That doesn't make you a coward."

Sky shot to his feet as if she's slapped him. He stalked away from the fire and stood with his hands on his hips.

"What does it make me, then?"

Lucie thought for a moment. "Perhaps a holy man."

Sky turned, looking absolutely stunned. "Holy?"

"Yes. A man that chooses not to kill and spends his days rescuing the four-legged ones. It seems a holy path to me, a true journey on the Red Road. That's what the People would say, I think."

He returned to her, dropping to his knees. "Could that be possible?"

She wanted to take his hand. Instead she smiled. He did not.

Hers faded as she looked into his troubled eyes.

"Sky? I'm sorry for what happened to your friend. It was an accident."

"No. I notched the bow. I aimed and shot."

"But you never meant to hurt your friend."

"Still, he is dead now."

"Yes," she said. Her words were small comfort indeed.

They stared at each other.

She wanted to tell him it would be all right, that she understood. But she couldn't. She couldn't understand his pain and loss any more than he could understand hers. But she wanted to.

At last she spoke. "Thank you for telling me this. Your burden must be heavy to carry."

He lifted his brows and his expression seemed to change from sorrow to astonishment. Had he expected her to diminish what he felt or to tell him all would be well? She had walked with regret too long to believe such fairy tales.

"Yes," he said. "Heavy."

He nodded. "We should go."

He repacked his saddlebag and threw it over the horse's haunches, tying it to the rings behind the cantle. Then he mounted and offered his hand.

Lucie lifted one foot to his, already resting in the stirrup, and accepted his help. Together they swung her up behind him. She slipped easily into the back of the wide seat, pressed between the molded leather and his body. Sky spun Ceta away. They cleared the cover of the spring, heading out over the prairie once more. As they rode Lucie felt a new understanding for him.

His avoidance of others and his sullen expression suddenly made perfect sense. Why hadn't she recognized a man who had lost everything? It was like looking in a mirror.

They rode through the morning and into the hot afternoon. Lucie found herself dwelling in the past on what Sky had told her about the Mormon. She had been rescued, returned to her family. While he had lost his family when he returned to a people he did not know or understand. How ironic; her race could not accept her and he could not accept them.

And all this time he had mourned the boy he had killed, punished himself for the life he had taken.

Sky's voice called her back to the moment. "I would like to ask you of your abduction."

How odd, she had been wondering about him, as he was wondering about her. He had touched on a topic she rarely spoke of and when she did, it was only with her family. She had learned early that others liked to exploit the details of her capture and captivity. She would not have her pain used as another's entertainment. Her silence did not keep men from writing the story. But Sky was different. He had been where she had been, walked a similar path. She braced herself to speak of that terrible day but Sky's next words brought her to an abrupt halt.

"How did your parents steal you from him?" asked Sky, his voice reflecting utter astonishment that such a thing could occur.

She frowned. By abduction, did he mean her rescue? After all she had told him did he still see her amnesty as merely another successful raid by the enemy? She was so rattled it took a moment to switch her mind to that bitter-cold day when her parents had come for her.

"Well, they tried to negotiate my release and failed. But Eagle Dancer's mother hated me so much she helped my mother."

"Ah. I never met her. Eagle Dancer mentioned his mother's betrayal, but I did not understand."

"Did he? The last time I saw him he was telling me to stay in his tipi and posting two warriors at the entrance. These guards saw two women enter and two leave. They did not notice that my mother had taken my place. Once we had been escorted out of the village, the guards were removed and Yellow Bird led my mother out of the village. But she gave my mother no horse and she nearly froze in the blizzard. My father didn't know what my mother had done. I didn't either until my father noticed me riding where she should have been. She never spoke to me, never looked at me—I never knew." Lucie was glad Sky could not see the tears wet her cheeks again. Telling this brought all the emotions up like rocks heaving to the surface of a pasture after the freeze. "He went back for her in that storm. The blizzard that nearly killed them also prevented Eagle Dancer from catching us."

"Your mother has a warrior's heart. Just like her daughter."

What did he mean, like her mother? She was nothing like Sarah West. Her mother was a fighter, while Lucie had survived by doing as she was told and not making trouble. Why would Sky think she was brave when all she had done was run from her marriage and from her parents and now from the school? He thought he lacked courage for leaving the People, while she was certain she did. She had never stood and fought. And that was exactly why she made no objection now at his words, avoiding the conflict of an argument as any proper coward would do.

He glanced back at her. "Were you glad to leave him?"

It was a hard question to answer. "I was happy to be reunited with my mother. I didn't realize then that so many people would hate me for what had happened. My mother knew and so she defended me the only way she could, by keeping me safe at home, until that became a kind of imprisonment. It was so gradual that I didn't understand, at first, that my life would never be as it had been."

"In that we are alike. Nothing is the same now. What did you do there, in your mother's home?"

"I attended school. The other children were not kind, especially the boys." She held down a shiver at the memories. "Names, pranks—I told myself that this was nothing compared to the life I had lived before I came under Eagle Dancer's protection."

"But it wasn't easy."

"No."

"You never loved him?"

She did not pretend to misunderstand and spoke in a clear, certain tone so that he would not misunderstand, either. "Never."

"Yet here we are, riding to his rescue."

Lucie thought Sky's voice held a note of resentment. She recalled that look of possession he'd cast her last night. Did he battle with his desires for her, just as she had been fighting hers? That thought gave her a little thrill, caused her heart to quicken.

"Yes. It is an obligation, a debt I must pay and then I will speak the words before a witness. Perhaps I then…" Her words trailed off. She drew a breath and tried again. "Perhaps then, I can think of him without remorse."

She wondered what would have happened if last night, instead of drawing away, she had kissed him. She recalled those hungry eyes again gobbling her up. The initial thrill died as she cautioned herself. Despite her attraction, this was not the time and this was not the man for her to become infatuated with. Sky was reckless, wild and completely unmanageable. He had told her he preferred his own company and kept himself apart from everyone. Yet, as he had said, here they were—together, alone, both battling a secret desire. He couldn't kiss her, of course, not without betraying a man he respected. But perhaps he was trying to share a different kind of intimacy.

She wrapped her arms about his middle and pressed her head to the wide space between his shoulder blades. She felt the muscles of his stomach jump and his spine straightened with new tensions. But she held on just the same, closing her eyes to savor the contact. He did not warn her off. Gradually his muscles uncoiled.

"Have you ever had a wife?" she asked.

He made a sharp should that could have been a laugh. "I frighten women."

"You don't frighten me."

"I did the night I jumped through your window. And you ran from me the first two times I tried to speak to you."

All true. "But that was because you spoke to me in Lakota. I had a bad feeling about you."

"Most women do." He lifted his water skin and offered it to her.

She drank then and passed back the skin. Their fingers brushed and the tingling excitement rushed through her. She wrapped her arms about his middle again.

"Feelings change."

She felt his stomach muscles cord. Was it her words or her embrace that caused his reaction? It pleased her to believe he felt the same warm glow that filled her whenever she touched him. Lucie bit her lip as she contemplated stroking the fine contour of his stomach. What would he do if she did so? In the end, the action was too bold and that was not her way.

Silence stretched. At last she filled the gap with an attempt to continue to get to know him a little better.

"What about before. Did you have a sweetheart?"

"Then, I was not interested in girls and now…I can't stay on the reservation because my skin is white."

He talked as if the only kind of woman he could marry was Indian. That possibility zinged like an arrow into her heart. Lucie grew cautious.

He glanced back at her and then continued. "I don't want marriage. My life is not the kind to share."

Lucie was about to disagree when she realized that to do so was to show her hand, as her father would say, and in so doing, give Sky a glimpse of her mad infatuation. But what if it wasn't mad? What if he felt it, as well?

"But still, Eagle Dancer suggested I marry."

Lucie's eyes narrowed. "Did he?"

"He thinks it will help heal my heart if I take a Bitterroot woman."

Her mind grasped the first objection she came upon and threw it back at him.

"But you're Bitterroot."

Sky nodded at her reasonable objection. But if he knew that men went outside their clan to marry, how could he consider a woman from the tribe?

"He says since I am not of their blood it was permissible. There are many widows, since the Battle of the Greasy Grass."

"But you just said you didn't want to marry."

He said nothing to this, but his muscles stiffened as he straightened his spine. Lucie frowned and chewed on her bottom lip as she tried to think past the unexpected blast of jealousy that blew through her.

"Someone you know?"

He nodded. She hated his silence. Why must he make her pull each strand of information from him?

"Do you love her?"

His laugh was devoid of humor, a mere cough of descent. "When I last saw them they were babies listening to stories at their grandmother's fire. I don't even know them."

"I don't understand. Why must you marry? What good will it do?"

"Some good, I hope."

She caught it now, the plural form he had used, and with it, the implication that he would become a bigamist.

"How many?"

He held up two fingers, as if he could not find the energy to say so aloud.

It was the way of the People to allow more than one wife. But Lucie had seen it only twice. Once when the first wife was sick with the wasting disease. The new wife cared for her and saw her passing was made easier. The second time, a brave married his sister-in-law at his wife's request after she lost her husband to a riding accident. It was expected for a man to take care of his family.

Lucie's eyes widened at the possibility. "Who are these widows?"

Sky sighed. His chest expanded and then contracted before her.

"Eagle Dancer suggested the daughters of Joy Cat."

She stiffened. He meant the sisters of his friend, Sacred Cloud, the widowed sisters. He felt a duty to provide for the siblings of the friend who had died. Lucie's mouth hardened into a thin line. Why did she care? He owed her nothing and yet, for a time, she had forgotten that she was ugly.

But why had he looked at her like that? A hateful, cynical little voice called out the answer. *The look he gave you last night—was just the look of a man who wants physical gratification.* And today? *Trying to be kind to the wife of Eagle Dancer.*

Lucie pressed her fist to her mouth. She had lived through many disappointments and she knew that she would survive this one, as well. But for the moment, she felt deflated as a fallen cake. It seemed she had still not learned her lesson.

Her head hung and if she did not sit the horse, she thought her knees might fail her.

"Eagle Dancer has offered to speak to him and see if he will accept me," said Sky.

A tiny hope flared, tinder ignited by a dying ember. Joy Cat might still refuse the match.

"Doesn't he hate you?" she asked.

"I do not know. But he has good reason to." Sky steered Falcon around a colony of prairie dogs who barked a warning and then disappeared as they passed. "But if he agrees, Eagle Dancer says I should take them with me. That way we all would have a better life."

She tried to think past the threatening storm cloud now hovering over her.

"Will he accept the match?"

"I do not know. I would not."

She wrapped her arms about his middle in a caress she prayed felt tender and sympathetic, rather than like the clinging hold of a woman who has lost her last hope.

Lucie pressed her cheek to the warm wool of his shirt and heard her voice crack. "It's a terrible reason to marry."

"No worse than yours."

How true.

Chapter Ten

Lucie wondered if marrying the sisters would help Sky's heart heal. Somehow she did not think so.

They forded the shallow James River on horseback, without even getting their feet wet.

Upon reaching the other side, Sky dismounted and helped Lucie down. He loosened the girth on the saddle and removed Falcon's bridle. His stallion gave a deep sigh of relief and then tossed his head. Sky chuckled and scratched behind the horse's ear and rubbed beneath his stubbly chin. Then he walked along the gravel beds that lined the river. She and Falcon followed behind him like ducks in a row.

"I would put our camp there." He pointed back toward the line of cedar.

Lucie nodded her approval at the choice.

"Would you set the camp?"

She brightened, happy to enter into this kind of partnership, the division of what must be done. She immediately gathered his bags and her bundle and headed for the area he indicated. He carried the saddle behind her, placing it over a dry log beneath the pines, and handed her his flint.

Sky cut a forked branch from a willow and sharpened the ends to make a fine trident. Then he headed toward the river. She watched him remove his blue jeans and lay them aside. She had a fine flash of his taut square backside before his shirt covered him to midthigh.

The man was beautifully made, that was certain. Lucie continued to watch him as he stood completely motionless, the spear just above the river's surface. There was always the possibility she might have another look at him. She wondered about the other side of him and then flushed at the curiosity that she had never experienced before.

Of course, Eagle Dancer had taken her body. She recalled the pain and terror of their first coupling. Later she'd endured a discomfort during their joining that was less than that of the tattooing experience but worse than a willow branch across her thighs. She knew her parents enjoyed bed sport. That was obvious from the number of children they had but more so from the sounds that came from their room in the wee hours of the night or the early hours as the birdsong foretold the dawn. The sounds filled her with disquiet, because it made her long for things she would never have—a husband, children, a home of her own. Since leaving Eagle Dancer, Lucie had not had the least inclination to couple with a man, until now.

He made her curious and reckless. She wondered what it might be like to share the tender caresses with a man whose touch ignited her skin with currents of sensation instead of dread. How different would it be to lie with a man, now that she was a woman and this time, a man of *her* choosing? And not just anyone but a dangerous and exciting warrior, with a raw power that caused her fingers to tingle and her stomach to twitch.

What would it be like to bear his child?

The butterflies in her belly erupted into flight, sending a chill of excitement down her arms and legs that turned her skin to gooseflesh. Was this desire? Longing? Both?

She thought of the others she had known in her life. None excited her the way this one did. She knew that was rare enough, but there was more. He looked at her as if he wanted the same thing. Lucie knew how infrequently that occurred. This was her opportunity to taste what her parents savored.

Once they reached the fort, they would no longer be alone and her chance would have fled. She was not foolish enough to believe he would stay with her. Even if he weren't Eagle Dancer's friend, even if there were no widows who needed him, he would not want her. No one did.

But she was foolish enough to think that she might convince him to have her once and if she were very lucky, he might leave her with a child.

Lucie watched him, all poised sleek potential—still as a coiled snake. His arm exploded into action, striking with a speed that was only a blur to her eye. He kept the lance imbedded deep in the soft gravel and mud of the river bottom and she knew he had succeeded. The water beneath the trident erupted with a wild flurry of splashing as the impaled fish tried vainly to escape. Sky was quick as he grabbed it by the gill. One twist and the fish suffered no more. He bowed his head a moment and she knew he was thanking the fish for giving its life so he might feed her.

She bowed her head, as well. After she had finished the prayer, she set to work gathering wood. She used her skinning knife and the flint to send a shower of sparks onto her tinder. Today she had found river reeds. The dead leaves shredded into fine dry fibers that caught the sparks, glowed for an instant and then went out. Eventually she had a curling finger of smoke. She knelt to blow cautiously and coaxed a flame.

She sat back in triumph, grinning at the smoldering tinder. She fed the fire on little sticks, as a mother robin feeds worms to a hungry chick. Her tiny flame grew, but it would be some time until she had the coals needed to cook his fish.

When he finally left the river, she had a nice pile of glowing embers. She enjoyed watching him push his lithe, muscular legs into his denim dungarees. He raised his shirt to fasten the rivet and her eyes consumed the sight of his ribbed stomach as easily as the fire devoured the dry wood.

He walked gracefully up the bank with his trousers in place, but his shirt was untucked and open. She didn't think she'd be able to keep her mind on cooking the offering he carried in his hand—four good-sized log perch and a very large catfish. The man was a good provider.

Sky set to work gutting and scaling the fish, except the catfish, which, of course, had no scales. His activity raised the attention of two otters, one of which was brazen enough to enter the camp and beg for scraps as if he were a spoiled pet dog.

Sky laughed and tossed him the fish heads. This prompted the second to try her luck and she received a fish tail. This equal treatment caused the two otters to wrestle furiously in a battle for the other two tails. The male won and Sky sent him a tail at the same time he tossed the last one to the defeated challenger.

He felt Lucie staring and looked back to find Lucie's attention not on the otters but on him. His smile faded and the churning tension filled his middle again.

"What?" he asked.

"I've never heard you laugh before."

"Yes, you have."

"Not like that. Before you sneered or gave a laugh of derision at some comment of mine. But that." She pointed at the otters, now engaged in a tag game in the river. "That was a joyful sound. You should laugh more often."

He allowed himself to smile. "Haven't had much cause."

"That's a pity. I'll see if I can talk the otters into joining us."

That made him laugh again and this time she joined him. It felt good being here with her. He speared the fillets on green branches and staked them in the earth. Lucie raked out a fine bed of coals. She certainly knew how to keep a camp. He set the pink meat in place and watched it begin to turn white.

She flipped them once and then waited for the pink to disappear from the underside. They ate in silence, but he could sense her eyes still roving over him.

He drew the edges of his shirt together and finished his meal.

Lucie washed her face and hands in the river. He waited until she had finished before doing the same. This avoidance game could not go on forever. Soon they must place their blankets and lay down to sleep. He glanced up at the darkening sky, knowing the greatest challenge of his life would soon come. At least there would be no rain, so he could rest away from her instead of enduring the torture of holding her in his arms. He delayed as long as he could, but eventually he had to return to her. He found her sitting by the fire, gilded by the orange flames. Behind them she had laid out his bedding and her blanket, near, but not touching. He could not seem to keep his eyes from the few inches that separated them. Did she choose such proximity for safety or...

"You're avoiding the roads, aren't you?"

He glanced up to find her studying him again. Those lovely blue eyes seemed to see inside him. It was just as hard to stay where he was now as it was to stay still while she watched him fishing from the bank. Did she know what she did to him with those direct stares?

"It seems wiser."

"And you are avoiding me."

He was about to deny it and then he looked at her. There was that direct stare again. His stomach twitched and down lower, he felt the blood rush of excitement pulse as he met her stare with one just as bold. Lucie bore a startling resemblance to a hunter on the prowl. Was he the quarry? Oh, he hoped so.

"Do you think of me like you do all whites, then?" she asked.

"You aren't one of them."

"But not an Indian—like you?"

"You float between both worlds, like a flower on a pond."

She laughed. "A frog, rather."

He met her gaze now, held it, hoping she could see that his words were true. "You are the most beautiful of women. Time has only made you more so."

Her expression hardened, like a blade of grass covered with frost. "Do not mock me. I have a looking glass."

"But somehow you cannot see."

She glanced away. "If I am so beautiful, why haven't you tried to kiss me?"

Her gaze flashed back to him, holding a challenge. Did she think he did not want to?

"I am trying to treat you with the respect due the wife of a head man."

"A station I will not hold for long. When I see him safe, I will break the union that was forced upon me." Her mouth turned down. "What excuse will you give then?"

Is that what she thought, that he secretly despised her?

"I'll wager all that once I am a free woman, you'll find some pressing business in another state."

"Lucie, why do you say such things?"

She shot to her feet with a speed that startled him. There she stood with her fists balled at her sides and her arms out stiff and straight. High color flooded her face and her lips grew bloodless as she pressed them flat. She trembled with a fury she barely contained. What was happening?

"Because I know what I am. I've come to terms with it. And then you come along with your lies and pretty flattery. Do you think I am some imbecile to be coddled and sheltered?"

He cocked his head, unsure what to say or do.

She glared at him as if she hated him and spat out the words. "Ruined, that's what. A spinster who is past all hope of marriage and children, because I did not hide as I was told to and because I could not run fast enough to escape."

Sky was shocked into stupefied silence and could only gape. It was madness. Wasn't it? And then he thought of the teasing boys, who mocked his accent and the men who cut his hair short and dressed him like all the other boys. Whites were very hard on those who looked or acted differently. They had no tolerance. He stared at Lucie's chin and then lifted his attention to find her glaring.

"Do you think I have not tried to rub them from my chin? But I can't and I can't disappear. I know. I've tried. And you have the nerve to lie to me. To pretend it is Eagle Dancer that keeps you from me when we both know it is your contempt."

She was right about one thing; Eagle Dancer was only a convenient excuse to avoid taking what he wanted. He tried another tactic.

"I don't want any woman."

"Yet you have proposed to two." Her narrowing eyes dared him to deny it.

It all came back to that, back to the reason he accepted a proposal not of his choosing, back to why he needed to take care of what remained of the blood of Sacred Cloud, to act in his stead.

He hung his head. "That is an act of duty, not love."

She made a disparaging sound. Clearly she thought this just another excuse.

"So you prefer to wed a stranger than to accept a 'beautiful' woman, like me."

She used his words against him, calling his bluff, challenging him to prove what he said. He could remain where he was and let her believe all she said was true or he could show her that, to him, she was the most beautiful of all women. His insides froze, cold as the sap in the cottonwoods during the Deep Snow Moon.

Lucie stood, fists bunched, jaw ridged, eyes narrowed, ready to receive anything he threw at her. The woman was magnificent. Her eyes glittered and she sneered.

"I knew it." Lucie turned away.

Sky grasped her and spun her back to face him.

"Eagle Dancer is my friend. I can't—"

She cut him off by wrenching free. "Don't. Don't you dare give me one more excuse. This is not about him or honor or duty. This is between you and me."

"Why do you want me to kiss you?"

The hard lines around her mouth eased. He noted her labored breathing and wondered what it was she tried so hard to hold back.

"I just want the truth," she said at last. "Either you can see past my face or you're a liar like the rest of them."

"A kiss will tell you all that?"

She nodded.

He should have walked away, but instead he reached forward, needing her to know what was in his heart. He clasped her neck in his hand and drew her in. He felt unworthy of someone so pure of heart and fully expected her to call a halt to this game. But her grim face made it plain she was going to follow through. Did she think he'd stop?

He wouldn't. Not now. Not for anything in the world. She'd goaded him into this, but it was exactly where he wanted to be.

Sky gathered her in his arms, still not understanding why she would want him. He held back one moment longer, to brush his thumb over her chin. Her smile was bittersweet.

Lucie allowed him to draw her near. It was hard not to fight the possessiveness of his touch. Over the years, a few men had tried to use her. One man had enslaved her, but none had loved her. She did not expect Sky to love her, but the way he looked at her made her imagine he might be capable of making love to her. It wasn't enough to fill a lonely life, but it would have to do.

Lucie longed for far more than a kiss—more, perhaps, than any man could give her. She wanted a man who could see the girl she was and the woman she might have become; pretty, normal, whole.

As she stared up into his eyes, she recalled that he had claimed to be the only man alive who might understand her. But understanding and acceptance were distant cousins.

Lucie's heart pounded a painful rhythm. She could scarcely breathe past the hope welling inside her. He had caressed her chin as if there were nothing damaged about it.

She melted against him, hoping that afterward he would not mock her for her naivete. His arms were strong and his hold tender. He took slow possession of her, cradling her head and pressing her body close to his. He gave her time to draw back, but she was committed. *In for a penny, in for a pound,* she thought and closed her eyes.

His lips brushed hers in the merest glancing of flesh, yet the light caress sent a shiver of anticipation dancing over her skin. She rested her hands on his hips and slid them upward, until her fingers gripped the taut shoulder muscles. She used her leverage to flatten her breasts to his chest, inhaling at the sensual contact.

His mouth found hers again, only this time the pressure was firm. She opened her lips at his insistence and his tongue stroked hers. Her body seemed ablaze now, the heat melting her against him, but no matter how close she held him it was not close enough. Like Tantalus, her thirst was unquenchable, her need unrelenting.

She was grasping at him now, clawing in a vain effort to remove his clothing, to revel in the pressing of naked flesh to flesh. His shirt was still open. She reached under it now, feeling the luscious play of his muscles as they contracted beneath her questing fingers. But it was not enough. She needed more than this kiss, more, so much more.

Lucie knew what she wanted, what she would take if she could.

She released him and unfastened her blouse. Deftly she released the white shell buttons at her wrists and then the invisible closures at her throat. One by one she opened the hooks and her blouse fell from her shoulders. He stood back, releasing her with everything but his eyes. As she opened the garment, his gaze shifted to her neck and he fingered the small indentation about her collarbone, his thumb falling into the hollow at her throat. Then he pressed his lips to the cording muscle beneath her jaw and worked upward, capturing the lobe of her ear in his mouth.

This caused Lucie to release a long, tortured moan of pleasure. He did this to her. He made her whisper his name between clenched teeth. If she could just keep him kissing her neck for a moment longer, she might keep him from noticing the other tattoos that ringed her arms like some hideous bracelet of ink. She dropped the shirt, feeling exposed in a way she rarely allowed. Not even her family saw her bare arms. For her this was more private than any other part of her. She might rather walk down the thoroughfare bare-breasted, than without her shirtsleeves. But for him she allowed it, praying she had not underestimated him. It was a simple matter to unfasten her skirt, petticoat and bloomers, allowing them to pool about her ankles.

Now only the thin white veil of cotton covered her torso. His hands were on her waist, stroking, caressing and moving steadily upward toward her aching breasts. And still he had not seen the tattoos, for his mouth remained on her neck. His teeth scored the flesh, leaving a cool trail of moisture on the hot surface of her throat.

She drew the shiny ribbon that threaded through the eyelets of her camisole, pulled loose the tiny row of buttons and released the last barrier that shielded her. She needed Sky to see her now, accept her with all her scars. If he could only do that, even for one night, she would know there was hope of finding another who could do the same. It would mean it was possible. So she gently eased back. His grip tightened, and for an instant she thought he meant to hold her captive. But his grip relaxed and he allowed her to draw back.

If he accepted her, loved her even for one night, he might unwittingly give her the proof of one night's devotion. Lucie trembled with the possibility. She might still have a child of her own, to love and raise. Up until this moment she had been playing house, first in her parents' home, where she pretended that her brothers and sisters were her own children. She had come to teach for the same reason, to fill this ache she could no longer ignore. And now fate had given her Sky, handsome, troubled and physically perfect. If Sky was willing to look past her imperfections, she might still have this one great joy.

She stood stiffly, waiting for him to see her as she was.

Chapter Eleven

Sky looked at her, naked, gilded by the firelight. Lucie stood before him waiting. He had only meant to kiss her, just once. He was a fool to think he could be satisfied with that. A lifetime of kisses from this woman would never be enough. She had stripped off her clothing, exposed herself to his eyes. She must know what such a sight would do to him.

But why, then, did she pull back?

His need for her pulsed in the most obvious of places. He took a step forward. She did not retreat. Instead she looked to the tattoo ringing her upper arm. He glanced at the row of even spikes bisecting her slim bicep. And then he stared at the lovely curve of her breasts. They were full and round and he knew her skin smelled so sweet. He reached for her, his fingers encircling her arms. He forced his gaze back up to her face and saw she bit her lower lip. Her expression reminded him of something, but he couldn't place it. Not fear exactly, but neither was it desire.

He looked to her for guidance, unsure what game she thought she was playing, but knowing that he would very shortly lose his ability to think coherently. He'd never been so tempted. He prayed silently that this was not some horrible trick, a test of his honor, for he knew he would fail.

"Lucie?"

"Do you still want me?"

Did she really think it possible that after seeing the perfection of her form, the beauty of her face, the courage of her spirit, that he wouldn't want her? He shook his head, positive that he did not understand women.

Her breath caught and he realized by her shattered expression that he had sent her a signal of rejection. He tried not to laugh at the idiocy of this situation.

"No, Lucie, wait. Of course I want you. That's why I couldn't even speak to you back at the school. You take my breath away."

She closed her eyes then and drew a deep breath, as if preparing to dive into water.

"Prove it." She held her arms out to him.

He dragged her forward, pressing her naked torso to his bare chest. His eyes closed as well as he offered a prayer of thanks to the Great Spirit for placing Lucie on the earth. Then he nuzzled her earlobe, gradually traveling south, over the pulsing vessel at her throat to nibble along her collarbone. She sighed and made a tiny humming sound.

Sky kissed the upper curve of her bosom. Her head fell back and she pressed herself more tightly to his mouth. His hands splayed about her waist holding her captive for his sensual assault. She trembled and quivered, but he did not hesitate. His tongue flicked over her rosy nipple, sending the flesh into a hard little nub which he took in his mouth and sucked. She cried out his name at this and clung tight, forcing him still closer to the soft bud of flesh. He trailed one hand over the tempting swell of her bottom and down the satin of her thighs. When he lifted her she only fell back into his arms in complete surrender.

He carried her to the blankets, wishing he had a fine robe of rabbit skins on which to lay her. It was the only thing he could think of that was softer than her skin. He knelt beside her and looked at the bounty she offered. Her hair fanned out about her in a red storm. Her skin glowed golden in the fire. He trailed two fingers over her lips and chin, down the column of her throat, veering to sweep around the outer orb of one breast and then the other. He continued along the center of her flat stomach, wanting to place his seed within this fertile field and watch it grow. She could give him strong sons and daughters and he wanted them. He, who had resigned himself to live and die alone, had found a woman who could give him—everything, everything that was, except absolution. He clenched his jaw and buried his face in the warm satin of her hair.

Sky's fingers delved into the tight mat of curls at the juncture of her thighs. She opened her legs, letting them fall to the blanket in an invitation.

But she did not stop there. She reached out and lay a hand on him, low at the juncture of his bare stomach and the jeans. Then her palm stroked the ridge of flesh, barely restrained by denim. She rolled to her side and released the rivet, peeling away the fabric, releasing his erection. When her fingers encircled him, he closed his eyes at the rush of pleasure. She stroked him once and then released him to strip his trousers off his hips.

Sky sat to remove his moccasins and toss aside his dungarees. Then he knelt beside her. Lucie slipped one foot behind his legs and pulled. He allowed himself to fall forward, catching his weight on his outstretched arms. Lucie wiggled beneath him, aligning their bodies, and stared up at him, her face as serious as a deacon's. She stroked his shoulders and then used her nails to rake across his flesh in an action that was painful and arousing as hell.

He gripped a hank of hair and pulled, forcing her head back so he could kiss her exposed throat, taking what he wanted. Her breathing came fast now and she could not keep her hips still. She called to him, with upward thrusts, pressing his engorged flesh between his belly and hers. He reached between her legs and found her honey-wet and ready.

Sky kissed her lips as he drove inside her and still it was not close enough. Their tongues warred, greedy and frantic to have each other. Lucie locked her strong legs about his back and lifted up so he could drive more deeply into her. They rocked in opposition, striking each other in a pounding motion that reminded Sky of the waves on the Great Lakes during a winter gale. She clutched his shoulders now, throwing back her head. His Lakota name issued from her lips in a long tortured cry. Now she threw herself away from him, her arms flung wide. Her body slackened as she surrendered to the internal storm that shook her. He had given her pleasure, but he knew he did not deserve his own. He must be careful or she might conceive.

His heart ached as longing obliterated desire and he

realized that he wanted that, wanted for Lucie to carry his child. Wouldn't it be amazing to have a baby with Lucie?

Sky's mind flashed an image of Sacred Cloud, dying in his arms. His friend would never have a woman, never smell the sweet musty odor of sex. Guilt consumed him. How could he enjoy such bliss after taking everything from Sacred Cloud?

He wasn't worthy of Lucie. And she deserved a man of honor, someone better than him.

He pulled out.

But his orgasm was already coming. He tore himself from her just in time, clenching his erection as his ejaculation spilled onto the blanket.

"What are you doing?" she cried.

Then he fell like a bull charging off the cliff of a buffalo drop, but instead of landing broken on the rocks, he landed on the soft mounds of her breasts. He did not want to crush her, so he tried to roll to his back. Lucie pounded his chest. He stared up in astonishment at her flailing fists.

"What did you do?" she cried.

"Lucie." He raised his hands to deflect the blows that rained down on him. "Stop now."

She pressed her hands to her face. Kneeling now, she curled in on herself as she began to weep.

Sky reached. "I'm sorry, I never meant to…to…"

She threw her hands down and glared at him. "To what—love me?"

She stood and yanked the blanket about herself.

"You are just like all men! Worse," she hissed. "Because you made me believe you were different. I hate you! And I hate him for sending you to me."

He filled with self-loathing at her words. "You can tell him so tomorrow."

She glared.

He could not meet her eyes past the shame that welled inside him like poison.

"I never want to see you again." The venom in her words pierced him like the fangs of a rattler.

He nodded his acceptance. "You'll have your wish tomorrow, when we reach the fort."

Lucie did not see Sky for the rest of the night, but felt he was near. When he returned, the stars were still out. She rose when she realized he was saddling Falcon. He did not speak to her as he offered her a hand up. But once she was mounted he lifted his gaze and stared up at her.

"I'm sorry, Lucie, for what happened last night."

"Of course you are." Humiliation burned her cheeks and the chunk of regret in her throat choked out her words.

He regretted it. Still his regret made that tiny diamond crystal of hope go dark.

"I never meant to hurt you."

It took all her resolve not to cry again so she nodded her understanding.

Sky swung up before her and lifted the reins. When the sun burst free of the land to the east, they were loping through the tall grass as if Sky could not wait to be rid of her. She felt stupid and used. Of course he'd taken her. After she'd stripped down and offered herself to him like a soiled dove, what had she expected him to do? She had become exactly what some men had called her.

She had gotten what she'd asked for, just once she had lain with a man who excited her, felt him moving inside her. But instead of making her life complete, it filled her with a longing. The knowledge of what would never be hers. And he was so disgusted with her that he had pulled himself from inside her before spilling his seed.

She closed her eyes at that final humiliation. After her escape from the Sioux she had thought that nothing could ever shame her like that again. How wrong she had been.

Had she really thought he might share her desire to create a baby? For one moment last night, she entertained the fantasy that he was trying to spare her from a pregnancy. But she could not delude herself any longer. Perhaps they were all right and she was unfit as a mother, ruined as so many had called her.

She scowled as the rays of light set the prairie ablaze with color. The sooner he left her, the better, for she could not even look at him without feeling the hot rush of humiliation and fury.

Even though they left before dawn, they did not arrive until after midday. Fort Sully sat on the east bank of the Missouri. Unlike Fort Laramie, Sully had no surrounding battlements. From a distance it appeared to be a low, squat collection of stone houses stretched along the wide flat bank of the river. The opposite shore was some one hundred feet higher, which made Lucie wonder why they would choose the lower ground.

They checked in at the guardhouse and were escorted to the commanding officer's residence, just beyond the officer's two-story residence and across from the barracks. Lucie's appearance caused quite a stir among the enlisted men. Sky had dismounted and now led Lucie, still seated on Falcon, across the open parade grounds. She now wore her hair in twin braids. Her skinning knife hung from about her neck and her moccasins were clearly visible from her seat astride his horse. Her skirts had worked themselves up to her knee, but she did nothing to adjust them. It was not her legs that drew the soldiers' stares, but what always made her the center of attention—the facial tattoos.

Sky was shocked to see the men whispering behind their hands like young girls. Some even pointed at Lucie in a manner he found offensive. Sky's dark mood turned black as he glared at the men.

Lucie rode with her chin up and eyes forward as if she were a condemned prisoner. He admired her courage. Lucie had the heart of a warrior inside her. Sky dismounted at the gate and now led Ceta to the hitching post before the commander's quarters.

He met them out front, having been alerted by a runner of their arrival.

"Welcome to Fort Sully. William Reilly here." He extended his hand to Sky, who took it for the briefest time possible. "And you are?"

"Skylar Fox."

"Ah, a pleasure. And who is your companion?"

Lucie dismounted unassisted and stalked up to the officer like the wildcat he knew she could be. Sky found himself smiling.

"I am Lucie West."

"West? Of course you are. But we didn't expect you. Your brother is David, isn't he?"

She nodded.

"But he didn't say a word."

"He doesn't expect me. I am here to see my husband."

The officer's eyebrows rose. He scanned the gathering of off-duty soldiers who were within earshot, but all took pains not to catch their commander's eye.

"Is that so? He is among my men?"

Lucie shook her head and her braids thumped against her back. "He is in your jail."

He laughed and lifted a hand in protest. "Madam, I can assure you that all I have in my jail are a few Sioux Indians and I hardly think…" He stared at Lucie's chin.

Lucie did not blink or look away.

"Husband, did you say?" His brow wrinkled in confusion.

"Eagle Dancer. You are holding him, are you not?"

"I am. *He* is your husband?" He motioned to an enlisted man. "Corporal, fetch David West, on the double."

Lucie persisted. "What crime has he committed?"

The man's face brightened. "There has been a murder."

"Of the truant officer from Sage River. Yes, I know. I was a matron there. Is Eagle Dancer charged with the crime?"

"We are leveraging—"

"So you are holding innocent men as hostages."

Now his face reminded Sky of the Artist's Paintbrush flower that sprinkled the prairie in the late summer.

"Detainees." Reilly could no longer meet her eyes and Sky marked the win in Lucie's favor.

"May I see him?"

He shifted uncomfortably. "I doubt that will be possible."

"I see. Where is your telegraph office?"

His eyes narrowed. "Why would that interest you?"

"Because, sir, I have several contacts, ones who have written about my travails as a captive, who would be very much interested in this story, both authors and members of the press. Also I will telegraph my father, who was honored to have President Hayes dine in our home during his campaign. They quite hit it off, you see, and not only because my father helped him win the election."

The man's face now matched the color of the underbelly of a bull frog. "I'm quite familiar with your family's connections. They won your brother this commission, I believe. But I wonder if you really know what you are playing at, Miss West."

Lucie stared imperiously at him. "Well, you do still work for the president, I presume?"

Reilly's brows dropped low over his eyes. "You are making threats, madam. I would not drop names unless you plan to use them."

"Have you ever seen a prairie fire, sir? Because I assure you it is nothing compared to the storm I will rain down upon you and this fort."

The courtyard was silent now except for the ring of a blacksmith's hammer.

The two combatants faced off. Sky wondered how Lucie could ever have thought herself a coward. The woman was magnificent. Sky was glad he did not have to count her as an enemy.

He thought about last night and then reconsidered,

his heart heavy. He had hurt her, though that was never his intention.

Reilly turned toward the man beside him and barked an order. "Take Mrs.…Mrs. Dancer to see her husband." He eyed Sky. "And *just* her. And call me when you find her brother. Perhaps he can take charge of her."

With that he spun on his heel and retreated back into his office. Did anyone but Sky see Lucie's shoulders sag?

"You'll wait?" she asked.

Sky smiled and nodded. She captured a large breath, straightened her spine and marched after the escorting officer.

Lucie's step did not falter until she was past the inner chamber of the stockade and approaching the solid door set with three vertical iron bars, which included one small window the size of a bible. She had expected to have Sky beside her when she faced Eagle Dancer once more. She had not realized how much she depended on his quiet protection until it was taken from her. And she'd thrown it away with her own reckless stupidity.

"He's in here, missus, with two other chiefs—Iron Bear and Joy Cat."

Joy Cat? The head man from the Bitterroot people, the one whose son Sky had accidentally shot?

"In there." The soldier pointed to the square hole high in the door.

"It's dark."

"There's no window but that one."

Lucie's heart sank. How long had they been trapped in this dank, airless crypt? She glared at her escorts and the soldiers shifted uncomfortably. But did not lower their rifles.

"Well?" she said. "Open it."

It pleased her that her voice did not reveal the tremors that now shook her as the doubt and uncertainty still sloshed about inside her like water in a pail. She straightened, determined to not show that to these guards.

The man who held the keys stepped forward and Lucie noted he had only a soft covering of down on his chin. "Can't. Just speak though the bars."

She scowled but then turned and stepped to the opening. *He can't do anything to you. He's locked up.* Still her fingers trembled until she gripped the cold iron bars.

Lucie held down the sudden dread. She had not faced Eagle Dancer since the day he set her in that tipi and told her not to move.

He has no power over you now.

She pressed her face to the bars, peering inside. Gradually her eyes adjusted to the gloom and she saw two of the men staring at her. She remembered Iron Bear, now head man of the Village-at-the-End, although he now had hair more gray than black, but she did not know the second. This must be Joy Cat. Yes, he had the lined face and the weary eyes of a man who had known much grief.

Both men rose, their eyes wide in astonishment. The third figure remained huddled in a ball, wrapped in a blanket.

Something was wrong.

The cramping in her stomach changed from trepidation to worry. She switched to Lakota. "Husband, I have come."

The hunched figure moved. He turned to her now. For a moment she did not recognize him. His face was drawn, pale and covered with tiny beads of sweat. But on seeing her, his smile appeared, transforming his features. She reconciled this stranger with her memories of Eagle Dancer. The years and the losses had been unkind. Whatever her wounds, his were greater and still he smiled.

His gladness gave way to a fit of coughing. His face turned purple and he used a dirty bandanna to cover his mouth. She saw the fabric was crimson with blood. The sound was a wet, rasping sound that reminded her of a man spewing water from his lungs.

She turned to the officer. "How long has he been like this?"

"I don't know, ma'am."

"Fetch your doctor."

He didn't move.

She motioned for him to go. "Quick, now."

He took a step to obey and then hesitated. "I can't leave you without permission. I have to ask the captain."

"Then do it."

The man jogged off. Since reaching the fort Lucie had been intentionally acting exactly like her mother, all bluster and bluff, and it seemed to be working.

Eagle Dancer had finally stopped coughing as he shuffled to the door. He reached for her with one hand, keeping the other clutched tightly around the blanket at his throat.

"Sunshine," he whispered.

His hand covered hers. The heat of his skin told her immediately he had a high fever.

He gazed from the darkness like a wolf in his den, his eyes glassy from the illness, but his smile was joyful.

"My prayers are answered. I have seen you once more."

She did not like the tone of his voice. It had the ring of a man preparing to leave this world.

Lucie hardened herself. "I did not come all this way to bury you. I have sent for the doctor."

"It is the white man's coughing sickness."

Consumption, she realized. Many of the students had this, as well. It spread quickly among the Sioux and weakened the lungs.

He squeezed her hands. "Sky Fox found you?"

She nodded, feeling a pulsing of shame at Sky's rejection of her. Lucie pressed back her emotions, walling them away to look at another day. What had passed between them had nothing to do with Eagle Dancer. She would do her best to keep Eagle Dancer alive to repay her debt. And then she would secure her freedom and say goodbye.

"He told me of the trouble here."

"I am happy for any trouble that brings you back to me."

"Rest now, until the doctor comes."

The doctor did indeed come and seemed a sincere young man. He was permitted inside the cell, but Lucie was not. She watched as he listened to Eagle Dancer's heart and took his pulse. He examined the bloody rag and confirmed what Lucie had known.

"But, in addition to consumption, I am afraid he

has also contracted pneumonia. With his lungs already weakened, well, the prognosis is not good."

"Can you do anything?"

"I'll recommend he be moved to the hospital."

"No, allowed to recover at home."

"I'm afraid he needs real medication, not smoke and eagle feathers."

Lucie did not inform the good doctor that many of the healers used medicinal treatments that were effective and unknown by whites because she knew from experience the effort was futile. She stepped aside as he exited the cell and tried to reassure him.

"I can administer any treatment you might deem proper."

"Are you trained as a nurse?"

Lucie looked him in the eye and lied. It was a skill she had perfected during her captivity and one that she could manage as smoothly as a bird taking flight.

"Yes, I am."

The man in charge locked the door and Eagle Dancer faced her through the small opening, filling her heart with pity.

The army doctor buckled his medical bag. "I'll speak to the commander."

"I'll go with you."

Eagle Dancer held her wrist. She glanced down at the strong fingers imprisoning her and skin prickled. "You have to let me go."

"Not again." His expression turned threatening.

She recognized that look. It was how he appeared to her every time she had begged him to return her to her mother, take her to the fort or deliver her to the soldiers—grim, determined. Always he had refused to release her and nothing had changed. Her sympathy died and she lowered her chin.

He can't keep me this time.

She returned the look of determination and pulled his hand from her. Then she turned her back and followed the doctor down the corridor and into the receiving room. She found Sky outside. He paused his pacing at the sight of her. His worried eyes pinned her and she shook her head, offering no reassurance.

"He is very ill and it is cold and dank in there."

Sky accompanied her as she waited for the commander. The doctor was speaking to Major Reilly. She and Sky were instructed to wait in the outer office.

She had barely taken her seat when the entrance crashed open, causing the young corporal seated at the desk to bolt to his feet. And Sky, quicker and more experienced, had Lucie behind him and his knife drawn at the potential threat.

Lucie peeked around Sky. For an instant she did not recognize the young captain. His sideburns were so thick and his face so dour. But when his eyes met hers she knew.

She sprang forward to greet her little brother. "David!"

Lucie stretched her arms wide. But her little brother made no move in her direction. Instead he turned toward the corporal. "Get out."

The man scurried off, closing the door behind him.

"David?" Lucie felt the coiling apprehension in her belly. His scornful expression was familiar, but she had never witnessed it from a member of her family before. Even so, his look of disapproval was clear enough.

"Who the blazes is that?" said David, motioning his head at Sky, who had sheathed his knife.

"This is Skylar Fox, the man who escorted me here from Minnesota."

David's brows sank lower still. "Will you excuse us, Mr. Fox?"

Her brother had fairly spat the words between clenched teeth. Lucie had never seen him so angry. Sky looked at her and she nodded her consent. Sky walked toward David, forcing her brother to step aside to let him pass. It was a clear act of dominance that had Lucie scowling at both of them.

Sky paused in the doorway. "Call if you need me."

She nodded her understanding. As the door clicked shut, she turned her attention to David.

"That was very rude," she said.

"Rude?" His laugh was harsh and humorless. "You come here, to *my* post, and tell my superior officer that you married the animal who held you captive. What the devil are you playing at?"

"You don't understand."

"I can see that." He dragged off his hat and raked his hand through his thick red hair. "And you clearly don't understand. Otherwise why would you make me a laughingstock among my men? How am I to keep order when they are snickering? I'm tired as hell of defending you, do you know that?"

Lucie lowered her head. She feared this would happen. That by trying to help Eagle Dancer, she would hurt her brother.

"So I ask you," he continued, "have you lost your damned mind? What would make you tell such a lie?"

"But it's true."

His face turned pink as cooked salmon. "What!"

"I married him. I had to—"

"Don't say another word. When they brought him in here, it took every ounce of restraint I had not to shoot the bastard who befouled my own sister. And now...I want to hang him and then shoot him."

"You have to help me get him out."

He turned his back. "Damned if I will." He rounded on her. "Why didn't you tell me any of this?"

Lucie felt her calm unwinding. The shock at his indignation gave rise to a surging anger of her own. "What business is it of yours? It happened before you were even born."

"You're making a spectacle of yourself."

"Yes, I do, everywhere I go. But I never expected my own brother to condemn me."

"You've embarrassed me, jeopardized my promotion."

Lucie's throat began to burn and she knew the tears were imminent. Her voice, what was left of it, emerged as a hoarse whisper. "David, I'm sorry. I would have died without him. He kept me alive. I have to do this."

"He ruined you for decent men. He's the very reason you're a spinster. My God, Lucie, he raped you."

Her head bowed. She knew all that. "He married me with my consent."

David's jaw dropped. If she lived to be a hundred, she hoped never to see that look of disillusionment again. Then his features turned hard.

"I'll kill him." He turned toward the door and Lucie grabbed his arm. She shook him off as his fury turned on her. "How could you?"

Lucie clenched her numb fingers into a fist. "David, please. You have to help me."

"If you mean help you get home, I shall most certainly do so. But I will do everything in my power to see Eagle Dancer faces the justice he deserves."

Lucie had never felt so alone in her life. In the past, even in her darkest times, she always had the love and support of her family. But now…what if her parents felt the same way? What if they also were ashamed by what she was trying to do? She knew it was right, but what would this decision cost her?

The door to the inner chamber opened and the doctor stood in the entrance.

"The commander will see you now, Miss West."

Lucie nodded, trying to gather in her pain. But David seized her arm in a hold that was commanding and painful. Her eyes flashed to him. This little boy, whose nappies she had changed and whose nose she had wiped, had the gall to try to bully her?

"My sister has made a mistake, sir. She's changed her mind. I'll take charge of her."

"Very good, Captain." He tipped his hat to her in dismissal. "Miss West."

Lucie watched him retreat inside the office. David was going to make her choose between her family and her duty. Lucie tugged her arm free.

"Wait."

The doctor turned, his brow quirked. She glared at her brother, who scowled back.

"Lucie, don't. I'm warning you."

"David, I will not take orders from you. I'm sorry you disapprove, but do not presume to speak for me again."

He spun on his heels and stormed off.

Lucie watched him go and felt a little piece of her heart break away with his parting.

Then she turned and followed the fort physician into the commander's office. There, Lucie negotiated to have all three men released to allow the head men to investigate the murder and see to their people. The doctor set the lynch pin when he mentioned that, in the absence of the head men's leadership, the whiskey-ranches just beyond the reservation's border were doing a bumper business. Thus far the young men, idle and bored, were only trading their food rations for alcohol.

"But I'm fairly certain, Captain, that a territory filled with drunken Indians is more of a threat than these three men."

"Damned whiskey-ranches spring up as fast as we close them down," said Reilly.

"And we can't send them off now because they married squaws. Lots of desperate men willing to take on a squaw or two for the acreage now."

Lucie felt her heart ice. Was that why Sky wanted to wed Joy Cat's daughters? She had read about the offer of grants for each Indian, man or woman, who would farm the land. But it seemed her people had found a way to exploit even this.

Major Reilly lowered his eyebrows. "I still think holding their leaders is the best way to get our man. Don't fool yourself, doc. They know exactly who killed Carr. Wait until I get those arrows, then we'll see."

Lucie saw her chance slipping away. So she gave him something else to chew on. "I wonder what the braves at the Great Sioux Reservations will do if their chief dies in your fort?"

Major Reilly gnawed the end of his mustache until it was as wet as a muskrat's tail, before he finally consented. "But I'll be coming to check on Eagle Dancer's recovery and the progress of their investigation. I'll have no more whites attacked and murdered in my territory. Not on my watch, no, sir, I will not. The guilty will be punished. Do you understand?"

Lucie spent the next hour with the doctor as he prepared various tinctures and rolled pills from his medicinal supply.

"I could give you the laudanum. It is excellent for suppressing coughs, but very dear and I can't give our supplies to Indians."

Sky drew his saddlebag off his shoulder and retrieved a pouch which he tossed at the doctor. The man missed and the pouch clanked to the floor, spilling silver dollars in a fountain of wealth.

"Maybe you can sell it to me, then," said Sky.

Lucie held her breath. She realized that Sky had not said the doctor might sell it to a white man, but rather just "to me," which only Lucie knew that Sky did not consider himself to be white.

The physician hesitated, then lifted the purse. "I'm only taking what they cost to replace. You understand."

Sky nodded and the doctor scooped up the coins, removed three and returned the rest. "I'll make up a cough syrup then, shall I?"

Lucie nodded, pleased that this physician, at least, seemed more concerned with the welfare of the sick than the rules that were forced upon him.

Sky left her to rent a wagon for Eagle Dancer. They would take a ferry up the Missouri, stopping first five miles north at the Cheyenne River Reservation, the southern reservation and then continuing north. Eagle Dancer's home was far up river in the Standing Rock Reservation.

By the time the mules were harnessed and ready, day had given over to dusk. Iron Bear and Joy Cat helped Eagle Dancer walk from the cell to the wagon. It was not until they were lifting him onto the buffalo robe that lined the wagon that Joy Cat glanced up to recognize Sky.

"You!" he said in Lakota.

Sky froze, his eyes growing huge. Lucie tensed as the two men faced off. Joy Cat looked murderous with fury as he glared at Sky and Lucie prepared to throw herself on the head man if he took another step.

Eagle Dancer clasped her wrist as he called to the other head man.

"Brother," he said to Joy Cat, "I spoke about this one. Do you recall? He is interested in marrying your daughters."

Joy Cat's breathing came in fast angry bursts. "First he takes my son. Now he would have my daughters, as well?"

Lucie glanced to see Sky's reaction. He stood still and pale as a condemned man.

Chapter Twelve

Eagle Dancer still held Lucie's wrist as he grasped the arm of Joy Cat. Sky could not meet her eyes. His pain spilled out before him, like the innards of a gutted fish. All his adult life, he had longed for and dreaded this meeting.

Sky braced himself to face Joy Cat's wrath. He longed to receive the punishment denied him by his flight. Eagle Dancer had tried to save him, but he had not foreseen the burden Sky carried as a result. So the guilt had rotted his insides like a cancer as he had searched vainly for a way to make amends for the life he had taken.

Now that he stood here, he could not even lift his head to meet Joy Cat's gaze.

He was prepared for whatever the head man would do, knowing that no payment was enough to compensate a man for his son. Sky waited and finally lifted his gaze to the father of his friend.

Joy Cat's eyes glistened with pain and sorrow. "I

want to know what he has to say for himself, this coward who runs in the night."

Again Eagle Dancer intervened on his behalf. "This one was also a boy, only fifteen winters."

Sky did not want Eagle Dancer to shield him any longer. Many times he had imagined he had stayed, taken responsibility and then fought for and regained his place.

Joy Cat snorted like an angry buffalo. "Old enough to shoot my son and flee like a rabbit."

Sweat ran down Eagle Dancer's face. Only then did Sky understand what this negotiation was costing his mentor. "You were mad with grief. What justice would he have found in your heart?"

Joy Cat clamped his lips together. So Eagle Dancer had been right about Joy Cat's urge for his blood. Well, let him have it.

Sky cleared his throat and prepared to speak.

"I carry him with me each day and I think of the life that I took from him. I wonder if he would have been a great leader, like his father, if he would now have a wife and children of his own. In tribute to him, I have taken no wife, sired no children and tried each day to live a life that would honor his memory."

Joy Cat's eyes grew glassy and he looked away.

"I would gladly give my life to bring him back. So I accept any punishment you choose, for no amount of punishment is enough to settle this debt."

Some of Joy Cat's rage ebbed. He looked baffled now.

Iron Bear spoke into the void. Sky recognized the deep voice of the head man and third hostage. The old war chief did not speak often so when he did it was best to pay close attention. "It is good that the hoop has spun and brought you two together. We will talk some more and see what is to be done."

Joy Cat nodded stiffly and then walked to the front of the wagon, climbing aboard. Sky tied Ceta to the back and then assisted Lucie up to the bed. She looked as if she wanted to say something but Eagle Dancer was now sagged back in the wagon, exhausted. Lucie took her place beside him and Sky felt a squeezing sorrow in his heart.

She glanced back at him with wide eyes. Was she still afraid of Eagle Dancer, of returning to the Sioux? Perhaps she still thought the head man could hold her against her will. But only because she had not seen the way they were forced to live now. When she had left, the Sioux were at the peak of their strength and numbers. War had taken so many good men and disease and starvation had cut down the rest. Standing Rock comprised fewer than two hundred families and Cheyenne River had fewer than that, according to the officer he had spoken to while Lucie reunited with her husband.

Sky walked to the front of the wagon to find Iron Bear regarding him with a strange look. Iron Bear had taken the middle place between him and the father of his best friend. He glanced back to find Lucie sitting on the buffalo robe directly behind his seat with one hand on her husband's brow and her face drawn in an expression of concern.

Sky took up the reins and released the brake. On the ride to the river, Iron Bear peppered him with questions about his time away from the People. Sky spoke of the Mormon and their school and how they had beaten him for his beliefs about the Great Spirit and the earth that sat on the back of a turtle. And how the Mormons believed that only their way was right and all others evil, and that there was but one road to the Spirit World and it was not the way of the People. He told them how Falcon had saved his life, by stomping a rattle snake that was coiled to strike him, and how he caught wild mustangs, in order to save them from the bluecoats and the passengers on the iron horse who thought it good sport to shoot the ponies out the windows of the moving train.

At last he had no more words. Iron Bear nodded and remarked, "It is good you come back to those who understand you. You are a stranger among them. Like us, you find their habits and beliefs perplexing."

"That is true. They are as unlike me as a bluebird from a fox."

"It is why I send my son to their school, so he can understand them better," said Iron Bear.

Sky hesitated before speaking. Iron Bear noticed him glance toward him and then away.

"What, brother? Speak."

"Be careful that he does not learn their ways so well that he forgets ours."

"You have seen the school?"

Sky nodded and met Iron Bear's eyes. "Bring him home if you can."

Iron Bear pulled his blanket across his back and said no more. They reached the Missouri and boarded a steamship heading upriver. Sky bought their passage as Eagle Dancer was carried aboard. They waited on deck as black smoke billowed from the twin stacks and then the engine engaged, making the deck vibrate. Joy Cat took his leave at the first stop, a trading post and whiskey camp across from the Cheyenne Reservation.

Because they were traveling with Indians, they could not secure a place below decks, so Lucie bundled Eagle Dancer in blankets and carefully administered her husband's pills, finding the laudanum caused him to sleep. Iron Bear moved himself closer to the rail, so he could see the stars past the black smoke belching from the stacks. This left Sky and Lucie alone for the first time since they reached the fort.

"I'm sorry your brother did not come to say goodbye to you," said Sky.

Lucie nodded. "He is very angry at me."

"He is a little boy. A man would have looked past his needs to see yours."

She stared at him in silence then. He could see the questions in her eyes and wondered if she still hated him for what they had done.

"What do you think Joy Cat will do?"

"He has the right to see me outcast, though I am outcast already."

"You are a white man. He has no power to punish you."

Sky spoke more sharply than he intended. "I am not white!"

He glanced down at Eagle Dancer to see if his outburst had disturbed him, but his old friend did not stir. Was Iron Bear right about the wheel spinning back around? He was tired of this half life, tired of his joyless existence. He lifted his gaze and looked into the open concern written on Lucie's beautiful face.

Sky motioned toward the rail of the steamer and she followed. There he could see the dark water of the Missouri and the golden light from the steamer, rippling across the boat's wake.

He stared down at her earnest face. Was the Mormon right? Was he damned for all eternity for what he had done? Sky clenched the rail and stared sightlessly across the water as the murmur of other passengers mingled with the sound of the engine and the slap of water on the ship's bow.

"Sky?"

He lifted his brow in response.

"What did you mean when you told Joy Cat about siring no children?"

Sky gazed at Lucie and knew she was remembering their night together and how it had ended.

"I decided long ago that I would not seek what he could never have."

Her mouth pinched into a frown. "Yet you will marry his sisters."

"If Joy Cat agrees."

"If he does, what will you do?"

"Marry."

"Out of duty to your friend, or for the land grant?"

He was so surprised at her words he made no effort to defend himself.

"Is that what you think?"

"I think you have found a way to ease your conscience, continue to be miserable and gain a horse ranch all at the same time." With that she turned her back on him and walked away. He followed her with his eyes, wishing he were free to pursue Lucie and seek the happiness he did not deserve.

* * *

The journey upriver took much of the night. Eagle Dancer slept until they loaded him into the wagon and then he roused only briefly. They stopped at the home of the agent from the Bureau of Indian Affairs. Sky presented him with the letter from Major Reilly giving them passage to the reservation. The agent, called Livingston, seemed diligent enough.

"Have to check the wagon for whiskey," he said. "They set up a new camp right across the river. We run them off and set up somewhere else. Devil's own time keeping them out."

Sky set the break as the man checked the flatbed, finding only Lucie and Eagle Dancer. Sky heard him speak to her in English.

"Miss? You white?"

"Yes, sir."

"What's your business here, then?"

Sky was about to present the paper again but Lucie intervened.

"I'm listed in the letter. Lucie West, Eagle Dancer's wife."

He pulled himself upright and stared at her as if her words made no sense. "Married?"

She nodded.

"That's a switch, I'll say. Lots of men are marrying squaws, for land grants. But never seen it the other way around."

Lucie glared at Sky.

"You staying?" asked Livingston.

Silence stretched.

"Ma'am?"

"I'm here to care for my husband. He's got pneumonia."

"All right, then. I'll check on you in a few days, make sure you're all right. Not supposed to be anyone here but Indians. Not sure you can stay for long. Indians only, you understand?" He glanced back at Sky and his companions. "This your own choice, Mrs. West?"

Lucie did not answer. Livingston was now regarding Lucie intently as he rubbed his chin.

Sky cut in, certain that the pause raised suspicions. "She's answered that already."

"I'm not asking you. Now hush up." He turned back to Lucie, his voice changing from irritation to a gentle hum.

"Ma'am?"

"Yes, my choice."

"See you shortly, then." He stepped away and waved them on. Sky lifted the reins. They rolled past.

Eagle Dancer had lay quietly until they reached his cabin, but had another coughing fit as he left the wagon and bloodied another handkerchief on the way into his house. When he could speak he turned to Lucie.

"You see? I have a fine white man's house now. You don't have to tan hides or move this tipi. It is like your parents' house—yes?"

Sky saw Lucie look away. Lucie's father was a very successful man, according to Mr. Bloom at the trading post, who had heard that from Mrs. Fetterer, who had quizzed Father Dumax about her background, and Lucie had mentioned that President Hayes knew her father. If it was true, surely her home put this one to shame. Sky found himself holding his breath as he waited for Lucie's reply.

Lucie nodded. "It's very nice."

Eagle Dancer turned to Iron Bear. "Call my nephew and tell him it is safe to come."

Iron Bear went to the door and gave a high piercing whistle. A few minutes later the boy appeared.

Sky watched him as his gaze scanned the room, noting surprise at seeing Iron Bear, then a smile when he noted Eagle Dancer being helped to bed by Lucie and then their eyes met. No Moccasins's smile vanished. Next came a quick shifting of his eyes as he looked to Eagle Dancer again, but seemed to find no answers there. Back to Sky now. Was that alarm because Sky had witnessed his humiliation or guilt because No Moccasins had killed the truant officer?

Sky was certain he recognized an expression of shame, having lived so closely with the emotion for so long himself. What had No Moccasins done after Sky had left him?

"Your uncle is home," said Iron Bear. "Send word to the elders and bring White Bull. Tell him that Eagle Dancer has a fever."

No Moccasins left without a word and with a speed that struck Sky as unseemly. He had not even greeted his uncle.

With help, Lucie made Eagle Dancer comfortable on a pallet near the fire. She doled out the cough medicine. His face was flushed and his eyes stared up at her with a glassy glow.

"Do you see this house I have built you?" he asked again.

"Yes. It's a lovely house. Rest now."

His eyelids drooped and he dozed.

Not long after this, White Bull, the medicine man,

arrived with a tea that helped lower Eagle Dancer's fever. He breathed more easily now. Gradually, his flushed face grew pale. Only then did Lucie leave his side to inventory supplies. Sky tried not to flinch at the twinge of jealousy he felt. What would he give to have such a woman care for him this way—his life?

But even that was not enough. Why couldn't he have died that day?

Lucie gave a gasp as she stared into the last empty parfleche, seeming horrified by the lack of food.

"No rations while he has been in the white man's fort," said White Bull. "His nephew has lived like a widow, on handouts and scraps." He gave Lucie instructions on the tea and promised to come tomorrow with a rub for his chest and to pray for Eagle Dancer's recovery.

Iron Bear departed, promising to return the following morning.

Lucie and Sky stood side by side in the doorway as head man departed on foot. Lucie hesitated in the entrance and Sky thought she might say something. But Eagle Dancer's cough caused Lucie to glance back to find him resting with eyes closed.

Sky stepped out into the dusk. He glanced back to see Lucie's worried face, trying to commit her features to memory, knowing he would never succeed in picturing such loveliness.

Lucie stopped him. "Where are you going?"

"Mexico."

She rushed out to him. "You can't, not now."

"Why not? I've delivered you to your husband, as I promised. My duty here is done."

She stiffened, as the panic made her heart buck like

one of his wild horses. She knew without question that if she let him go, she would never see him again. And although she was still furious for the way he had treated her, she did not want that.

"You have not heard Joy Cat's answer?"

"I will stop at Cheyenne River before I leave. If he agrees, I will take the sisters with me."

Jealousy spurted through her, straightening her spine.

"Sky, please. Don't."

Sky softened his voice. "You said you wanted me to go."

"That was my anger talking."

He nodded. "And now it is your fear. I don't need you, Lucie. He does." Sky motioned to Eagle Dancer.

"And here I am. But this isn't about him and you know it. This is about your proposal, one hundred and sixty-eight acres, and it is about your terrible tribute. Is that really what you think Sacred Cloud would want, for his sisters to marry a stranger who doesn't want them, so you can ease your conscience?"

"Don't speak his name."

"He wouldn't want this. No one would ask that."

"He didn't ask for his death, either."

"Convenient, isn't it? This shield of duty you hide behind. It keeps you from having to face me and what happened between us."

Lucie held her breath and waited. Sky turned to go, but before he could, Eagle Dancer roused and called him back.

Over the next week, Lucie had her hands full and Sky avoided the house as much as possible. This morning she watched him chopping cord wood, swinging the ax so hard that it sent the split pieces jumping in two directions as the ax head sank deep into the block. At least he was still here. His presence gave her peace, because she trusted him to protect her.

She had meant to speak the words that freed her as soon as they secured Eagle Dancer's release. But that had not worked out as she intended. As he grew stronger, she prepared to tell him the truth and say goodbye. When that happened, Sky would see her safe and then leave her.

Lucie held no illusions about that.

She searched the yard for the boy. His nephew had been like a ghost, avoiding the house. She found No Moccasins at the stove one evening eating what was left of her cornbread.

The rations, she had learned, were pitifully inadequate for two people, but for four they were vastly insufficient. A pound and a half of beef, of the poorest quality, a half pound of corn that was rough, not even ground to meal, and a half pound of flour each day made for a monotonous menu.

Sky had purchased extra beef, bacon, coffee and pinto beans, but the others had no resources beyond what was provided.

Today White Bull visited Eagle Dancer, checking his progress and bringing him news from his people. After the healer had departed, Eagle Dancer asked Lucie to call Sky, because he had something to discuss with him. Sky spent most of his time out of doors, entering only for meals. He even slept outside, but he came at her insistence.

Eagle Dancer waited until Sky had settled beside

him on the buffalo robe before speaking. Lucie soaked the corn that she would serve mixed with the beans and leftover beef for a stew, making as little noise as possible, as she wanted to hear their conversation.

"White Bull has delivered Joy Cat's answer to your proposal to wed."

Lucie frowned.

"He will bring his daughters here for you to meet. If they are agreeable he will approve the match."

"What dowry?"

"He can no longer own horses, so he asks for food, a cow, five pounds of coffee and two of sugar. It is a large dowry, but he reminds you of your debt and that you will gain two good wives."

Lucie found herself before them, without even recalling crossing the room.

Sky stared up at her as he spoke. "I am pleased to meet them again."

Eagle Dancer smiled and then glanced at Lucie. "No Moccasins tells me they are journeying here and will arrive today. Do we have coffee to offer them and sugar?"

She stood glaring at Sky. This was wrong.

"Sunshine?"

She roused herself and glanced at Eagle Dancer, who was looking with confusion from one to the other. She returned to the kitchen area. "I have brown sugar and coffee."

The party arrived shortly thereafter. The women wore colorful shirts, one peach and one pale blue. Their skirts showed they had trim figures and that the lack of food had not diminished their charms. They were both younger than Sky but did not look it. Perhaps the years and hardships made them appear older. Lucie hated them both on sight. It took all her restraint not to slop coffee on them or order them out of her house.

But it was not hers. She never had a home of her own. And even if she did, a tantrum wouldn't keep Sky from doing as he promised. He would marry them both and become a squaw-man. There were many whites already, across the river, married to Indian women in order to qualify for a government land grant to begin the newly opened tracts.

She watched Sky as he spoke politely to the women. His posture seemed stiff and his jaw tight. Lucie felt sick. Her coffee tasted burned in her mouth and she set it aside.

After what seemed like hours, Sky bought them passage on a riverboat for their return, so they would not have to walk the fifty miles south. Joy Cat would not speak directly to Sky, but did sit beside him in the wagon. They set off after supper. Later, Lucie checked his usual sleeping place and the corral where Falcon slept, but Sky had not returned by midnight.

She knew that Eagle Dancer had looked forward to spending time alone with her as much as she was dreading it. She did not know what he intended, but she planned to tell him she would not stay. As it happened, the illness made him tired and he fell asleep after supper.

Tomorrow, she promised herself, but when she woke she discovered Sky had returned, wearing a wide grin that darkened her mood. No Moccasins appeared as if Lucie had rung a supper bell and she served the meal, being sure that Sky's biscuits were black on both sides.

He glanced from the biscuit to her. She waited for

him to say just one word. Instead, he lifted one hard
nugget and took a huge bite, his eyes never leaving hers.
Lucie pressed her lips together and stalked away, angry
that he would not accept the gauntlet she had thrown.
Why did she care what he did? If he wanted to toss his
life away, then what business was it of hers?

Lucie was honest enough to realize that she did care
for him, but was not fool enough to long for a man who
did not want her. Was she?

The floor seemed to drop from beneath her feet as
she realized that she did, with her whole bruised heart.

She did care because…she loved him.

Lucie lifted her hand to her mouth to cover her startled expression as she stared at Sky. She loved him, this
man who avoided others because of the pain he carried
in his heart.

Lucie was so distracted that she did not note the
sound of horses and the rattle of tack. But No Moccasins did. He sprinted to the rear of the house and
slipped out the back window.

Eagle Dancer needed help to stand, but he walked
to the door unassisted. There sat William Reilly and a
contingent of soldiers, beside Mr. Livingston from the
Bureau of Indian Affairs. David sat his chestnut horse
beside Reilly, glaring at her with a fury that turned her
stomach.

Lucie slipped out and stood beside Eagle Dancer.

"Ma'am," said Major Reilly, "would you be so good
as to translate? Our usual translator is…incapacitated."

"Drunk," furnished Sky. "I've met him. He can
barely speak Lakota."

"More reason to use a trusted source." Reilly faced
Eagle Dancer, but did not dismount.

Lucie had a bad feeling. Were they going to arrest him again?

"We have made no progress on the murder. Eagle Dancer has not found the culprit and delivered him as he promised."

"He is still very ill," she said, defending him.

"Translate, please."

She did.

"So we are ceasing all rations to all members of both the Sweetwater and Bitterroot tribes on the upper and lower reservations until we have the man in custody."

Lucie gasped and Sky scowled. She repeated the message.

Eagle Dancer's face remained placid, but Lucie noted a slight tick at his jaw.

"We do not know who has done this thing," he said.

Lucie relayed his words.

"You deliver the guilty brave."

"This food is promised us by the Great Father in Washington."

Lucie repeated what he had said.

"As you have promised to keep our laws. A murder has been committed and we will have justice." Reilly paused, waiting for Lucie to stop speaking and then continued. "Rations cease as of tomorrow morning. No hunting outside the reservation. If you want to avoid privation, we will be back in the morning for the culprit. Rations recommence on delivery of the man in question."

Lucie delivered the ultimatum.

"You will kill our women and old people."

She was still translating as Reilly shouted to his men and wheeled about. The men thundered away, leaving a fine cloud of dust to settle over them.

Chapter Thirteen

Sky tracked No Moccasins to his hiding place by the river and was about to confront the boy with his suspicions when No Moccasins surprised him with a confrontation of his own.

"Why do you pursue the wife of my uncle?"

Sky went completely still as a blast of cold air seemed to blow around him. If it was obvious to a boy, was it also obvious to his uncle? He did not want to embarrass Eagle Dancer and he had not intended to...

"I do not pursue her."

"Your eyes do. I watch you and it is so."

"I did not come to speak of Sunshine, but of the man I shot."

No Moccasins dropped his gaze.

"I will not tell the bluecoats, but I must know. Did you go back?"

No Moccasins nodded once.

"Alone?"

A shake of his head.

"Did you kill this man?"

No Moccasins lifted his chin. Tears streaked his face. "Their arrows brought him down, but it was my blow that finished him."

"Whose arrows?"

"Running Horse, Red Lightning and Water Snake."

"Sweetwater?"

No Moccasins nodded.

"Older or younger?"

"Sixteen and seventeen winters, so they do not have to go to school." No Moccasins sighed. "I broke my uncle's war club."

"Where is this club?"

"I've hidden it well."

"Is it far?"

No Moccasins shook his head.

"Show me."

He followed No Moccasins down a dry gulch. The boy made for the abandoned hole of some rabbit and knelt. He used a stick to avoid a run-in with a snake and fished out a bundle of tied grass. He stood and offered it to Sky.

Sky unwrapped the club, seeing the broken point immediately. Dried blood darkened the smooth wood and coated the brass studs nailed about the head. The boy had killed a man and in so doing kicked a hornet's nest of trouble.

"Did you tell my uncle?"

"No."

"But there will be no more rations because of me," said No Moccasins.

So he had heard what the soldiers had said. Sky

looked at this boy's defeated posture and saw another, racked with guilt, unable to change a terrible mistake. There was no question that Reilly would make an example of the boys. But would he hang them? Sky feared he would. No Moccasins looked at Sky, his face determined. Once Sky had stood before Eagle Dancer in the same way—alone, riddled with guilt and uncertain what to do.

"I have to surrender myself."

The very words Sky had spoken. Sky felt a prickling down his spine as if he could feel the hoop rolling back around to the beginning, moving in the circle that was the way of the universe.

"No. Let me speak to your uncle. This is a decision for the elders."

No Moccasins nodded his acceptance. "Yes. They will decide."

But Sky knew what must be done, realized now he had not come here for Lucie or to wed the sisters. He had come back for this.

Eagle Dancer spent the day in discussions with the other head men over the issue of rations. The next morning Lucie woke to the buzz of many voices. Overnight their yard had bloomed with tribe members who had come to witness the confrontation between their leaders and the bluecoats.

Sky was not among them and Lucie feared he was again visiting Sacred Cloud's two sisters, but could not believe he would leave them here to face the soldiers alone.

Lucie left the solemn assemblage to gather water at the spring that fed into the river and found Sky waiting for her there. Lucie drew up short at the sight of him. The thrill of excitement rippled through her. He had sought her out in this private place. Her anticipation died when she took in his somber expression.

She forced herself not to show her eagerness for the sight of him, grasping the handle of the bucket before her as she waited for him to speak.

"Lucie, I came to say goodbye."

His words struck her like a blow. How could he leave her now, when the soldiers were coming at any minute? Didn't he care what happened to the people he professed to love?

A little ugly voice scoffed at her. *That's not why you want him to stay and you know it. You'll say anything to keep him with you.* Her next words proved the voice was correct.

"Eagle Dancer needs you."

He nodded. "I want you to understand, before they come. Lucie, it's the only way I can repay my friend and give meaning to my life."

So he was going to marry the sisters, regardless of the cost.

She turned her back so he could not see her shatter before him like ice. Lucie's throat ached. His life with her would have no meaning, no purpose? Why had she allowed herself to believe he might be different, that he could do what no one else could do and love her for who she was?

Lucie dashed the tears from her cheeks, resigned to the truth now: that everything between them had been a terrible mistake, that her love was one-sided. She ignored everything he had told her in her effort to convince him, to force him to share her feelings.

Her breath caught as she realized that she acted exactly like Eagle Dancer. She was trying to keep Sky against his will, force him to feel what he clearly did not. Her stomach cramped as she recognized the similarities.

No, she would not be like him.

She straightened, forcing her face to placidity. Somehow she managed to meet his gaze.

"Go to them, then. I hope they bring you joy."

"What?"

"Forever Flower and Dragonfly. And I'm sorry for the cruel things I said. You should do what your heart tells you."

He stared at her in stunned silence. She turned to go, hoping her legs would carry her up the small incline.

"Lucie, wait. You don't understand."

Somehow she kept moving. At the top of the rise her tears were falling hard and she could not see where she was going. She only knew she had to get away from Sky. His voice pursued her, closer now.

"Lucie, listen."

She ran into someone. Eagle Dancer caught her. She stared up into his frowning face as he glanced from her and then to Sky. She ducked her head and slipped away, dashing past him and leaving both men behind.

Lucie reached the yard only a moment before Eagle Dancer and paused as she saw the dust that forecast the imminent arrival of the military. Iron Bear and White Bull stood before their people, somber as deacons.

Was that why Eagle Dancer had been seeking them out, to tell them the soldiers were here?

The women huddled closer, shifting nervously at the

army's approach. They knew exactly what the cavalry were capable of and Lucie knew they had good reason to be afraid.

All the people waited silently to witness what the army would do, standing unarmed and helpless as stalks of wheat before the scythe. Lucie stood with the women, in a group behind the men.

Major Reilly drew up before the elders, reining in his black horse. He had brought a show of force uninvited onto land that the government had promised would be patrolled by Indian police. They stood behind the riders and infantry men.

"Are you prepared to turn over the man responsible?" asked Reilly in a voice of a born commander.

Some of the women around Lucie flinched at the barked question.

The translator had come with him today. He dismounted and wobbled forward as if still recovering from a Saturday night. Lucie was prepared to step in if he misinterpreted his words, but he did not.

Eagle Dancer remained where he was, looking handsome and fierce in his formal attire—leggings, war shirt and a single sacred eagle feather, wrapped in trade cloth and tied to one of his long braids. The group fell silent as any congregation.

"This white man was killed far from our lands and without our knowledge. You punish us for something that is not our doing. You break your own treaty and the word of the Great Father in Washington and come onto Lakota land to take what we cannot give."

The translator got that right, except he said president instead of Great Father and he changed Lakota land to reservation.

"Maybe this will help." Reilly leaned heavily on his saddle horn as he spoke and then called to a man behind him. "Sergeant, bring up the arrows."

A lanky officer hurried forward holding a bundle sheathed in canvas.

"Show him," ordered the commander.

The soldier approached Eagle Dancer as Reilly sat his horse, watching. His man unwrapped the folds to withdraw several arrows.

"These were taken from the corpse," said Reilly. "Just got them from the school yesterday. You expect me to believe you don't know exactly who these belong to?"

Eagle Dancer leaned forward and then straightened too quickly. He knew. Lucie was certain he recognized the marks. His face remained placid but his eyes searched the men beside him. Others in the group were less careful with their expressions.

"They dug this out of his skull." Reilly lifted a white lance point and held it between his index finger and thumb. Then he lowered his voice. "You can't protect him, chief. He's got to come with us. We know there were three, but we'll settle for one—the one who carried this lance."

The translator leaned in and Eagle Dancer turned his face away in disgust.

"Your man stinks of whiskey," said Eagle Dancer.

The translator said, "He ain't saying."

Sky stepped forward. Lucie thought he would correct the error but instead he extended a war club. Lucie saw at once that one of the two points were broken.

Where had he gotten this? Reilly accepted the club

and fit the point in his hand against the broken edge. He smiled.

"Good work, Mr. Fox. You found the murder weapon."

Lucie held her breath as a premonition of doom soaked her body in a cold sweat.

Reilly leaned toward Sky. "You know who's responsible?"

"Yes. I am."

Reilly's smile dropped.

"I found him molesting a boy and I stopped him."

This is what he meant earlier—what he had tried to tell her. He wasn't talking about marriage. Sky hadn't rejected her for the sisters of Sacred Cloud. He had found a way to regain his honor by accepting the blame for something he did not do. And when he said goodbye...

Lucie opened her mouth but nothing came out.

"Mr. Fox, do you know what the hell you are doing?"

Sky nodded. "I shot him."

Lucie's voice returned. "No!" She ran forward, throwing herself into Sky's arms. "No, no. Don't do this!"

Reilly called to his men. "West, Selman, secure this prisoner."

David's jaw was set in a look of determination Lucie recognized. The two dismounted and grabbed Sky by each arm. Lucie clasped her fingers behind Sky's neck and clung to him with all she had.

"Lucie," David said, the disapproval ringing in his voice. "Have you no shame?"

No, she had no shame left. Instead, she had a love for a man who would give his life away to save...who?

She fought and it took three men to dislodge her. Sky stood straight and silent, refusing to look at her.

"Let him go!" she howled.

She struggled in the arms of the soldier holding her, kicking at them and trying to wrench free as they tied Sky's wrists behind his back.

Eagle Dancer stepped up to him and spoke. Lucie could not hear the words, but she heard Sky's reply.

"Friend, let me do this."

Eagle Dancer stepped back and Sky was led away. They were leaving.

"No!" she howled. "They're not his arrows!"

The men released her. But the others had already thrown Sky upon a horse. Lucie flew to Eagle Dancer.

"Save him. Please. It's a lie. You know it's a lie. He didn't do it."

"He has made his choice."

Lucie released him. "You will let him take the blame?"

Eagle Dancer said nothing. She turned to follow Sky, but Eagle Dancer grasped her arm and drew her back. "Lucie. Don't go."

She saw the hurt in his eyes, reflecting her own. They had each lost the one they loved today and the understanding and grief flowed between them. But still he would not give her up, even knowing she loved another.

"Let go," she whispered.

"I have waited my whole life to see that look in your eyes and when I see it you are looking at another man."

Her heart broke again. "I love him. Please help me."

Eagle Dancer released her. When he finally spoke his voice cracked. "If it is your wish." He cleared his throat and spoke to his people. This time his words were clear and strong. "I divorce this woman. She is no longer my wife."

The crowd seemed to give a collective gasp and the whispers began.

Lucie stood dumbstruck. The man who had done anything to possess her had finally given her up. She thought of all the times she had begged him to release her. Why now? Was it because he knew he had no power to prevent her leaving? That she would go with his permission or without it?

Eagle Dancer aged before her eyes. His shoulders slumped and his expression seemed bereft. When he spoke, his words were low and gentle, like a caress. "It is all you ever wanted from me, isn't it, Sunshine—your freedom?"

She could not speak past her tears and could only nod. She turned to go, but he stopped her again, this time with a gentle touch.

"Sunshine, why did you come back?"

"To repay you for keeping me alive and to tell you that I forgive you."

Eagle Dancer's dark eyes swam with tears. "Where will you go now?"

It was a very good question.

Lucie had three choices. She could backtrack to the school and beg for her position, return to her parents, or go to Fort Sully and try to get Sky released. She had no illusions that they would let him go as easily as they had discharged Eagle Dancer. Sky was their scapegoat and they would definitely put him on trial in a military court.

The arrows did not belong to Sky, but Lucie was

certain that no one cared if they had the right man as long as they had a convenient culprit. He would be painted doubly the villain as he was white. Lucie considered that her sensationalized story would pale by comparison.

She still did not know how Sky felt about her, but she was certain what lay in her heart and that was enough to decide the matter. She was going to Fort Sully. But first she would discover the real guilty party, for she would not see Sky punished while the guilty one went free.

The morning had fled and she had done little but cry herself sick and pack her belongings, while Eagle Dancer was out conferring with the elders. He called a greeting before entering, as if it were a tipi instead of his house.

She did not try to hide her red eyes or puffy cheeks. They suited her mood. She rose to speak to Eagle Dancer, hoping he would help her save Sky.

"You know who did this. The man responsible must step forward."

"The *man* responsible?" Eagle Dancer shook his head. "Did Sky tell you of his friend?"

"The boy he killed with an arrow? Yes. But I don't see what that has to do with this."

"They are joined together in the spinning hoop. One action, and now another—linked."

Lucie shook her head in confusion.

"This boy that was Sky Fox has lived in guilt and shame over his action. He never faced the council of elders, he never accepted punishment for his crime. What is more, he is responsible for the death of a good boy, brave and strong."

"A tragedy, to be sure."

"I knew then that he should not die for doing this one bad thing. But I did not foresee how he would suffer by not being able to pay for this act." Eagle Dancer shook his head. "He has told me that he has never taken a life since that day, not even to defend his own. Yet he has survived gun battles, thieves who would steal the cattle he guards, attacks by Comanche. How is this possible?"

"He is very lucky, I suppose."

"He went searching for death on many occasions. He has told me this." Eagle Dancer continued his train of thought. "We once had a warrior who was impervious to bullets. Only one of his own people could kill him."

Lucie realized that he was speaking of the great war chief the whites called Crazy Horse.

"He was protected by strong medicine because he was a holy man. He gave his life for others. Sky Fox follows this path."

Lucie's spine prickled as she recalled having a simi-lar thought. "Even a holy man should not be asked to protect a murderer."

Lucie opened her mouth to speak, but Eagle Dancer raised a hand to stop her. Then he stood stiffly and walked to the door. He called to his nephew, who appeared a few minutes later.

"This boy is not yet fourteen winters old," said Eagle Dancer. "Nearly the same age Sky Fox was when he killed the son of Joy Cat."

Lucie stared in frustration at Eagle Dancer.

"The arrows belong to others, three boys. But the war club this boy used to avenge himself belonged to me."

"To you?" But how could Eagle Dancer have killed

Carr? Lucie glanced at No Moccasins in confusion. In that moment, seeing his flushed face and downcast eyes, she understood it all.

The boy returning for vengeance, his friends trying to capture the glory of battle they would never know and the man who could not save a boy killed by his carelessness, given the opportunity to save three young lives. Of course he accepted the blame. It was a way to atone for the act for which he could never make right.

Lucie stood. "Oh, my God in heaven. Sky did it to save him."

"And most surely, he has."

No Moccasins's head hung.

"And the lives of three others, as well." Eagle Dancer held up two arrows. "Running Horse and his younger brother." He added a third to the group. "And Red Lightning."

No Moccasins lifted his head, staring with eyes made glassy from unshed tears. Eagle Dancer spoke as he stared at the boy.

"But this one will not live his life filled up with shame and guilt, for he will make up for his mistake. He must be like Sky Fox and make a life worthy of such sacrifice."

No Moccasins looked at his uncle.

"But his way is not the white man's way. So, he will not go back to the mission school. He must gain a different kind of education. He will be a keeper of the language, the rituals and rites to remember what his brothers and sisters are forced to forget. Like Sky, he will not be a warrior, for he will also be a holy man who serves his people."

No Moccasins straightened. He no longer looked

defeated and ashamed. Eagle Dancer had given him back his dignity and delivered a purpose. Eagle Dancer had seen what had become of Sky and would not make the same mistake twice. No Moccasins would have a time of penance and then gain absolution. Then perhaps he would not also feel the need to sacrifice himself.

The head man pushed his nephew toward the door. "Go and speak to Iron Bear. Tell him that you wish to learn all he can teach you."

No Moccasins ran out the door.

Lucie found her throat burning and the tears she had held back now fell.

"If Sky tells the truth, they'll kill the boys." Eagle Dancer stared at her. "You will go to him now?"

She nodded and he clenched his jaw as he looked at her with a longing that constricted her chest and made it hard to breathe.

"My heart knew that once I opened the cage door, this little bird would fly away."

"Yes. But I am not the only caged bird. You should remove your niece from that school."

Eagle Dancer's brows rose. "This you say after working there?"

"She is a captive, just as I once was. Bring her home." She gathered her blanket bundle and Sky's possessions while Eagle Dancer watched her with sad eyes. At last she stood in the doorway. "Goodbye."

He didn't speak or move, only stared after her until he could see her no more.

This time Eagle Dancer did not have the lie to shield him. He had to face the truth and it cut his insides like flecks of swallowed flint. She did not love him, had never loved him and nothing he could say or do would change her mind.

He looked about at the white man's cabin he had built for her. The straight walls and careful chinking all erected on a delusion.

Eagle Dancer walked slowly to the glowing oil lamp and hoisted it over his head. Then he threw it with all his strength against the wall.

The glass shattered in an explosion of flaming oil that instantly ignited the furs upon the floor and the blankets before the fire. Black smoke billowed, forcing him to retreat. He banged into the wall, missing the door and falling to the floor, choking on the smoke.

Someone grabbed hold of his war shirt, dragging him backward. He breathed fresh air, but his eyes stung from the smoke and it took a moment to open them. When he did, he looked up into the face of the one who had saved him, his nephew—No Moccasins.

Chapter Fourteen

Lucie stepped from the riverboat to the dock, thankful that Sky's saddlebag had provided her more than enough for her passage downriver. She also had his gun and gun belt. The horse she had left in No Moccasins's care. She walked to the fort, but upon arrival, discovered that the major would not see her. She considered telling Reilly who was really responsible, but could not find the nerve to condemn four boys, so she went to her brother.

David left the officers' quarters to speak with her, but instead of the help she had sought she got only an angry tirade.

"I've telegraphed Mother and Father and written at length. They know…everything."

David was still tattling, just like he had always done. Had he expected her to hang her head in shame? Well, she wouldn't. "Will you help me to see Sky?"

"Are you chasing after him now? What about your husband, the chief?"

"He divorced me."

David took a step back, to absorb that. His voice lost its condemning tone. "Lucie, go home. You don't belong here."

"No, David, you're wrong, This is exactly where I belong."

He sighed. "You can't save him."

"But I can at least see him."

David pressed his lips together. "I'll see what I can do."

Lucie squeezed his upper arm and left him to return to his fellows. She knew she was making David's life difficult. But she was determined to do anything she had to do to reach Sky.

She was not granted access to Sky on the second day. She needed an excuse to remain in view of the stockade so she took up the task of darning socks and mending uniforms for the soldiers. She stationed herself directly across from the guardhouse with her basket. There she waited and watched. The morning detail included three soldiers, a cook who brought meals—two a day—an afternoon detail that stayed until the sun set and then the night watch took over until daybreak.

One week had passed when Eagle Dancer arrived with the B.I.A. agent, Mr. Livingston. How had he journeyed all the way from the northern reservation? She hoped he had not walked, for such exertions were bound to aggravate his consumption, but she knew he could little afford the boat passage. She watched him across the yard, noting that his hair was singed and his face burned, as if he had fallen into his fire. What on earth had happened?

She stood to cross to him and his step faltered as he

noticed her, but did not change direction or signal recognition. Lucie hesitated, unsure if she should approach or not. What had she expected—that he would be her ally after what she had done to him?

She watched the men check Eagle Dancer thoroughly before they all disappeared into the guardhouse. It was not until after he had vanished that she thought that he might also be under arrest.

Sky glanced up at the sound of boots that arrived too early for dinner and too late for lunch. Something had happened. He stood peering out the square window set high in the solid door as Eagle Dancer was escorted forward.

"Have they arrested you, brother?" asked Sky.

"No."

One of the soldiers spoke to Livingston. "What's he saying?"

"Asking if he's arrested," said Livingston.

"Not yet," said the soldier, fingering the trigger of his rifle.

Eagle Dancer stared steadily forward, accusing him with his gaze. Sky looked away and then back.

Lucie's outburst at his arrest had certainly left no doubt about her feelings. Sky regretted the hurt this caused his friend, nearly as much as he regretted not being able to explain to Lucie what he had done.

"Will you make her understand?"

Eagle Dancer shook his head. "She knows all."

Sky's head sank forward in relief. Eagle Dancer's words called him back from his musings.

"How did you get her to come? Did you tell her I

was sick, miserable, in prison—dying? Did you take all my manhood to bring her to me?"

Sky thought of lying, but had too much respect for this man. "She would not come at first. When you were arrested, she changed her mind."

Eagle Dancer's eyes squeezed shut as if he were enduring some torturous pain.

"What they saying now?" asked the guard.

"They're talking about Miss West."

The man leered. Sky's hands balled into fists around the iron bars. He set his anger aside and stared at Eagle Dancer, who had recovered himself somewhat. He waited.

Eagle Dancer breathed deeply and then spoke. "We will not forget what you do here. I will see to it."

"I do nothing but give back the life I have taken. The hoop was broken that day and now it is whole again."

"What'd he say?" said the guard.

Livingston translated. "He is confessing to the crime."

"Will you take care of Lucie? None of this is her fault."

"This I cannot do," said Eagle Dancer.

He pressed his hands flat to the planed cedar as his stomach dropped at the possibilities.

"Why?"

"I have spoken the words. She is my wife no longer. If you die, I think she will cut her hair and that would be a pity, as she has such beautiful hair."

Sky felt his eyes burning and could not speak.

Lucie breathed a sigh of relief when Eagle Dancer finally emerged from the guardhouse. As before, his face revealed nothing, but this time, instead of walking past her without so much as a glance, he made straight for her. Livingston had stopped to speak to the guards, leaving them alone for a moment.

Only when he was before her did she notice that his face was burned. She blinked in shock at the burns across his forehead and jaw. Before she could ask what had happened he began to speak, quickly, urgently.

"I am not permitted past the door. There are two guards with rifles, who never leave. Who has the keys? I don't know. No Moccasins rides Ceta south and will wait for you across the river on the land of the Bitterroot. Send word to us with any of the People who trade here and it will reach me."

Livingston caught up with them, just as Lucie understood that he was passing her intelligence, like a scout. He was trying to help her help Sky. She stared up at him in wonder, gratitude welling up inside her.

"All right, chief. You seen him. Now you got to go."

Eagle Dancer nodded and held her gaze for a moment more. "Remember the trick of your mother."

And then he was gone.

Her mother? What the blazes?

What had Eagle Dancer meant about her mother's trick? She thought back to all Eagle Dancer knew about Sarah West. Had he met her when she had visited their camp, trying to rescue her daughter? The day Lucie escaped....

She sat upright. The day she escaped, her mother had taken Lucie's place. Draped in blankets against the cold, not even her daughter had known what Sarah had done until hours and miles later. Sarah had played a trick. She had changed places with Lucie. The guards saw one white woman enter and one leave.

But Lucie couldn't take Sky's place, even if they did let her in his cell.

"But I can't…" She recalled Mr. Livingston's presence and fell mute.

"I have brought you corn bread." Eagle Dancer turned and motioned to a woman who carried a folded piece of red wool trade cloth. As she approached, Lucie noted it was Joy Cat's daughter, Dragonfly. Lucie accepted the bundle, recognizing it was too heavy to be bread.

Eagle Dancer turned and walked with Dragonfly and Livingston through the gate. Lucie recalled a time when he rode a fine horse and was the epitome of power and masculinity. The grace and pride were still there, but the power was gone.

Lucie waited until she lost sight of him before opening the trade cloth and discovering a loaf of cornbread resting upon Sky's holster and pistol.

She was so preoccupied that she nearly missed David striding purposefully toward the guard house. She dropped the bundle in her mending basket and dashed after him.

"Where are you off to, brother?"

"Lucie, you need to go home, now. There's nothing for you here."

Except her world. She stepped in front of him, searching his face for some sign of his mission.

"You promised you'd speak to the commander about allowing me to visit."

He exhaled heavily though his nose and gave her a

look of sympathy. "No visitors. He's guilty. He admitted it. There is nothing I can do."

Her stomach dropped and she understood. She grabbed the pristine lapels of David's uniform. "When?"

He broke the contact of their eyes. "We'll hang him on Saturday."

Lucie's knees gave way.

David caught her. "Oh, for the love of…corporal, get over here and help me!"

She regained her footing and he released her, waving off the help he'd called for. "You have to let me see him, to say goodbye."

"No, I don't."

"If I promise to leave?"

"You'll go home?"

"I—I can't go back there."

David's features hardened. She recognized the look. In a moment he'd be intractable, so she hurried on.

"But I'll go. I swear. But you have to let me see him. May I bring him some little comfort?"

David's eyes narrowed. He knew her too well. "I'll speak to the commander. But, Lucie, you'll be searched."

She tried to look flabbergasted.

"I'm just trying to protect you."

Lucie nodded. "Thank you, little brother."

Lucie had never been one to fly by the seat of her pants, as her mother had done. Sarah West had told her daughter about the day of her rescue many times. Her mother had said that she had not preconceived the switch, but when the opportunity arose, she had taken it. But Lucie had no confidence in luck. And her experience with fate had been all bad, until the day Sky appeared carrying a message that had changed her life.

Now she approached the guardhouse clutching written permission from Major Reilly. David had done it, somehow, getting her inside the blockhouse. She also carried a bible and a large apple pie.

She made sure to learn the names of the guards who covered the late afternoon detail. Pritchard and Fink. Fink was larger, more closely proportioned to Sky and he carried the key on a hook in plain sight on his leather belt.

Pritchard stood, nervously handling his rifle as she faced Fink with her paperwork. He looked her up and down. Reilly said she would be subject to search. But what kind of a search?

"Any weapons?"

"Of course not." She was glad she had not brought her skinning knife—this time.

"What about under them skirts?"

She lifted her chin and stared him down. "None, I said."

He looked tempted to check but instead he only ordered her to turn around. When she turned back he had his nose under the cloth covering the pie. He drew the knife from his holster and sliced the pie in half and then into quarters. He lifted out a quarter and placed it on the tin plate she had brought. Then, he took the rest, tin and all.

"Gotta check for weapons," he said and grinned.

"Of course." She covered the remains of the pie and then paused. "I wonder how he is to eat the pie without utensils?"

"He can use his hand, miserable bastard. Turning on his own, I'd like to shoot him myself."

Pritchard's glance shot from Lucie and then back to Fink as his face turned a bright pink. She decided she liked him better. Lucie stared at the pie, lying on the snowy center of the cloth.

"Corporal Pritchard, could you fetch me a plate?" she asked.

Pritchard turned to go.

"He stays here," said Fink.

Lucie accepted the defeat with a smile. The man was her only adversary here.

"Very well, then." She turned to Fink. "I'm ready."

Fink unlocked the door. Lucie waited for him to open it but he just stared at her.

"The door?" she asked.

Pritchard glanced back to his commander.

Fink shook his head. "He needs his hands free."

Lucie was forced to juggle the pie and opened the door herself. She proceeded down a short hall that had three cells on only one side.

"Last one," said Fink, speaking with his mouth full.

She walked slowly down the hall. "It's quite dank, isn't it?"

The men followed her with rifles, as if she were the prisoner. She stopped before the cell and turned to the men, waiting.

"You'll speak to him from outside the cell."

She gaped. "What about the pie? I can't fit it through the bars."

The opening in the door was only six inches wide and perhaps eight inches high.

"I cut it fer ya. Pass it through."

Lucie seethed, but she only nodded to the men. So she would have no help from Sky until she had the door open. She called to him and waited. Someone moved inside the dark cell. A moment later she saw his face, streaked with dirt, his hair in wild disarray and she thought she had never seen a more welcome sight.

"Hello, Mr. Fox." She wanted so badly to touch him, to kiss him through the bars. She drew on a mental image of her mother and stiffened her spine. The men had not searched her thoroughly. That meant she could bring his gun under her skirts the next time.

"Lucie?" He sounded so shocked.

"I have permission from the major to bring you comfort and to pray with you."

Sky looked confused.

"I brought you some apple pie."

She fed the slice through to him.

She glanced back to see Pritchard holding his rifle upright and Fink lounging against the wall with one hand on the revolver holstered at his hip. She smiled at them.

"You shouldn't be here," said Sky.

"I'll be coming tomorrow as well and Friday. What would you like me to bring you? What about steak and potatoes?"

He cocked his head, obviously confused by her false vibrato.

"Try the pie," she urged.

She waited while he did. Then he came close to the bars.

"Lucie, what are you up to?"

"Being a good Christian, like my mother."

He lowered his brows over his ghostly pale eyes and he dropped his voice. "You can't save me."

"Something from the gospel, then." She opened the bible and read from Luke 15:4. "'Suppose one of you has a hundred sheep and loses one of them. Does he not leave the ninety-nine in the open country and go after the lost sheep until he finds it?'"

"Lucie." His voice was low and threatening.

"Perhaps this one, then. 'Father, hear us as we ask You to rescue the lost from the domain of darkness and bring them into the kingdom of Your Son.'" She read on for a few minutes, then closed the bible and glanced up at him. "I hope that brings you comfort, brother."

She wanted to speak to him in Lakota, but she knew that might raise suspicion. So she lifted one finger and stroked one of his. He released the bars and their fingers hooked together. His eyes begged her not to act and her eyes begged him for understanding.

"I'll be back tomorrow evening, then." It was hard to release him, but she did and managed a self-righteous smile for the guards. "Sinners need to hear God's words even more than the holy."

Lucie walked calmly down the corridor with the guards following her. The door leading out was also locked. She made careful note of which key Fink used to release her.

"Thank you, gentlemen. I'll see you tomorrow night."

Twenty-four hours to figure out a way to send one of the men away and overtake the second. She worried about what Eagle Dancer had told her. Was No Moccasins really waiting across the river with Falcon? Could she really send a message with any of the Sioux that traded with the customers on the ferries?

Chapter Fifteen

Lucie arrived the following evening carrying a tray with steak and potatoes and a fine bottle of wine that she had laced with enough laudanum to drop a horse. She wore her moccasins, inside which she had her skinning knife and beneath her skirts, where a woman might wear a garter, she had strapped Sky's pistol.

She knocked on the door, stepped back and waited. Behind her came the sound of hammering. She flinched at each one. The gallows rose in the yard with terrifying speed.

The flap in the door opened and someone peered out at her.

"What's your business?"

Her heart sank. She did not know this guard.

"That the one the Indians marked? She's cleared." That voice she knew. It was Fink.

The door swung open and she was confronted by a giant of a man. He scowled down at her as she took in the wide chest, arms thick with corded muscle and a uniform that included a pin with two shining silver swords. The officer was a prime side of beef. Lucie's stomach began to ache in dread.

"I brought Mr. Fox some supper."

"He's eaten," said the unknown mountain of a man.

"She's got permission to visit, Captain."

The man moved aside, glaring at her as if she had just slapped his mother. Lucie's step faltered. She stopped before Fink, who also seemed cowed by the officer.

"I'm Lucie West," she said.

"I know who you are. You're the one they captured. Heard you married one of them."

"Yes."

"Country'd be better without them lying, thieving—"

She interrupted. "Yes, I think I understand your position."

"You went back to him, didn't you? That means you're worse than them, betraying your own. Lost a brother to those savages. Like to kill every damn one."

He loomed and Lucie stepped back. He took the tray. "No food to the prisoner."

Fink eyed the wine as the officer thumped the tray on the table. Neither seemed inclined to taste the wine.

Lucie struggled to come up with a new plan. She had intended to become suddenly unwell. That would cause one man to run for help and leave her alone with the other. She had been certain that Fink would send Pritchard, which suited her as Fink had the keys. But now…she could likely faint dead away and the monstrous man would merely kick her aside.

Lucie chewed her lip. Tomorrow was Sky's last sunrise. The terror nearly blinded her, so she set that aside. She needed to think. The chaplain would come and the major. Security would be more stringent than usual. It had to be now. But how could she do it?

She eyed the two men. Fink was a coward; that was certain. He had bossed Pritchard yesterday and today he was groveling to do the captain's bidding. Between the two, she would rather face him. That meant that she had to subdue the captain.

Her mind stretched but she could not think of anything she might say or do to cause him to leave his post.

That left only one option, really.

Lucie knew she would likely fail, but it did not stop her. She was going to free Sky or she would be occupying the cell beside him.

"Open the door, Fink."

"Yes, Captain." He hurried to comply. Lucie moved toward the tray.

"Just a minute, sir. If you think I am leaving an expensive bottle of wine here with you, you are mistaken."

The captain stepped closer. "He's not getting that bottle."

She stood on her toes and raised a finger to point at him. "Well, neither are you."

His eyes narrowed on her as if he was sighting her down the barrel of his rifle. What Fink was doing, she could not say, for she was completely focused on the captain.

"The major will hear of this." She grasped the heavy glass bottle and pressed it to her bosom.

The captain's mouth twitched in an ugly smile at her feeble threat. Then he folded his arms before his brawny chest and leaned against the table, which clunked against the wall under the force of his weight, lowering his head several inches closer to Lucie's. He stared coldly at her.

"I'll be back in a few minutes." She turned away and let the bottle slip from her hands. It crashed onto the floor and rolled. Lucie crouched, as if to retrieve the bottle, but instead she reached under her skirts and drew Sky's heavy revolver, secured to her leg with a series of ribbons, tied in pretty bows.

Fink crouched to help Lucie collect the spinning bottle.

She stared wide-eyed at Fink, who now gazed at the revolver pointed at his nose. He dropped the wine and stood blocking the commander's line of sight.

Fink lifted his hands and stepped back, giving the captain a clear view of her pistol, which she now swung to aim at his chest. She held her aim steady.

He tensed and raised a hand to go for his own weapon, calculated he'd be too slow and paused. "Miss West. Don't be a fool."

"Walk through that door."

He licked his lips and glanced at the door in question and then back to her. "If you shoot me, Fink will shoot you."

Lucie didn't even glance at the man who was inching away from his commander in an effort to save himself. "I doubt that."

"The others will hear. They'll come a running."

"But you won't be here to greet them. So, Captain, are you willing to give your life to warn them?"

He hesitated a little too long, so she cocked the trigger. The click had the desired effect.

The captain's voice was more growl than words. "Fink, do what she says."

"Through there," she said, motioning to the open door leading to the row of cells. Lucie was surprised at how icy-cold her voice sounded.

Fink hurried down the hall, but the captain stood to the side. Hoping she'd step in and be trapped?

"Both of you," she ordered. It occurred to her that she had never ordered a person around like this. All her life she had accepted orders, obeyed them. Now, with the help of this gun, she had a grown man nearly wetting himself in his hurry to do her bidding.

She didn't like it, not the sensation of power or the fear she caused.

The captain gave her a murderous glance.

"You won't get far."

She motioned with the end of the pistol.

"First cell, Captain," she instructed.

Fink slid the key in the slot, pulled open the heavy door and his superior inside.

"Lock it," she told Fink.

He did.

She instructed Fink to walk ahead of her to Sky's cell and unlock it. When this door swung open Sky sprang out. On seeing Lucie, he paused.

"What are you doing?" he asked.

"Freeing you." Then she turned to Fink, motioning with the gun barrel. "Inside."

He switched places with Sky.

"Now, strip out of that uniform and those boots."

Sky stared in disbelief as Fink peeled out of his clothing, stopping only when he stood barefooted on the cold earthen floor dressed in nothing but a dirty pink union suit. Fink did not have the wide shoulders or trim waist that Sky did and Lucie waited anxiously as Sky tugged on the soldier's discarded attire. She breathed a sigh of relief when he finally managed to complete the transformation. If one did not look too closely, you might not note the straining buttons down his chest.

Lucie handed the pistol over to him. She locked Fink inside Sky's cell.

Only then did Sky turn to face her. Instead of a look of pride or joy, he continued to scowl.

"You need to leave now," he said.

"We both do."

He didn't move. A cold premonition of tragedy trickled down her spine.

"Sky?"

He spoke in Lakota. "I'm staying."

"What?"

"I can't have your life on my conscience, as well."

She answered in Lakota. "But we can make it. I have it all worked out."

"I have to stay." His eyes implored her to understand. "Don't you see? My death will save four boys. It's payment for the life I took."

Lucie's mouth dropped open. He made no sense.

"But you've already saved them. Everyone thinks you killed Carr. There is no reason to hang. Isn't it enough that you'll be wanted for a crime you did not commit?"

"Is it?"

Now Lucie was scowling. It took a moment longer for her to understand what was happening.

"This isn't about the boys. It's about you."

He did not deny it.

"You're running again."

"No. This time I will *not* run."

Her frustration boiled to the surface and she pushed him with both hands. He took only a small step backward.

"You *are* running—have been all your life because if you stop, you might just love someone again and then you'd have to face the possibility of losing them, too."

This time it was Sky who gaped as he realized her words were true. He didn't want to love her. He had been ready to face the scaffold, but this…this wild gamble that they might escape, that he might actually have Lucie. No. He couldn't go, couldn't gamble Lucie's life because…he loved her.

Oh, Great Spirit, he loved this woman and to be with her he must risk both their lives.

"No, you have to go." He wondered if begging her would help.

"Why?"

"Because…" He could barely speak past the lump now choking him. "I need to see you safe."

One glance told him she wasn't going. She was as stubborn as any woman he'd ever met, and brave and foolish. And she'd stay here with him if he didn't go. Behind her Fink started shouting. Lucie prayed the thick walls would contain the cacophony.

"Come on!" She grabbed his arm and tugged.

But he wouldn't move. Couldn't. He was paralyzed by the realization that despite all his efforts to guard his heart, he had lost it again—to this woman. And he was more terrified now than any other moment in his life. What if they caught her, killed her? That would be his fault, too.

He had to get her out of here.

He fell into step with her. They walked silently out to the entrance. Sky looked around.

She handed him a wide-brimmed hat. He frowned.

"Put your hair up under your hat and pull the brim low over your eyes." She told him the plan and he nodded his acceptance.

"If they catch you, I will never forgive myself."

She lifted up on her toes and kissed him hard on the lips. "Then you better be sure they don't catch us."

Outside, Lucie tucked the pistol under her shawl, praying she would not have to shoot. Sky clasped her elbow gently as he escorted her toward the gatehouse. Behind them, she heard the howl of the captain and prayed that the soldiers would assume it was his prisoner for just a few minutes longer. Before them, the gate loomed.

As they neared the checkpoint, Lucie's heart began a wild pounding. Sky would have to speak to the guard. If he failed to convince them, they would not reach the river.

Sky's actions were slow and confident as he stopped before the entrance. Lucie stood between him and the guard.

"Corporal Fink, escorting this one to the ferry. Major's orders."

Sky reached in his jacket but the soldier waved him on and returned the way he had come. "Ferry's leaving. You best hurry."

Sky set them in motion. She listened for some sound

of alarm as they continued down the hill. Many long, tense moments passed before they were out of sight of the fort.

They hurried down the incline away from the dock.

He glanced at her. "They'll soon be on us. Ferry is the first place they'll look."

"We aren't taking the ferry." She glanced into the darkness. "Can you hoot like an owl? I told him that would be the signal."

Sky hooted. A reply came and a moment later No Moccasins appeared from under the dock, gliding silently beside the larger ferry in a narrow canoe that had been scooped out of a single log, barely slowing as they scrambled aboard. A few minutes later they were halfway across the river.

"Someone will have seen us," Sky warned.

Despite his nay-saying, they reached the opposite shore, somewhat down river. There No Moccasins led them to where he had hidden Falcon and a second horse.

Lucie's eyes rounded in surprise. "But how?"

No Moccasins grinned. "Sky Fox is not the only man who can whisper to horses."

Sky clapped him on the back. "Is he saddle-broken?"

No Moccasins shrugged. "I am better at catching them than training them."

Lucie stepped back from the unpredictable mustang. She was a pretty filly, buff-colored with a darker mane and tale. Her saddle was the smaller Sioux version, a wooden frame that seemed to be only two pommels connected by dual crosspieces. Sky approached the unfamiliar horse, with hands raised. He moved slowly, chanting as he placed a hand on the mare's neck. Over the course of the next several minutes, he led the horse, waving the reins in a slow circle. When, at last, he swung up into the saddle, Lucie could not breathe. The mare tried a few crow hops, but could not lower her head far enough to buck, because of the short rein Sky kept her on.

No Moccasins shook his head in disgust. "She threw me every time I tried that. Took me forever to get her saddled."

Lucie and No Moccasins mounted Falcon and they were off. Sky sang softly to the wild horse, who kept one ear turned forward and one back as he followed Falcon into the heart of the Cheyenne River Reservation.

They headed north. All along the way, members of the Bitterroot tribe stood, waving and cheering.

Sky pulled his hat lower over his eyes, as if trying to disappear. "Why are they all out here in the middle of the night?"

"I told them you would come," said No Moccasins, his voice loud with pride. "And so they have."

"But why are they happy? The bluecoats will follow. It will bring more trouble."

"And we will be gone by then," said Lucie. "They want to see you, Sky. You're a hero now."

"Hero?" He made a scornful sound.

"Yes," she said. "You are the man who saved the lives of Running Horse, Water Snake, Red Lightning and No Moccasins. Sky Fox the brave, who outwitted the Wasicu and walked through prison walls."

Lucie saw that Sky was nothing but baffled by this. Had he been so long in shame that he did not recognize that all had changed the instant he had admitted to the crime?

Sky blinked at the crowds with disbelieving eyes, flinching as the women patted his legs, shouting congratulations and blessings.

"I will tell the story for many, many winters and my children will also know of this," No Moccasins promised. "And the People will protect you and guide you through the land of the Bitterroot. Joy Cat has promised his help. We are going to his lodge now."

Sky pulled to a stop.

No Moccasins kicked Falcon's flanks to no avail. His voice grew petulant. "You must go or you will dishonor the head man."

Sky looked at Lucie. "I have promised to wed his daughters."

His face held such torment, it touched her heart. Was this an obligation he would be happy to be done with or was it as she feared, that he preferred to rejoin the People? No Moccasins interrupted.

"You are too late for that. Eagle Dancer is courting both."

Sky looked at Lucie and she nodded. Was that relief she saw flickering there or just her own desire to see him happy at this turn of events?

No Moccasins cut in. "Hurry now."

The shouts continued as they rode on through the night. Even at the remote houses, the People were there, mothers with babies in their arms, men and grandmothers. All but the children. Lucie sighed at their unnatural absence. They should be educated here, on their land, near their homes. Why had she thought to help their children to make a transition that no child should be forced to make? Their bondage was no different than her capture, except they had no hope of rescue. She was ashamed to have ever been a part of such a place.

They rode swiftly now, reaching Joy Cat's home before the guards had even changed back at Fort Scully. Joy Cat stood before his tipi, flanked by Iron Horse and then Eagle Dancer and the two daughters of Joy Cat, Forever Flower and Dragonfly, each holding an arm possessively, as Sky dismounted and then helped Lucie to the ground.

Joy Cat stepped forward and placed both hands on Sky's shoulders. "The People of the Bitterroot welcome back their lost son. He has journeyed far and been absent from our fire for too long." Joy Cat pulled Sky to stand beside him. "He cannot stay for he is pursued by the bluecoats who would take his life. This life that I once wished to take."

Lucie watched Sky's head sink again. How sad to finally have all he ever wanted, readmission to the tribe he had lost, only to have it snatched away from him once more.

"The head man of the Sweetwater people was wiser than I all those years ago when he stole this boy away. He knew that vengeance does not return the lost."

Beside Lucie, No Moccasins shifted restlessly. Was he thinking of the price of his own vengeance?

Joy Cat continued on. "If he had failed, four boys would now be locked up in the Wasicu prison awaiting their death. We do not always see the threads that connect us like the web of a spider. But they are there. Sever one and many strands break." He clamped Sky's shoulder. "I know that there is one who is not here today who would be proud of his friend's bravery. In his honor, I take the place of Ten Horses as your father.

From this day forward, this is my son." Joy Cat raised his voice still louder and spoke to his people. "He is one of the People and welcome at my fire. He is Sky Fox of the Bitterroot People once more."

Joy Cat fell silent and the people cheered. Old friends who he had not seen in more than a decade stepped forward to welcome him. His new sisters, Dragonfly and Forever Flower, gave him a beaded medicine wheel pendant as a gesture of welcome.

Dragonfly motioned to the large tipi. "This is our home. We will paint a blue fox on the lodge to tell all that you are part of this family and to help you find us."

Finally Eagle Dancer stepped up to speak to Sky Fox. The group fell silent.

"Goodbye, brother. Take good care of her."

Sky murmured his farewell, his voice barely audible.

Eagle Dancer faced Lucie. She braced for his words.

"Forgive a man who tried to capture Sunshine."

They shared a smile, but inside, her chest grew tight, for she knew he still loved her.

"Thank you for that," she whispered and kissed his cheek.

Supplies were hurriedly gathered. Water skins, a knife for Sky. Lucie accepted parfleches of foodstuffs. The folded rawhide was brightly painted, light, sturdy and easy to tie behind her saddle. Soon the people had offered too much. Lucie knew they would need their blankets and food for the winter far more than she and Sky ever would.

Sky was diplomatic in his refusal. "We need to be light and quick to outrun the army."

"They will expect you to move north on the great river. Instead, go west and hide among the Black Hills.

They will protect you from your enemies as you make your way north," said Joy Cat.

Sky nodded at the wisdom of this. "Thank you, father."

The men embraced.

Sky turned to Eagle Dancer. They each rested a hand on the other's shoulder for a moment. No Moccasins stood bravely waiting for Sky to look to him.

"Thank you, little brother, for this fine horse," said Sky.

The boy nodded. "And I thank you for my life."

Sky smiled.

No Moccasins held Falcon as Lucie mounted. She turned to Sky, who was already sitting on the wild mustang.

"What about our tracks?" she asked Joy Cat.

"By tomorrow they will be erased by the tread of many moccasins."

"They will ask about us and search our homes. We will help them look." He grinned. "And look." He held his hand up over his eyes, peering this way and that. "And look!"

The People's laughter filled the air.

Eagle Dancer smiled. "Perhaps this search will take days and days."

Lucie nodded her understanding. "Walk in beauty," she said and they answered in kind.

The next moment they were loping out of the village, heading west along the Grand River. Lucie longed to turn north toward the Canadian border some three hundred miles away, but they followed Joy Cat's advice, heading west from the Missouri.

They rode hard through the night, stopping only

when Lucie nodded off and nearly fell from her horse. Sky tied the filly to his horse and set her before him. She leaned back against him and let the rhythm of Falcon's steady gait lure her back to slumber.

For the next three days they rode, with very little rest, eating what the People had provided and stopping only to let the horses graze. Once Lucie woke from a doze to see Sky singing a song to the new mustang. When he turned and walked away, the horse followed, stopping just when he did. To Lucie's tired mind, they seemed to be dancing.

All too soon, they were riding once more. Lucie knew the army could catch them, but with each passing day, she grew more hopeful. They were heading north now.

On the following day, Sky decided to ride during the night. He did not like the open stretch of prairie ahead and there was a quarter moon and no clouds, giving them enough light to see the ground before them. This night ride reminded her of the time of her capture, only now she rode her own horse and her wrists were not bound. There were other differences. Then the sight of a rider with a blue jacket would have meant her salvation, where now it would mean the death of her. She did not know if they hung women and hoped she would never find out.

Lucie's thoughts were interrupted when Sky stopped the horse and cocked his head. Lucie heard the buzz of insects and the ceaseless wind, but nothing more.

"Hold on," he whispered.

Lucie had time to grip the pommel before they were galloping toward the dark line of trees. Streaks of crimson reached out across the wide sky, making the woods seem a dangerous place.

Once in cover, Sky drew her down off Falcon. She looked about and saw he had stopped in a dense pine forest. A poor place for grazing, but good cover, should they need it.

She opened her mouth to speak and he pointed. She peered out into the tall grass emerging now in the light of the rising sun. A carpet of wildflowers was sprinkled like confetti across the unending prairie. She was about to comment on the lovely sight when she saw movement and froze like a rabbit before a coyote.

The cresting sun glinted off of something, making it look like a row of mirrors, flashing in the pink light. The minutes passed and the light increased.

A line of thirty riders crested the ridge in a single-file line. The jingle of their tack and the murmur of voices now reached her, increasing in volume like a drum roll.

"You heard them?"

"My horse did." Sky stroked Falcon's neck.

"Soldiers," she realized.

"Must have wired Fort Buford. That's east of here."

"You think they are looking for us?" Lucie's voice broke on that last word. She glanced back and Sky met her gaze with a single nod.

He watched until the men rode into the forest ahead of them. "They're waiting for us to cover that open ground. If it had been any lighter, they would have seen us."

"What do we do? They're in front of us now."

"Wait for them to move south."

"What if there are more ahead?"

Lucie flinched at every twig the horses broke with their feet. She followed behind Sky, who was leading Falcon and the little filly through brush and branches. He took a circuitous route that confused her so thoroughly that she did not know what direction they were now heading.

Finally, when her legs were trembling from fatigue, he found a mossy patch beside several fallen trees. Their passing had opened up a small gap of blue sky above them. The forest below had responded by growing a fine, thick grass, different than what they found on the prairie. It was pale green and soft.

"We'll rest now," said Sky.

Lucie sank to one of the logs as Sky removed the saddles and threw them over the log beside her. He hobbled the filly and unbridled them. The horses were more hungry than tired and proceeded to yank the grass out by the clumpful.

Lucie rallied and set out her blanket for them. The moss beneath made a fine spongy bed. Sky offered her water and she drank. They shared the last of the pemmican, given to Lucie by the daughters of Joy Cat. The mixture of dried, pulverized buffalo meat, fat and crushed dried cherries filled the hollow in her belly. She could not finish her second piece because her eyes kept closing.

Sky packed away their food and guided her to the blanket. They stretched out there in the circle of sunlight, listening to the horses munching their meal.

"It seems so peaceful," she whispered. "It's hard to believe that they are out there, waiting."

"We won't give them a reason to venture into the

deep cover. We'll have to stay here all day, be certain they pass."

She thought of the stretch of treeless prairie he did not want to cross in daylight. His decision had saved them both. It took a moment to realize he had called a halt. She could rest, sleep.

She sighed in relief. But what if they had seen them and were searching or if…

"What if they hide in the woods and wait? How will we get by?" Lucie thought of the horror of being caught on the open land by the larger group and shuddered.

"I'll find them and we'll get past. They figured we weren't on the river but misjudged our speed." Sky gave her a look of appreciation. "Didn't figure a woman could keep a pace like that."

That look of admiration did more to lift her flagging spirits than anything she could imagine. They sat in silence, for a time, propped against the log, watching the birds flitting through the branches and listening to the steady grinding of grass between the horses' strong teeth. The rhythmic sound and dappled sunlight lulled her. Her head began to nod.

He drew her down beside him in the tall grass. How long had it been since they had rested? She could not keep track of the days. They rode all night and still they were nearly caught. Her head jerked up and she glanced about the quiet grotto.

"Are we safe here?" she whispered, fighting hard against the sleep that pursued her as relentlessly as any army. She knew that she must surrender soon, whether she wished it or not.

"We're as hard to spot here as that needle everyone is always searching haylofts for."

"Haystacks," she corrected and yawned.

He nodded then leaned close, whispering in her ear. "You're safe with me."

Lucie sighed, feeling the uncertainty seep away. She looked up, wanting to capture his face in her mind. His cheeks were now dark with stubble, but his eyes were the same vibrant blue.

He smiled. "Sleep."

She lay on the mossy carpet, tucked her head on the crook of her elbow and closed her burning eyes. Sky would watch over her, protect her and wake her before the soldiers came.

Chapter Sixteen

Sky slept until the sunlight left them in shadow. Lucie now curled on her side, breathing softly. He rose and searched for the horses, finding them still hard at work filling their bellies. It did not take long to set a few snares for rabbits. The animal paths were clearly evident in the underbrush and they would be active as the night came upon them. Locating a spring was more difficult, but he found one, by following the ferns and moss to the crack in the earth that bubbled with fresh, clear water. Sky hurried to fill the water skins and return, fearing Lucie would wake and find him gone. When he returned she was still asleep and had not moved. She was so still that he checked on her.

Even in slumber she was beautiful, her full lips gently parted to allow her soft breathing. She was curled about herself as if she were cold. Sky collected wood and set a fire, knowing he must wait until full dark before lighting it. Smoke was harder to spot at night, but even so, he would keep the flames low and hot.

Finally, he retrieved her blanket and covered her.

He closed his eyes and slept hard for several hours. He woke at an unfamiliar sound. The night had closed in about them. The horses were still and, judging from their breathing, they were asleep, as well. But something had roused him. He reached for his pistol and cocked the trigger.

"Sky?"

He turned to see Lucie raised up on one elbow, holding very still.

"I have to excuse myself."

"What woke you?" he asked, still cautious.

"My bladder, I suppose." He saw her raise her hands. "I just flipped back the blanket and then I heard you cocking that gun."

He released the hammer of his pistol. "Sorry."

They faced each other in awkward silence.

"Don't go far."

"I won't." She rose and then paused, looking back over her shoulder. Her hair shimmered in the moonlight and her face seemed carved of bone. "Don't shoot me when I come back."

He lifted both his hands, showing they were empty. It was the very reason he did not like to carry a gun. Perhaps when this was over he would put it away forever.

She nodded and crept away, lifting her skirts to midcalf. He watched her until she vanished into a pine grove, then he listened hard for anything else amiss, but heard nothing.

When she returned, he was sitting on one of the felled logs.

"I have to check my snares."

She stopped in her tracks. He could not see her face, but she clasped her hands before her, massaging the base of her thumb with the opposite one in a worried sort of motion.

"I'll come, too."

"No need. I'll be within hearing, all the time," he assured her.

She nodded and returned to her blanket. But this time he noted that she sat up against the log, waiting.

He was surprised at how hard it was to walk away, but their food stores were nearly gone and he could not leave the snares there. It was wrong to kill without reason and all animals that died at his hand deserved to be valued, not left to rot. He drew a deep breath and slipped along the animal trail, cutting between the ferns to his left.

He found two of his traps had snared rabbits. He lifted the limp bodies one after the other, thanking them for their lives and all rabbits for being so plentiful. When he returned, he found Lucie sitting up on the log, waiting. Her shoulders relaxed at the sight of him. Her relief warmed him. For a moment he could imagine what it would be like to return to this woman, to keep her always, protect her, care for her—love her.

But here was a woman who did not want to be kept. A captive who had been owned as property and treated with all the scorn and abuse of a slave. How did he convince her that she would never be ill-treated, that his love would not confine her?

He couldn't. Because it wasn't true. He wanted to

own her—just as Eagle Dancer had once done. What if she would not have him?

Suddenly, he felt as lifeless as the rabbits he held. He needed to tell her all that was in his heart. But he feared that she would turn from him as she turned from Eagle Dancer. Perhaps she only saved him because he had saved the boys.

But she had clung to him when they tried to take him and then risked her life to bring him out of the fort. Didn't that mean she had some feelings? After what had happened to her, could she ever trust a man again?

He entered the clearing where she waited and offered his kill to her. Lucie accepted the rabbits with a smile.

"Something fresh." The smile faded. "Can we have a fire?"

He nodded. "Small one."

She drew her skinning knife as he set to work on the fire. When the hardwood had burned down to coals, he sat beside Lucie, to find she had skinned the two rabbits, gutted them and skewered them. She had already made two hoops from the pliable pine branches and was sewing the green hide inside the ring.

"I haven't done this in years," she admitted.

He lifted one skewer. "You'd never know it."

Her smile brightened and Sky felt something flip in his belly. Suddenly food was the farthest thing from his mind. Lucie was hungry, he told himself, and he must see to her needs. He took the carcasses and staked them over the coals. The sizzle of fat dripping to the coals and the smell of roasting meat aroused a powerful appetite in Sky and judging from the way Lucie now sat forward on the log and stared at the rabbits, he supposed she was famished, as well.

He sat beside her, wondering how to open his heart. It had been closed for so long, he hardly knew if he was capable of tenderness. If she would accept him, she would want to live in the white world. A world he had rejected for so long. How could he have her if he did not understand the role she would expect him to play?

"This reminds me of all the times we had to move north, away from the wagon roads," she said. "The women in the front and the men guarding our retreat."

He nodded, thinking back to those days. His father was head man and a war chief. He had allowed Sky to ride between the women and the men on the first pony Sky had ever caught. Actually, his first pony, Follows Home, had done just that. He had been a yearling chased off by the new stallion in the herd. Sky had taken him home on a bridle he'd woven on the spot out of prairie grass.

"You've got a far-off look in your eye," said Lucie.

"I was remembering my first horse."

The meat that was getting crispy on one side, so Lucie left her place to turn it. The hissing of blood and juices hitting the coals began again. "The white one with the brown blanket?"

Sky grinned. "Yes, that's right."

"He had knobby knees," said Lucie. Her smile told him she was teasing.

"Oh, but he was fast. Riding him, it was like flying."

Lucie struggled to hold her smile and he knew her memories were not so fond.

Sky's smile faded. "I miss that horse."

"What happened to him?"

"I don't know. I had to leave him behind." He had

lost his horse along with everything else he had loved. What if he lost Lucie, as well?

They sat side by side, but Sky feared they were drifting apart, pulled by memories to distant shores. The aroma of roasting meat filled the air about them.

Lucie checked one of the rabbits and then offered him the stick. She took up another and the next several minutes was spent pulling tender meat from the bone and blowing on scorched fingers. Lucie claimed she was full before she had finished her rabbit. He ate the second, but would not take any of hers and she ended up finishing it.

"When will we be safe?" she asked.

He was reluctant to tell her, for he knew that once they reached a town or village, she could leave him if she chose. He would have no right to stop her.

"If all goes well, we will make the border before the next moon's rising."

She set aside the remains of the carcass.

"So close?"

Was that regret in her voice? He felt a moment's hope.

The night had closed in about them. The horses were still and, judging from their breathing, they were still asleep.

"They won't cross?"

He shook his head. "They might not even know we got by them for a week or so."

"And the Canadian police, they'll allow you to stay?"

Why had she said *you* instead of *us*? Would she leave him once they crossed the border? Was he just one more of her humanitarian projects, no different than the girls she had tried to make over in a white image?

He had been years on his own, but he'd never known her then, never tried to fill a day and night without hope of seeing her again.

"Sky?"

She waited for his answer. He danced around the issue, hoping she might tell him what she intended. "They might order us out of the country, but they won't turn me over to the US Army."

Her shoulders relaxed at this reassurance.

Would she stay with him? She was a free woman now, free to stay, free to go. He frowned.

"You can't go back either, Lucie. You're wanted, too."

"I know."

She said nothing further, just stared steadily at him. Why had he said that? Why didn't he say something to ease her mind, instead of adding to her burdens?

He wanted to tell her that his heart's desire was to love her every day of her life, if she'd let him. And that if the Great Spirit blessed them, he would build her a fine home where they could raise horses and children. And in that instant he knew that his fear of losing her was not as powerful as the need he had to love her. He would build her a white man's house, if that would make her happy. He would go and sit in the confinement of a church once every seven days to please her. She could teach their sons and daughters to read and write the English letters and he would teach them Lakota and tell them stories of the Bitterroot People and how they had two grandfathers, Ten Horses and Joy Cat. Three, he recalled, thinking of Lucie's father, Thomas West. His smile slipped. He recalled her father as a fearless man, relentless as his wife. He had been the reason Sky had avoided Lucie at the fort, after her rescue. The man was a human watchdog. What would West think of him as a potential son-in-law?

Sky's head hung.

"Perhaps it is bad luck, when we are so close, to speak of Canada." Lucie used some of the grass to clean her hands and then sat beside him in silence.

Sky stared straight ahead. He'd never felt this kind of terror. Not even when Eagle Dancer had pointed him toward the fort and given him a little push with the word, "Go." Yet then he had been able to speak, to reason. But now, faced with losing Lucie, he was paralyzed with fright.

The words she had spoken to him in the block house came back to him like a curse. *You are running—have been all your life because if you stop, you might just love someone again and then you'd have to face the possibility of losing her.* She was right. He did love her, enough to risk his life to save her and to fight all comers to have her. But that was child's play compared to opening his heart and speaking the words he needed her to hear.

What did he have to offer? He was a vagabond, a drifter with no home, no family. Joy Cat's words came to him. He was Bitterroot again. But Lucie did not want to be one of the People. She needed a white man's home, with straight walls and sharp corners. She would want a man who would give her the things a white woman needed. But what were these things?

He had money, after all, the silver and, sewn into the lining of his saddlebags, one hundred gold coins. Was that enough for a white woman's dowry? He knew that most fathers demanded at least three horses and some as many as twenty. But white men didn't take horses for their daughters. He knew that much.

The wife of the Mormon he'd lived with for three years was always talking about dowries and hope chests for her daughters. But he had never seen the chest or what the new husband was expected to fill it with. It must be gold. It was all the white men cared about. He thought of one hundred gold pieces and thought it a very small pile, not enough to prove his worthiness as a provider.

"Sky, I'm getting sleepy. Will we ride tonight or shall I go back to bed?"

He looked at her now, in the dim light of the roasting coals.

Her brow wrinkled as she stared at him. "What is it? You look worried."

He did not understand her world, but she knew his. Perhaps that was enough.

He captured her hand. She opened her mouth in a surprised little O and her gaze turned from concern to caution with just the widening of her eyes.

"I have traveled many years alone. I am not used to people, women especially. But if anyone could understand me, Lucie, it's you."

She pressed her lips together and he felt his chances slipping away. But the words poured out of him now, like water through a break in a beaver's dam.

"I know you were forced into marriage and maybe you don't ever want to marry again. But I also know you've been lonely, too. We're like the last two ponies in the lot. One's half crazy and the other is a paint and no one likes her markings."

Her brow wrinkled and he knew he had said the wrong thing. He hurried to recover.

"That's not the reason I'm asking, because nobody wants, I mean, or because I *can't* get anyone else. I want you because I don't *want* anyone else. Do you see?"

She gave a slow, cautious shake of her head.

"I'm hoping what you feel for me is more than just loneliness—because I already love you with everything I got."

She gasped. "What are you saying?"

"I want to marry you, Lucie. I want you to be my first and only wife."

Her eyes were round and full as the moon. As she stared in silence he felt his dreams burn up and blow away like ash. She was thinking of a way to escape him now and he'd have to let her go or be exactly like the man she never loved.

Lucie could only stare in surprise at Sky's proposal. During all the long stretches of silence and the excruciating pauses, she knew he was getting ready to tell her something. But she had assumed he was going to prepare her for their parting. She had been bracing for rejection, wondering why she was not accustomed to it by now, when he had asked her to be his wife. But more than that, he had shown her the honor of making her his *only* wife. Most women would not understand, but she did. Sky was prepared to devote himself only to her, have children only with her and provide only for her. No one had ever made such a generous offer.

And now his eyes reflected all the uncertainty that she had felt only moments earlier.

Say something, you idiot.

"Sky, I have been married once and I have been

asked by another to be his bride. But I have never had a man of my choosing and I have never been in love."

He nodded his acceptance of this and let her hands slide from his.

"Until now," she finished.

His head snapped back around and he grasped her shoulders in a grip that made her wince. He relaxed his hands, but his face remained taut as his eyes searched her expression. She smiled.

"You love me?" he asked.

She nodded. "I am afraid I do—desperately, foolishly and completely. I don't know what I would have done if you had left me at the border. I probably would have followed you."

"Left *you?*" His voice echoed astonishment. "Is that what you thought?"

"Well, you said yourself you're unaccustomed to women and you were so distant. I thought you were trying to think of a way to detach yourself without hurting me too badly."

"I was thinking of all the things *you* said, about not having any choice and wanting your freedom. I couldn't figure you'd give that up for me."

She laughed. "The only thing I'm giving up is my loneliness."

He clasped her hands. "I'll build you a ranch house with the tallest pine in Vancouver."

"Vancouver?"

His smile slipped. "It doesn't have to be there. Anywhere you say. I just thought we'd be closer to your family and still safe on that side of the border. The land is good for horses."

She nodded her acceptance of this.

"We can be married soon as we find a preacher and a church. Would that suit you?"

Her heart squeezed and she felt warm all over with the joy. He was offering her a proper wedding, the kind he'd expect her to want, when as far as she knew he'd never gone into a church by choice. It showed how much he meant to do to make her happy.

"I think that would be wonderful, but we don't have to wait so long."

Now his eyes rounded as she stood, tugging his hands, encouraging him to come to his feet before her. She gazed up into his eyes and spoke the words in Lakota that would bind them.

"I take you as my husband."

His smile spread from ear to ear. He had to swallow once to find his voice but when he spoke it was in a clear baritone.

"I take you as my wife. You will never go hungry and I will protect you always."

She stood on her toes to meet him as he swept down to claim a kiss from his bride. She clasped her hands about his neck and kissed him back, hoping he could sense the faith and joy that carried her into his arms. She drew back and saw her wonder reflected in his eyes.

"I can't believe it," he whispered. "My wife."

He reached to the ground and swept up the blanket, wrapping them both in the coarse wool. He knew Lucie understood the significance of this gesture. It was under such a blanket that all the Lakota newlyweds shared their first kiss as husband and wife.

Chapter Seventeen

The joy filling Sky's heart was so big he was afraid it might break through his chest. She rose up on her toes once more and kissed him again, but this time with none of the chaste reserve of a new bride, but with the wanting hunger of a new wife.

"Lucie." His voice was like a caress.

Her eyes opened wide as he drew back and she stared into the fluid blue of his eyes.

"I love you and I never want to be parted from you, but I'll honor the Lakota way. You are free to leave me when you will."

"I do not wish to be a captive, husband, but that does not mean I do not want to be possessed."

His eyes widened in understanding. His mouth slanted over hers and the pressing of lips quickly escalated into a frenzied dance of tongue upon tongue. His hands caressed her throat, then traveled down her shoulders and back, drawing them still closer.

The blanket slid from their shoulders. Sky paused,

waiting for her to decide what to do. She collected the blanket and laid it out beside the fire, then she unfastened her bodice and slipped it off her shoulders, leaving only her chemise. Sky copied her, dragging his shirt, still buttoned, over his head, revealing his wide, muscular chest.

The sight of him, half-dressed, frozen with that look of longing upon his face, did something to her insides. Her fingers grew clumsy as she struggled with the hook and eyes that closed her skirt. Finally it gaped enough for her to draw it down over the petticoats, which she removed one by one. They sat side by side on the log, he removing his moccasins and she removing hers. They placed them side by side as if they rested beneath their wedding bed, instead of beside an old rotting log.

Unbidden, her mind cast back to her wedding night with Eagle Dancer and her eyes pinched closed at the rush of dread and the shame of that coupling. Some of her ardor drained away.

Sky knelt before her, his hand upon her knee, just below the laced hem of her bloomer. His thumb moved in tiny circular strokes, but crept no higher. She opened her eyes to see him gazing up at her, his features now a mask of concern.

"Shadows of the past," she whispered.

He nodded his understanding.

"They leap upon you when you least expect them, like wildcats on a rock ledge." His smile was gentle and he showed no hint of disgruntlement at her admission. "I do not think they will go away, but perhaps if we fill our minds with other things, they will have no place to perch."

She squeezed his hand and nodded her approval of this.

His thumb swirled over the skin on the back of her hand. "Lucie, I know you have been a wife, but you have never been *my* wife. It will be different with us."

She nodded, knowing in her heart that he was right, that *this* was right. She stroked his face and he pressed his jaw into her palm—her mind now full of him. Then she reached for the ribbon tying her chemise and dragged the cord until the bow released. The fabric gaped. Sky's hands spanned her waist and he leaned forward to kiss the flesh she had revealed. Another tug and another knot slipped free. Sky followed the path down between her breasts to her navel, dipping his tongue into this shallow pool. Lucie trembled with anticipation as she slid her shoulders from the chemise. The cool air felt frosty on the wet trail he had blazed down the center of her body and her stomach twitched with delight as his tongue danced a circular path about her abdomen.

Sky captured her hand and brought her down upon the blanket. She lifted her hips to allow him to draw away her underthings. He crouched back on his heels to stare down at her, stretched out before him in the blue starlight. She was no longer embarrassed or afraid, for she felt truly beautiful and capable of pleasing him. The look in his eyes spoke of appreciation and a reverence that made her feel cherished.

"I've never seen a more lovely sight," he whispered.

She stretched out a hand. "Come…husband."

A smile flickered on his lips. He stood and shucked out of his trousers as if they were on fire, giving her the most tantalizing glimpse of his slim, muscular haunches before dropping down beside her and covering her body with his.

His mouth found her neck. The scraping of his teeth along the sensitive flesh caused her to throw her head back with a groan of pleasure. Sky captured the lobe of her ear and sucked. She closed her eyes to savor the erotic sensations. The rhythmic motion of his mouth stirred her, making her lift her hips against his and she heard him groan at the contact of her thigh to the thick shaft of his arousal. She rubbed against him, but he moved quickly away, gliding down her body to caress her breasts, first using his thumb and then his tongue to awaken her nipples into hard buds of sensation. Her entire body now pulsed and rolled like a wave, anxious to throw itself against the shore. Finally his hands moved lower, discovering what she already knew, that she was wet with wanting.

So this was what it was like to yearn for a man, to crave his touch. Her body knew these things and, although his fingers had never grazed her skin like this, she recognized his touch. How unshakable was the slow steady throb of wanting.

She reached for him, no longer content to passively receive what he would give and realized this, too, was different. When she was a young bride, she had waited and braced and endured. Now, she relished the warm velvet of skin that covered the bunching muscles of his biceps and the hollow to the right and left of his hip and the long cord that ran like twin ropes down his back to the firm buttocks.

His knee slid between her thighs. She needed no urging to open for him, for she was anxious to take him into her body. He held back, surprising her. He was ready for her, the pressing of her body to his told her that much, and her body was wet with the honey of desire.

His hand brushed her thigh and then toyed with the mat of curls that protected her most private of places. He found the cleft that separated her body. His fingers danced gracefully over her swollen flesh. Her urgency to join with him was halted by the exquisite pleasure of his touch. Her head dropped back and a cry came from her. Her breathing changed to an anxious little panting and her thoughts broke apart. All her being seemed focused on the liquid glide of his fingers over her flesh and with each passing moment the pleasure became more unbearable. She arched and writhed. He stilled her with the pressure of one leg thrown across her belly. His mouth found her throat. He whispered endearments in Lakota as he told her how beautiful she was—and she believed him. His words gave her the confidence to relax into the building wave that threatened to consume her. Sky would take care of her, protect her, love her.

The wave of sensation within crashed upon the shore, sending rivers of pleasure surging out in all directions. Somewhere deep inside her came the pulsing contraction and she cried out her joy at this gift that her husband had given her. Her body went slack as she fell back into the thick grass mattress beneath their blanket. She could not breathe the air fast enough now. He stroked her forehead and her arm as she lay trembling.

When she opened her eyes he was there above her, gazing down.

"My beautiful wife," he whispered and kissed her.

She pressed her lips to his, clutching at his hair,

to keep him from escaping. Her thigh slid along his until she came to the junction of his legs. She used her thigh to stroke his aroused flesh, causing him to groan. Her seeking fingers encircled him, drawing him closer, guiding him and stroking her wet cleft along his shaft.

His eyes widened and suddenly she was on her back again. She laughed at the strained expression on his face. She bent her knees, nestling him tighter against her body. He drew back and she guided him.

He held her hips as he arched, driving into her slick body in one smooth, masterful stroke. Now it was his turn to fight the rising desire. She glanced down at them. The sight of his body moving into hers did something to her insides and she found herself riding another upsurge. Each swift stroke of his body added to the momentum filling her. Faster he moved, with her clenching him tightly with each downward thrust. She arched into the contractions, stilling for an instant as the pleasure crested for the second time, only this was better for she felt her body gripping his, as if taking what he had to give. He gave a hoarse cry and thrust, locking them together in a moment of mutual bliss. The swelling pleasure receded her and she sank to the earth. Sky fell upon her a moment later, pressing her down, blanketing her with his warm, moist body.

It took great effort to lift her arm, but she succeeded, stroking his head as it nestled on her breast. His lips moved and he kissed her. They lay entwined until the night breeze chilled them. She shivered and he moved, instantly, rolling her up in the blanket and pulling her tight to his body. This was what it was like, then, to love and be loved. She smiled and nestled closer. He rubbed her back until the chill was gone.

"That was wonderful," she said.

He squeezed her tighter in response.

She gazed up at him, seeing the satisfaction glimmer in his eyes.

"I never knew."

He smiled. "Neither did I."

"You didn't?" She did not attempt to keep the astonishment from her voice.

"Lucie, I have laid with women, but I have never loved one. It changes everything."

Now it was her turn to glow with satisfaction. "Yes, everything."

He stroked her forearm. "You're pale as starlight."

"Not the sort of woman you had planned to have as a wife?"

He made a sound that was neither affirmation or denial. "I have not thought to have a wife for many years. Not since I left the tribe. But when I was younger I thought of it."

"What did you imagine?"

"Well." He stopped and shook his head.

She poked him in the ribs. "Tell me."

He drew a long, steady breath and then nodded. "I thought I would not be a warrior's first choice for his daughter. Three or four ponies wouldn't do. I knew I would need more and I was too young for raiding. So I learned to sing to the wild mustangs."

"I've heard you singing."

"Have you? In my song, I tell them of the new life they will have and how they are needed, because they are brave and strong. How we could not survive without them. And they listen. My first horse came to me in that way and many more since then. They come because they choose to come."

She sat up. "Wild horses?"

He nodded.

"I'd like to see that."

"You will." He tucked her back against his side. "So, I imagined a day when I would tie a string of fifty horses outside her father's lodge. A gift so large, her father might overlook that I was not the ideal son-in-law, but prove I could provide well for a wife. Her mother would come out and say, 'What is this?' and run to get her husband. His jaw would drop open as he stared at the riches and then he would lead the horses to his pasture, accepting the dowry. Then my bride, well, she would know I value her above all else."

Lucie felt her insides go soft.

"But what about the girl? What did you imagine she would look like?"

Sky laughed. "I was so busy catching horses, I never thought about that."

Lucie did not know how else to ask her question.

He lifted her chin and stared into her eyes. "If you are asking if I wanted a Lakota woman, the answer is yes. As a boy, I did. As a man, I decided I did not deserve the happiness of having a wife."

"Until now." She rested her head on his chest and hugged him.

He stroked her head. "I couldn't have imagined a woman like you, Lucie. I never expected this kind of happiness could be mine."

Lucie fell asleep with Sky petting her head and back in long rhythmic strokes, filled with a happiness she had not felt in years.

* * *

In the morning, they broke camp before dawn and crept through the cover of the juniper and sage, down to the cottonwood and willow that lined the bank. They continued into the morning, keeping clear of the open area and seeing no more soldiers.

For the next several days they traveled hard, taking short rests of an hour or two at best and then more riding. The horses were losing weight faster than she was, but Sky was determined to put them out of the reach of the army.

She saw no signs of pursuit. On the fifteenth day of their odyssey Sky stopped beside the river they had been following for days.

"What?" Lucie asked.

"The water in this river is running east."

She nodded, her tired brain finding no significance to this.

"Eagle Dancer told me once that the People would run all the way to where the river turned east to escape the soldier. This is that place. We've made it."

"Canada?"

"Yes."

Sky dismounted and pulled Lucie off her horse. She threw her arms about him.

"We're safe!" she cried.

"And no one will separate us again."

Lucie's smile was mischievous. "You haven't spoken to my parents yet."

Sky's smile dissolved and Lucie laughed.

Epilogue

It was nearly a year to the day since they reached the Canadian border that Lucie's father disembarked from the train in Vancouver. Lucie ran forward to meet him, hugging him fiercely. When she opened her eyes it was to see her younger sisters descending the steps. First came Julia, looking tall and lovely in a sky-blue day dress, straw hat and lace gloves. Nelly and Cary nearly knocked her off the steps in their hurry to descend, bounding off the train like foxes in high grass. In the rear came her mother, gripping the hand of her baby brother, Theodore, keeping him from tumbling down the steps.

Lucie kissed them all. The hugs and kisses she received proved they had missed her, too. She glanced back to see Thomas offer his hand to Sky, but her father's face remained threatening. She sighed. Her father and mother had protected her all her life. She must make them understand that they had been relieved of duty. But first they would see that she was safe and happy.

She talked nonstop all the way back in the wagon, telling of their spread and how hard Sky had worked to build the ranch house and fencing. They'd hired several hands, too, and were selling horses as fast as Sky could train them.

Sarah smiled and Thomas scowled as she extolled the virtues of her husband. She knew they were not happy to have missed her wedding, actually, both of their weddings, since she and Sky had married in the first church they came upon. Nor were they pleased with the reports from David on her part in Sky's escape.

At the ranch, she got the children settled in one room, except for Julia, who was already a grown woman and entitled to the privacy of the loft. Her supper was devoured. She was pleased at their appetites, but her siblings' excitement and the travel took its toll. Nelly nearly dropped off to sleep right at the table and Julia only just stifled a yawn, so Lucie showed her sisters to the loft and then showed her parents the guest room, which Lucie hoped would soon be a nursery, though it was still too early for her to be certain that she was with child. Sarah and Thomas wished them good-night shortly afterward.

Lucie turned to Sky. "Well?"

"What?"

"Did he say anything?"

Sky nodded.

Lucie gave him an impatient look.

Sky quirked an eyebrow as if he did not understand, so she shoved him.

He chuckled. "He said if I ever hurt you, I'd answer to him."

Lucie nodded. "Not so bad."

Sky's smile was sardonic. "But your mother added something about cutting out my liver."

Lucie gasped. "She did not!"

Sky's look convinced her of the truth of his words.

"She wouldn't." Lucie knew her voice did not hold the confidence she had hoped.

Sky gave a soft laugh. "She would."

Lucie nodded and then led him to bed. "Best keep me happy, then."

His smile was knowing as he pulled her down to the bed. She made an effort to be quiet, because of her guests. His lovemaking always helped her sleep, but tonight she was attuned to any noise due to her guests, and that was why she heard Sky rising far earlier than his custom.

"Where are you going?" she whispered.

"To the horses."

She dropped back to the pillows, intending to only close her eyes for a moment, but as it happened she woke to her mother's voice.

"Lucie? Are you awake?"

She slipped from the bed and quickly donned the nightgown she no longer wore to bed. A moment later she had the door open.

"I'm sorry, but something odd is happening. Is Sky going to an auction today?"

"No. Why?"

"Well." Her mother glanced back over her shoulder. "I'd better show you."

Lucie followed her mother out and saw the line of

horses. The first, a fine black mare, was tied to one of the upright beams supporting the porch. Her halter was tied to the following horse. The pattern continued, each to the next. They stretched from the house to the barn and out of sight. Her father stood scratching his head as he stared down the string of ponies.

Lucie laughed.

"What is this?" asked her mother.

"It's a gift from Sky to Father. Fifty ponies in exchange for his daughter."

Her mother's confusion hardened into disapproval. "Christians do not sell their daughters. You should know better, Lucie."

Lucie did not let her mother's censure spoil her delight. Instead she walked forward and stroked the front pony. It was fine and fat, with broad shoulders and a straight spine.

"It's my dowry, proof that Sky can provide for me." She turned to her father. "If you accept them, then you accept our marriage."

"But we already have accepted it," said Sarah.

Lucie turned and held her mother's gaze. "Have you?"

Her mother hesitated only a moment and then nodded. "But the dowry goes to the husband, not the father."

"Not in this case," said Lucie and then turned to her dad. "Do you accept?"

"It's too much," he said.

"What?" said Sarah, her voice sharp. "Too much for your firstborn?"

Lucie grinned. "If you agree, then take them to that

paddock. It's empty and by taking them you consent to Sky as your son-in-law."

Thomas nodded and untied the first pony from the post. "But what am I going to do with them?"

Lucie laughed again. "Whatever you like."

When all the ponies were in the paddock, Sky appeared atop Falcon. He rode into the yard with an air of authority that made them all straighten. He steered his stallion up to Lucie. She knew what happened next, so she lifted her arms to him. In one smooth motion he scooped her up before him and rode away.

"But what about breakfast?" called Sarah.

Lucie peered over Sky's shoulder. "Start without us!"

* * * * *

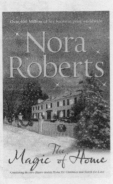

 *Have Your Say*

You've just finished your book.
So what did you think?

We'd love to hear your thoughts on our
'Have your say' online panel
www.millsandboon.co.uk/haveyoursay

- 🌹 Easy to use
- 🌹 Short questionnaire
- 🌹 Chance to win Mills & Boon® goodies